Heart & Soul

Brenda Meister

The characters and events portrayed in this novel have been conjured from the author's imagination. Any resemblance to persons living or dead, or to current or past events, is strictly coincidental.

Order this book online at www.trafford.com
or email orders@trafford.com

Most Trafford titles are also available at major online book retailers.

Printed in Victoria, BC, Canada.

ISBN: 978-1-4269-0232-1 (soft)
ISBN: 978-1-4269-0234-5 (ebook)

Our mission is to efficiently provide the world's finest, most comprehensive book publishing service, enabling every author to experience success. To find out how to publish your book, your way, and have it available worldwide, visit us online at www.trafford.com

Trafford rev. 11/30/2009

 www.trafford.com

North America & international
toll-free: 1 888 232 4444 (USA & Canada)
phone: 250 383 6864 ♦ fax: 812 355 4082

Prologue

∞

A Daughter's Last Good-Bye

Savannah, Georgia

1827

The winter wind blew cold and crisp to paint a cherry hue on Lara Kendrick's cheeks. The eleven-year-old girl looked into chestnut eyes as her mother knelt down to face her. Unspoken fears shadowed Lara's thoughts as she noticed again how dark those lines were around her Mama's eyes. How very tired Mama looked. Her mother was the most beautiful woman Lara had ever known, but the recent weeks from lack of sleep, little to eat, and a heart full of worries had taken their toll on Linette Kendrick.

"We must be getting on," Captain Dane Haley urged firmly despite the sympathy he felt for mother and child.

Lara looked passed the sea captain out to the merchant ship afloat in the harbor. This boat was to take her to Aunt Lyddie in Charleston, South Carolina. Lara had never sailed before, nor had she ever traveled alone. These, though, were extreme circumstances, and Lara, even at this young precocious age, was able to comprehend the seriousness of the situation, despite the grand efforts of those around her to conceal the truth.

"Be good for your Aunt Lyddie." Her mother's voice brought Lara back from her troubled thoughts.

"Yes, Mama," Lara replied in her usual obedient tone.

"I won't be waiting for you to board the ship. I must get back to Papa."

A silent nod in understanding. "He'll be much better soon," Lara offered as she tightened her grip on the handle of her father's violin case. The stringed instrument was his prized possession and had been given to her to play and take care of until her father was well again.

"Of course he will," Linette reassured her daughter with a loving smile. Lara had always been a strong child, able to take both the good and the bad in stride. Never had Linette Kendrick been more proud of her daughter than at this moment. "And when he does, we will sail to Charleston to fetch you and we will all be together again. I promise."

Lara wanted nothing more than for her mother's pledge to come true, but in Lara's dark and silent thoughts, she feared she would never see either of her parents again.

Dengue fever had erupted in Savannah, Georgia. William Kendrick had been struck hard by the fever and Lara had watched helplessly with her mother as the disease overtook him. Lara had deciphered the hushed conversations telling of the loss of many family friends and acquaintances. With the number of deaths climbing rapidly, there was talk of a quarantine that would envelope Savannah and the outlying plantations. With her father gravely ill, her mother had made the difficult decision to send Lara away. Now there she was, standing on the dock. Minutes from now, she would be taken into custody by a stranger with only his solemn word as captain of a merchant ship that he would safely deliver her to Aunt Lyddie in Charleston.

Lara's hair blew in her face. A shiver ran through her as she felt her mother's cold hand brush back her long tresses.

"Papa and I love you more than anything else in this world. You know that, don't you?"

Lara nodded once again, knowing it to be the absolute truth.

Linette removed her wedding ring from her finger. She placed it in Lara's palm and folded her daughter's fingers tight over the gold band. "Papa's gift to you is his violin. Mine is my ring," her voice faltered. She stopped to swallow the lump in her throat. "You take good care of them until we see each other again."

"Yes, Mama."

Linette held her daughter at arm's length. She forced herself to gaze into Lara's big brown eyes. The tears threatened to betray the young mother's courage. Linette knew her heart would shatter to shards if she were to let their goodbye go on much longer. "Be strong," she managed with a wide smile, the words meant just as much for herself as for her daughter. She wrapped her arms around Lara for one last hug.

"Go with the Captain now," Linette directed as she summoned the inner strength needed to let her precious Lara go.

Lara felt the love of her mother's last kiss and then the quick release from her mother's arms.

Seated in the longboat, Lara could only hear the shrill call of the sea gulls overhead, and the rush of salt water over the oars as the captain rowed them toward the ship. Through the next few strokes, Lara's eyes remained intent upon her mother who stood statuesque on the dock. Lara glanced down at the ring in her hand. Curious, she slipped it onto her finger. Too big. Then, after thinking twice, she decided it was safest to tuck it away in her pocket. When she looked again to the wharf, her mother was nowhere to be seen. Lara drew in a long, silent breath. Never before had she felt so alone. She felt like crying, but her mother's familiar words echoed in her head: *Be strong.*

Chapter 1

∞

Lost Heart

Brooklyn City, New York
September, 1835

*L*ike most everyone else in the grand ballroom, Lara's attention was focused upon the bride and the groom. She watched Irina lose herself in the arms of her new husband, Adam. A strikingly handsome couple, Lara remarked to herself for what must have been at least the hundredth time. The rhythm of the sweeping waltz could not be ignored and Lara surrendered to the music, her slender body swaying to each long, smooth note. The next minutes passed like seconds until the melody faded into the enthusiastic round of applause that broke out for the newlywed couple. Even before they could step off the floor, the pair was enveloped by a swarm of well-wishers. Lara laughed at Irina and Adam's feeble attempt to free themselves from the family and friends that surrounded them.

"May I have the pleasure of the next dance?"

Lara turned toward the deep, melodious voice. The stranger stood tall and confident. He flashed a bright and engaging smile that immediately drew her to him. She locked gazes with warm blue-grey eyes that shone bright in anticipation of the moments to come. His blonde hair was swept back and neatly tied showing off a strong jaw that enhanced the chiseled lines of his handsome face. His clothes hinted at his preference for the finer, more exquisite things in life. His linen shirt was crisp and white, and was a perfect contrast to set off his summer tan. His suit of black cotton was skillfully tailored to his broad shoulders and long limbs. Lara felt her pulse racing.

She had caught the stranger's attention from the other side of the ballroom. At first he had stood like all the others, content to watch his best friend, Adam Toews and his new wife. As he followed the couple through their first dance, he was drawn to the vibrant young woman standing alone, swaying gracefully in time with the music's rhythm. While all eyes were on Irina and Adam, his became fixed upon the striking brunette. He was bewitched by Lara's joyous smile and the sparkle of her chestnut brown eyes. Full of life, her expression was animated in joyful excitement. In the seconds it took for him to catch his next breath, he had become completely mesmerized by her enchanting manner.

In turn, Lara immediately became intrigued by the man before her. The stranger had caught her attention earlier that day at the church ceremony when their eyes met for the few brief moments it took for him to flash her a smile. She had overheard a telling conversation between two older ladies of the stranger's southern background, and the promise of an influential career in the banking industry. With little discussion, the women had easily determined that he would prove a good catch for any one of their unmarried daughters.

"You are bold, sir, to approach when the request for an introduction has not been made." Lara responded more in lighthearted play than in earnest for she couldn't help but wonder how concerned the man actually was with adhering to proper decorum and social etiquette. She coupled her reply with a teasing smile as if daring him to respond.

Amused by Lara's good humor, the stranger's smile broadened into a dimpled grin. "It is not boldness, but your lively charm that captivates me and compels me to intrude upon you. My apologies, but you seemed to be enjoying the music as much as I and I thought we could capture this extraordinary moment in our memories with a dance. May I suggest we surrender ourselves to the magic of this moment and leave the niceties to later?" He extended an open hand to repeat his invitation in silence.

Captivate. Compel. Surrender. His strong, suggestive words came quickly and easily. Lara's face lit up with a brighter, sweeter smile. Her eyes sparkled like gems in response to his suave manner. Flattered and charmed by the attention bestowed upon her by such a devilishly handsome man, Lara placed her hand in his without a second thought and, together, they stepped out onto the dance floor.

Feeling like a schoolgirl, Lara took a deep breath to quell her excitement. Calm and composed, she addressed her partner with a deep curtsy before looking up to meet his steady gaze. The folds of her silk satin gown billowed to a soft puddle on the floor. There, Lara remained poised, her eyes upon the man as he bowed before her. She noted a twinkle in his eyes and a hint of a smile on his lips. She placed her hand in his and rose upon hearing the first chords played by the musicians. Her heart quickened with the touch of his hand at the small of her back. His quiescent strength brought her forward into their first steps. A lively waltz, their bodies embraced its rhythm and the stranger held her firm in his arms to sweep her in long strides from one end of the dance floor to the other, from one corner to the next. So light and natural were his steps, so easy to follow, that Lara soon lost herself in his arms. The world around her disappeared and Lara knew of no one else but the charming stranger who was leading her so gracefully across the floor. Two as one they were: light, smooth, and timeless. Then before she realized, the chatter of the crowd drowned the last of the musical notes. Their dance had ended much too soon for Lara's liking.

"Thank you, Miss Kendrick, for sharing this extraordinary moment with me."

Lara responded with another curtsy. As she rose her face was lit up with surprise. "I'm flattered, sir, that you have taken the time to find out who I am. You have me at a disadvantage."

"Then I do believe it's time for those introductions." A quick look around and with a sudden wave of his outstretched arm the stranger was able to catch the attention of Adam and Irina. The newlyweds needed no other prompting to join them.

"Lara, it seems you've caught the eye of the most eligible bachelor here," Irina observed boldly, her voice ringing with happiness. The elated expression on the bride's face clearly showed her approval. "As it should be for you look even more ravishing than usual tonight."

"Indeed you do," Adam confirmed. "Lara, it gives me great pleasure to present my best of friends, Mr. Kyle Harrison. Kyle comes to us from Charleston, South Carolina and has been with us two years now in Brooklyn City. Kyle, you are indeed fortunate to have me for a friend for I have the honor and pleasure of introducing Miss Lara Kendrick. Lara, too, is from the south."

"Savannah, Georgia," Irina added.

"I'm pleased to make your acquaintance, Mr. Harrison," Lara responded with the formality of an extended hand.

"Lara's studying music and languages at the seminary," Irina disclosed.

"The pleasure and the honor are not Adam's, but most certainly mine. And I look forward to becoming more than just an acquaintance." Kyle brought her hand to his lips, barely touching. Even so, the warmth of his breath and the slight touch of his lips were enough to send a shiver through her body. It was a most unexpected and tantalizing sensation.

Several times over the weeks before the wedding, Irina had pressed Lara to allow an introduction to the eligible and debonair South Carolinian. Her friend had predicted without a sliver of doubt that Lara and Kyle would be drawn to one another for she believed the two shared much in interests, spirit and temperament. Abi recalled Irina's prediction: *He's charming and sensible, but not so prudent as to be boring. He shares your love of music and dance. What a perfect match he would be for you.* Yes, Lara would have to agree that there was an attraction between her and Kyle and it was strong and magnetic, but what had Irina revealed to Kyle?

"Irina has bestowed nothing but the most flattering of compliments," Kyle reassured her. It was as though he had read her thoughts. "I had serious doubts that any one woman could be so engaging. I see now that Irina has been nothing but truthful."

Lara caught Irina's look of approval and now she could sense her friend's excitement and keen interest. Lara cast Irina a warning glance in hopes of stifling her friend's expectations. "A word of caution, Mr. Harrison, I've never known Irina to speak anything but kindly of others. Her compliments flow freely especially for those she holds dearest. Thus she may have spoken laurels for which I may be undeserving."

"The fact that Irina treasures your friendship speaks volumes in itself. Still, I do consider myself a good judge of character, Miss Kendrick. Adam will be the first to tell you that I am seldom influenced by the impressions of others. I prefer to form my own opinion on most things. I hope you will allow me some time in your company so that we may become better acquainted."

Kyle remained by Lara's side throughout the rest of the evening. She wouldn't have been able to brush him aside even if she had wanted to. Together they shared every moment of the wedding supper. They explored each other's lives; they laughed; they sang; they danced. And sometime during that night, Lara fell in love. Kyle Garrett Harrison, a man whom only the day before was nothing more than a faceless stranger, had somehow captured her heart and touched her soul.

~ · ~

As Lara had dared hope he would, Kyle had appeared on her doorstep without any warning the day after the wedding, and each day thereafter until Lara was counting the weeks they had known each other instead of the days. Throughout that short time, Kyle and Lara were separated only by his responsibilities to work and her commitment to her studies at the female seminary.

Time spent with Kyle was chock-full of fun. He had a way of making Lara feel extraordinarily special, like she was the only woman in the world! Oh, how he could make her laugh! Around others, Kyle was proper and reserved, but more the fun-loving imp when he was alone with Lara. At first his jokes and teases were light and innocent. As they got to know each other better, he started picking up on the most innocent of her comments and turning them into sly innuendoes. Lara laughed at his game. It wasn't long before his suggestions grew more playful and more provocative. Teamed with more potent displays of affection, the holding of hands turned to possessive hugs and stolen kisses on the cheek. Never before had Lara been so fascinated by another man!

Time spent with Kyle was also chock-full of surprises. Each night, shortly after leaving work, he would come calling. Each night there would be something cleverly planned for the two of them. This day was no different as Lara settled comfortably on the bench seat inside the carriage. Her eyes gleamed with eager anticipation as she waited for Kyle to relay his instructions to their driver. His voice was soft and low and she understood none of what he was saying, but neither did she want to know his plans for fear it would spoil the marvelous surprise that was sure to come.

Just a few hours notice was all Lara had been given to pack some things for two nights away. She had thought hard, mulling over the perceptions and repercussions of accepting Kyle's offer, but still those insecurities remained with her. Two nights without a chaperone! Such an outing was unheard of in her small and tight circle of friends. It took some serious coaxing on Kyle's part, and it was only with his steady reassurances that Lara felt comfortable with her decision to join him.

"You haven't changed your mind, have you?" he asked one last time as he snuggled up to her.

"No." Lara moved to make more room for Kyle beside her. Her answer had come quickly and without any further thought about the propriety of their excursion.

"Good girl," Kyle responded with the broadest smile before bringing her hand up to his lips to receive his kiss.

"Remember, I have your word that you will be the perfect gentleman," Lara reminded him with a glowing smile of her own.

He slapped his hand twice against the wall of the carriage to signal the driver and almost immediately the coach started to roll. "Is there such a man?" he asked.

Lara's face was set aglow with her mirthful smile. "You are a wicked tease."

The next four hours in Kyle's company passed quickly and Lara found herself in a suite with two bedrooms in a mountain inn somewhere along the Delaware River. From their balcony, she took in the expansive view as her gaze followed the river below. The sound of the river swept through her, relaxing and soothing her. The serenity of the moment was broken when she felt Kyle's hand over hers.

"The rooms are small," he commented.

"They're comfortable enough." Lara replied, thinking about her own. Her response set Kyle's mind at ease for he had worried that their accommodations might not be to her liking.

"Beautiful, isn't it?" Lara asked as she continued to view the idyllic scene before her.

"I've never seen anything quite so breathtaking," Kyle replied with his eyes intent upon her. "Are you tired from our long ride? Do you need a rest?"

"Not at all," Lara replied, both amused and pleased that Kyle was so caring.

"Good, then how about a horseback ride? There are horses ready in the stable and I'm told that we can follow a path along the river to a small lake. It's about an hour away. We should be back in plenty of time for dinner. Would you like that?"

Feeling the warmth and humidity in the air, Lara looked to the heavens, wondering if the soft, grey clouds might turn darker.

"Come on," Kyle coaxed. "We'll come straight back if it starts to rain."

~ • ~

Rain it did. Lara and Kyle had not yet reached the lake when the sky grew ominous with rain clouds rolling over from the east. Lightning flashes could be seen in the far distance.

"Sorry, my love. It's best we head back," Kyle directed.

The pair had just turned the horses around when the rain clouds burst. The two sent their horses into a gallop, but there was no hope of outrunning the storm. Caught in the pelting rain, Kyle led them through the trees. There they remained only for a few minutes until it became clear that the cover of the branches would not be enough to shelter them from the rain.

It took the couple thirty minutes to find their way back to the inn. It was impossible for the two to not have been noticed as they dashed through the foyer to their rooms. The pair could not escape the chuckles and innocent teasing from the owners and other patrons who were lucky enough to have been saved from a good soaking.

Kyle closed the door to their suite and the two stood laughing at each other. They were quite a sight, both drenched from head to toe with puddles forming at their feet.

"Well, I've never had an outing quite like that," Lara admitted good-naturedly.

Immediately she went in search of towels. When she returned, she found Kyle in front of the fireplace. He had arranged some kindling deep in the hearth and was about to light a fire. She held out a towel for him.

"We should first get out of our wet clothes," Lara suggested as she set to drying off her hair. "We're getting water everywhere."

In the bathing room, Lara had removed her shoes and stockings and tossed them into the brass bathtub. Her day dress and petticoats were next, but the ties of her chemise refused to cooperate and she found herself struggling with a wet knot. The more she tried to loosen it, the tighter it became until there was no give at all. Frustrated, she tried to pull the chemise over her head, but found the opening too small. Perhaps she could cut the strings, but there was nothing around that was sharp enough.

Lara jumped at the knock upon the door.

"Lara, are you alright in there?" came Kyle's concerned voice.

"Not quite," she finally answered after seconds of hesitation.

"What's the matter? Is there anything I can do?"

Lara laughed aloud. "I'm not sure. I'm being held hostage by my chemise."

"By your what?"

"I have a knot in my shift and I can't get it undone."

There was a pause from the other side of the door. "Shall I try?" Kyle finally asked.

Lara could only laugh at herself. She pulled hard on the ties in hopes they would break, but the cotton was too strong.

"Lara?"

Feeling foolish, Lara wrapped herself in a towel before opening the door. Standing before Kyle so scantily clothed, the roguish grin on his handsome face was too much for Lara and her own face lit up with laughter. "You, sir, are a cad!"

Kyle came to her. Completely amused by her circumstances, he wrapped his arms around her waist and drew her closer to him.

Embarrassed, Lara felt helpless as she clutched her towel. "You are here to help a lady in distress," she reminded him with a shy smile of her own.

Kyle's kiss was soft upon her lips. "What would you like me to do?" he whispered in her ear. His nibbling of her lobe left her weak in the knees.

"The knot… in my chemise," Lara mumbled as she took a tiny step backwards.

"This knot?" Kyle asked as his fingers pulled the strings out from under her towel.

"Yes," Lara whispered.

The towel fell away as Kyle brought her hands down to her sides. There she stood looking wildly beautiful, clothed only in a wet cotton shift that clung to every curve of her svelte body. He tried hard to dismiss the devilish thoughts running rampant through his head in order to concentrate on his task. He fumbled with the ties without the slightest bit of success. Then holding on to the knot, he took it by his teeth to try to loosen the strings. His breath was hot against Lara's skin and she felt her own temperature rising. Still he couldn't separate the stubborn ties, and he found it increasingly difficult to concentrate. His lustful thoughts grew with his increasing desire for Lara. His passion and frustrations overtook him and he took hold of her thin garment. He ripped the shift down the middle leaving him with a tantalizing view of Lara's full, round breasts.

Lara's eyes widened with surprise. Moans of pure pleasure escaped her as his hands massaged her breasts.

Without warning, Kyle mustered enough restraint and willpower to step away.

"What's wrong?" Lara whispered.

"I'm sorry, Lara," he apologized with regret evident in his voice and by the sober expression on his face. "I shouldn't have."

Aroused by her own desires, Lara stepped forward to wrap her arms around his neck. "There's no such thing as a perfect gentleman."

Kyle unleashed his salacious hunger as his remaining threads of self-control melted away.

Lara tasted his kiss, sensual and exciting. Held tight in his arms, he brought her down to the soft, plush towels spread out on the floor. He swept her long tresses over her shoulders to leave himself with a full view of every sinuous curve of her voluptuous body.

Timid and somewhat nervous, Lara lay waiting and watching as Kyle stripped himself bare before her. He gave her nude body one long slow glance from toe to head. He came to hover over her, straddling across her hips with a knee on each side of her. His touch was almost a tickle as his hands moved over her stomach, around to her waist, and up to her breasts. Lara reveled in his touch as he massaged her breasts, his thumbs teasing her nipples. She reached up to cup his handsome face in her hands. She brought him down to her, reveling in the feel of his body molded hot against hers. His kiss, fierce and demanding, compelled Lara to respond.

Kyle's hands grew bolder in exploration of the most intimate parts of her body, waking her to new titillating sensations and newfound pleasures. The fire within her raged as Kyle's gentle hand moved between her legs. Lara closed her eyes to lose herself in the erotic sensations that overtook her. His slow, purposeful fondling drove her mad and her body writhed in response to his lovemaking. She didn't know if she could endure more, but neither did she want him to stop. His kisses and nibbling, sensuous stroking and massaging, teased and taunted her. He roused her carnal senses, taking her to unimaginable heights of blissful pleasure.

Near the edge of insanity, Lara felt the weight of him on top of her. She gasped as she felt him enter her body. She clung tight to him as he started to move. There was strength, passion and desire within his rhythmic movements, a fierce, but controlled power. Each thrust fuelled a mounting passion from deep within. Wrapped in each other's arms, their sensuous lovemaking sparked a frenzy until the intense and uncontrollable wave finally exploded at the height of their passion. The surging rush pulsing through them to leave the two lovers physically exhausted and emotionally complete.

~ · ~

It was eleven the next morning when Lara and Kyle found themselves back on horseback. With a blanket and a picnic lunch, their plan was to find the lake destination they never reached the day before, and to spend a leisurely afternoon exploring the countryside.

It was already the end of September and there was barely a hint that summer was coming to an end. The air was still hot and dry. And after the previous day's shower, the surrounding forest was never as lush with its variegated shades of green. The trail ran alongside the river, straying here and there, but never too far for the babbling sound of water was ever-present. The path was wide and well traveled. Even so, the pair found themselves alone with not a soul within sight or sound.

Upon reaching a fork in the path, Kyle veered to the right taking the narrower, steeper trail.

"Are you sure we're going the right way?" Lara was compelled to ask.

"I was told if we stay to the right we would eventually come to a waterfall. I thought it might make a nice stop for lunch. Perhaps I could coax you into a swim?" Kyle's raised brow and the lilt in his voice promised something more intriguing.

"Perhaps I can't swim," Lara replied in fun.

"Perhaps a cool bath," came Kyle's alternative suggestion.

Immodest thoughts and images ran through Lara's head. "Perhaps," she responded, silently wondering how daring and fearless Kyle could be.

A little further ahead, the water cascaded over a rocky river bed only to plunge into a basin five or six feet below. It was under the shade of a tall oak near the pool's edge that the couple spread out their blanket to enjoy their picnic lunch.

The little shade that protected them from the late morning sun soon vanished and they both began to feel the full force of the sun's hot rays. Taking advantage of the opportunity, Kyle was not the least bit modest and had stripped himself bare to dive into the deep, refreshing waters. He was like a fish dipping in and out of the pool, disappearing for a few seconds only to emerge at a distance moments later. Lara watched, fascinated by his long glides, and quick twists and turns. He had surprising speed and agility for a man with such a tall, broad frame! Each time when Kyle resurfaced, the water would stream off his body and Lara found herself ardently admiring the hard lines of his muscular form.

With his unrelenting coaxing to join him, Lara eventually gave in to temptation, but only to the point of removing her shoes and stockings. With her skirts gathered high into her arms, Lara waded knee deep into the pool of water.

"You, my sweet, have far too many clothes on to be of any serious fun," Kyle declared with a devious grin as he came out of the deeper depths to meet her. With that, his nimble fingers began working on the buttons to free her from her bodice.

"Kyle," Lara objected.

"What, my love?" He managed to steal a kiss.

"What if someone comes along?"

"The more the merrier," he teased.

Lara rejected his sly intimations and turned away. With layers of petticoats and the folds of her dress wrapped up in her arms, she started back to shore. Seconds later she felt the cool spray of water against her back. At once, Lara rushed to get out of the water to save herself from Kyle's playful splashing. In her haste she slipped on the wet, mossy rocks. Her balance lost, Lara shrieked. There was a great splash as she tumbled into the water.

She sputtered and choked as she took in some water. Her heart pounded inside her chest, the adrenaline flowing as quickly as the cool rush of the river flowing over her!

"Lara!" Kyle's voice rang out.

Drenched from head to toe, and all the layers of her clothes soaked through, Lara propped herself up in the water. Kyle rushed to her side. His stunned expression of shock and concern charmed her.

"You knave!" Lara laughed. Her gleeful attempt to scold was not the reprimand Kyle had expected. Quick to react, Lara gave as good as she got and sent a great spray of water full into Kyle's face. Her spirited and fun-loving response immediately started a feisty water fight that eventually left the two breathless. For that short time, the silence of the woods was broken by their playful squeals and roaring laughter.

That afternoon Kyle discovered Lara, indeed, knew how to swim. And later still, he proved how bold he could be when he made love to her in a secluded spot amidst the quietude of the forest trees. Here, Kyle taught Lara something of herself as well, for never would she have believed she could cast aside her inhibitions to allow such a brash yet exhilarating escapade.

It was early evening before the couple found themselves back at the inn. Knowing it would be hopeless to try to get to their rooms without being seen, the lovers braved the critical stares and chatter and walked through the lobby without a care. Both looking a little like rag dolls, their bodies were tinted a golden tan from their day under the hot Georgia sun.

An older gent peered over his newspaper as Lara and Kyle strolled near. The two recognized him as the same fellow who had given them a decent ribbing after being caught in the rainstorm the previous day. With Lara's dress not yet dry from their swim, the elder was compelled to ask, "Caught in the rain again?"

"No sir, not a cloud in the sky!" Kyle confirmed with a wink and wide, cheeky grin.

Needing no further hints as to how the two had spent their afternoon, the man was quick to respond. "My hat's off to you, son."

~ · ~

In the days that followed their weekend excursion, Lara continued to discover the physical and emotional pleasures of Kyle's love. Whether it was a formal night at the theatre, a romantic buggy ride through the countryside, a serious evening of work and study, or the sharing of his bed, Kyle was able to charm her with his gallant manner, and captivate her with his presence to make her feel like the remarkable woman he knew her to be. He had an uncanny awareness of her thoughts and feelings. Instinctively he seemed to know what would evoke her laughter, inflame her temper, or tug at her heartstrings. Her thoughts were often his and it seemed Kyle knew her better than she knew herself. He was in tune with her moods as she was with his.

Lara found in Kyle all that she had dreamt of in a lover. He was profoundly thoughtful, openly honest and proud, much like she remembered her own father to be. His touch was always tender as were his words. And yet, with even the slightest tease, Lara could arouse his own playful nature and he would wrap her in his arms to demand as little as a kiss or as much as a few precious hours making love to her. In so many ways, Kyle was her soul mate. He was the man she had fallen deeply, madly in love with and soon she found herself wondering if perhaps he might be that one unique and extraordinary man with whom she might share the rest of her life!

~ · ~

Aphrodite, the Greek goddess of love and beauty, could not have conjured up a more blissful romance. In the heart and mind of

Lara MacKenzie Kendrick, she had been living a dream come true for the last fifty-three days, ever since that enchanted evening when she met and fell in love with the dashing, charming, witty Kyle Garrett Harrison.

The crackling fire filled the small parlor with a cozy warmth. The red-orange glow cast its soft light upon the lovers as they sat cuddled up to each other on the settee. Lara's heart was light and carefree as she watched the flames flare and flicker across the logs.

"We really haven't known each other long, have we?" Kyle asked suddenly.

"Not yet two months," Lara replied, still mesmerized by the dancing lights.

"I suppose some would say we've barely had a chance to get to know each other, but I would think them wrong." Kyle pulled her closer to him, his arm possessively tight around her slim waist. "I think we've come to know each other rather well, don't you think?"

Kyle had gained her full attention for she couldn't help but wonder where this conversation was leading. "Quite well," she agreed.

"In fact, I know you well enough to want you to be my wife."

Lara's heart jumped and she sat up straight, both astounded and bewildered by his sudden declaration. Before she could find the words, a bright twinkle caught her eye and she stared in amazement at the diamond ring Kyle had in his hand.

"This was Mother's. I want you to have it," Kyle offered, "but it comes with one condition."

Lara could feel her pulse racing in hopeful anticipation.

Kyle moved in close to whisper ever so softly in her ear. "You must wear it as Mrs. Lara Mackenzie Harrison."

The thought left Lara breathless for this was too surreal to be anything but the most marvelous of happy dreams. Her eyes were wide, watching in disbelief as Kyle held her trembling hand.

Lovingly, he slipped the golden circlet onto her finger before bringing her hand up to receive his tender kiss. The polished facets of the solitaire diamond sparkled its brilliance as the stone reflected the flickering flames of the fire.

"I will love you, honor you and cherish you always and forever. Will you, Lara Mackenzie Kendrick, promise to love me, honor and cherish me as my wife?"

Kyle had spoken with absolute certainty and with utmost confidence. His marriage proposal ran through Lara's head a second time and then a third before she heard her own promise to him. "Always and forever."

Her pledge was barely spoken before she tasted love and passion in his kiss. In that one magical moment, the world was perfect and everything was as Lara had dared hoped it would be. Her fantasy was to become reality, one that would be hers and Kyle's to live out through the rest of their lives. He would love, honor and cherish her forever, and she would be forever his, heart and soul.

Lara rested her head on Kyle's shoulder as she nestled once again into his loving arms. She held out her hand to admire his ring yet another time. She removed it from her finger to look at the initials engraved on the inside. The lettering complimented the intricate engraving on the band and the delicate scroll claws that held the gemstone in place. It had been his mother's ring, he had explained: MH for Martha Harrison; now the M would be for Mackenzie.

Lara remembered how surprised she was the first time Kyle used her middle name. It began as a jest for "Mackenzie" seemed too masculine a name for a woman so young and with such a dynamic personality. Eventually Kyle shortened it to "Mack" for a more emphatic contrast. No one other than her father had ever nicknamed her that. She enjoyed hearing Kyle use her name so endearingly. It felt comfortable and so very right!

"We'll have your first initial added to Mother's," Kyle offered.

Lara's smile reflected the glow in her heart for Kyle's endearing sentiment of adding her L would make it her own: Lara Mackenzie Harrison. Yes, that would be perfect! "Thank you, Kyle. It is the most beautiful ring and I'm honored to be wearing it." The timbre of her voice was softly seductive and loving in his ear.

"Not as beautiful as you." He placed a kiss upon her head.

Lara looked up with smoldering brown eyes. Kyle needed no other prompting. Their lips met for a tender, lingering kiss.

"Is there anyone I need to ask for permission to marry you?"

Lara paused. The time had come and she knew she had to choose her words carefully. There was something Kyle needed to know, but she had not been brave enough to broach the topic. Now she knew she had to come out with it. "I suppose you should ask Aunt Lyddie, but she's going to love you the moment she lays eyes upon you. Just like I did!"

Kyle played with a lock of her hair for he liked how the glow from the fire set alight the reddish hues of her long, brown tresses. "Is this the same aunt you've talked about before?"

Lara nodded.

"And where would I find this Aunt Lyddie of yours?"

Lara hesitated, taking a deep and silent breath before speaking. "Aunt Lyddie lives in Charleston. Her name is Lydia Randall."

Kyle's abrupt shift in position forced Lara to sit up from her snug position. "You must be joking!" His voice was distinctively cool and she felt him withdraw from her.

The happiness Lara felt only moments ago began to vanish. "You've heard of Aunt Lyddie?" But she didn't need to wait for his reply. Lara already knew his answer for there was no mistaking his reaction. He knew exactly who and what Aunt Lyddie was!

"Everyone in Charleston knows Lydia Randall! Why didn't you tell me she was your aunt?"

"I've spoken of Aunt Lyddie before."

"Yes, but only in passing and nothing of consequence. You come from Savannah. Isn't that how Adam and Irina introduced you? There has been nothing to even hint that your Aunt Lyddie and Lydia Randall is one and the same person."

"I was born in Savannah and lived there until I was eleven years old," Lara confirmed. "I was sent to live with Aunt Lyddie in Charleston after the fever overran the city. My times there were always short for Aunt Lyddie arranged for my schooling here in New York."

"Why didn't you tell me sooner? How could you keep this from me?"

"There was no reason to tell you about Aunt Lyddie," Lara answered. She could feel the churning in her stomach and it was increasingly difficult to remain calm and composed. "Not until now. And why should it matter so?"

Kyle stared at her in stunned disbelief. "Mack, how can you ask that? Of course it will be a discerning factor! I have accepted the position as manager at the Bank of the State of South Carolina. This is a tremendous opportunity for me. For both of us. Social status, connections and appearances are vitally important, more so now than ever before."

"I see," Lara muttered. With her fears soaring, she rose from the couch. Her hopes suddenly dashed. She should have known to expect the worst. Thrice before she had been rejected immediately after her beaus had discovered the truth about her aunt. Now the same as those other times, she was suddenly no longer "acceptable." It didn't matter how intelligent she was, or what skills and talents she possessed. All that mattered were her lowly connections that could bring nothing but dishonor to anyone associated with her.

Lara remembered those torturous feelings only too well. Each time it had taken what seemed an eternity for her tender heart to stop aching. Although the wounds had healed, the scars remained and she had learned to build and strengthen her walls in protection of her heart. Introductions and invitations had been declined over and over again as she opted to share little of herself when it came to forming new friendships with men. To be so prudent would keep her heart safe. With Kyle, however, she had somehow convinced herself that he was different from the others and that it wouldn't matter to him about Aunt Lyddie. How could she have been so foolish and so very wrong?

Kyle rose, too. He reached out and caught hold of Lara's hand. With his gentle strength, he pulled her to him, but she remained stiff in his arms.

"I'm sorry, Mack. I'm surprised, that's all. It doesn't change how I feel about you." His next words were soft in her ear. "I love you and I want to be with you always. We'll go home to Charleston together. We'll find you a nice room until we're married."

Lara unwrapped his arms from around her waist and stepped away from him. She looked down at the sparkling gem on her finger then closed her eyes in an effort to control the ache growing inside of her. "Why would I need a room?" she asked, her voice melancholy with disappointment. "I've always stayed with Aunt Lyddie."

"Lara, you can't be serious!"

His disbelief was obvious. Standing aloof and hurt, she couldn't listen to any more. "What are you trying to say, Kyle? Do you want me to turn my back on Aunt Lyddie? Do you want me to pass her on the street and not acknowledge her existence? Aunt Lyddie has been everything to me since Mama and Papa died. I can't do that to her. I won't! How can you even ask that of me?"

"Mack, be reasonable. Think of our future and what we could have together."

His last words echoed loudly in her ears. Her anger flared as she listened to his stinging words. How could he accuse her of being unreasonable? Wasn't he the one being unfair and irrational? He had already made up his mind about Aunt Lyddie without first meeting her. How could he make such preconceived judgments based upon malicious gossip and stereotypes? He didn't know the "real" Lydia Randall and how generous and loving a person she truly was.

"We're both wrong, Kyle." Lara's voice trembled low, betraying her hurt and disappointment. "We barely know each other at all." Lara wanted desperately to run from Kyle. She didn't want him to witness the tears that were about to stream down her face. Inside, her heart was breaking, shattered like shards of a crystal vase smashed to the floor. She slipped his ring from her finger and held it out for him. "I can't wear this ring. I can't be the Mrs. Lara Mackenzie Harrison that you want."

Kyle stood motionless, stunned by the sudden turn of events, refusing to take back the ring.

Unable to stand much more, Lara closed her eyes. Be strong, she told herself. She opened her eyes again to meet his gaze. "I'm not the woman for you," she declared, her attempt at a brave front came across only as a weak façade. She placed the diamond solitaire in his hand and flew to the parlor door. Still she was not fast enough. Kyle's strong arm flashed in front of her and braced the door closed.

Lara summoned whatever courage and determination she had left, hoping it would be enough. She turned to face him. Her glistening eyes flashed the turmoil of emotions simmering within her.

"Mack, please! I love you! I know we're meant to be together. We can work this out," Kyle pleaded in desperation.

Lara shook her head. "No, Kyle. Your mother's ring demands too high a price! You're forcing me to choose between you and Aunt Lyddie. She's my only family," Lara choked. Her voice softened. "I have no one left in this world, but her. If you love me true, you wouldn't ask this of me, you couldn't!" She stopped to take a deep, calming breath. With a quick stroke of her hand, she brushed away the tears rolling down her cheeks. "Well, you can go home to Charleston and have your precious career, but I won't be going with you!"

Lara could feel herself rapidly losing her composure. Her eyes, which glowed with love and affection for this man only minutes ago, were now glazed as tears blurred her vision. Abruptly, purposefully, with her head held high, Lara turned away from him. Unfaltering, Lara reached for the door, refusing him completely.

Chapter 2

⚬⚬

A New Life

Savannah, Georgia

Three o'clock. August fifteenth, 1836. More than seven hours had passed since the pains started. Lara's doubts weighed heavier on her mind as she started to lose faith in herself, wondering if she had the strength and stamina to last however much longer this was going to take.

"Deep breaths, Lara. Deep breaths."

Lara responded to the coaching. She exhaled quickly only to draw in a long, cleansing breath. With her eyes closed, she concentrated on Aunt Lyddie's calm and soothing voice. The contractions had become almost unbearable, each growing more intense and lasting longer than the one before. Lara knew there would be little precious time to rest before the next wave would come and seize her body. Then seconds later, and like the times before, it began with the pressure in her back. The wave swept over her becoming ever more painful. Overwhelmed by the urge to bear down, Lara's hands tightened their hold around the spindles of the headboard. She screamed pushing with all her might.

"Harder, Lara!" Aunt Lyddie's voice rang out. "Push the baby out!"

There was an unexpected and powerful burning sensation from within.

"There's the head," the midwife exclaimed. "Hold steady now, child."

Lara panted. Quick, short breaths. She opened her eyes to see her aunt's face hovering above her.

"You're doing just fine," Aunt Lyddie encouraged. "Not much longer now."

"Good girl, Lara! Little pushes now," the midwife coached.

The contractions eased unexpectedly and with a few more pushes Lara felt the baby slip out of her body. Lara, almost to tears, groaned in relief.

"A boy!" Aunt Lyddie cried aloud as she bent down to envelope Lara in her arms. "Lara, you have a son. You have given me a grand nephew!"

The room filled with her son's first cry. Relieved and near total exhaustion, Lara fell back into the bed. The next minutes passed like a haze before the midwife came to place the infant in her arms. Instantly the baby's cry softened. Filled with maternal pride, Lara cuddled her son, kissing him, loving him, keeping him snug and warm against her tired body.

"Try putting him to your breast," Aunt Lyddie urged.

Lara gasped, surprised by the sudden and unexpected pulse that ran through her body when the babe latched onto her breast and began to suckle.

"He's hungry," Aunt Lyddie observed with a laugh. "Have you decided on a name for your son?"

"Gavin William," Lara answered, having chosen both her grandfather and father's first names.

"Gavin William," Aunt Lyddie repeated, beaming with pride. "Your mother and father would be so proud."

Overcome with emotion, happy tears rolled down Lara's face as she continued to stare down in awe, marveling at the very sight of the tiny miracle that lay nestled in her arms. Now forgotten were the endless worries and anxieties that had begun the very moment she had discovered she was pregnant. Would she be able to finish her studies and find work? How was she going to support her child? Such disturbing questions had filled the last eight months of her life, but all of that was put aside for the moment. None of that mattered right now. Nothing, but the health and well-being of her beautiful infant son.

~ · ~

"You must tell him," Aunt Lyddie advised.

Lara sighed. She gazed down into Gavin's little face as he lay sleeping in her arms. She listened to the sound of his breathing, soft and smooth. Since the birth of her son, Lara had come to relish these quiet moments with Gavin, but tonight she was not able to enjoy this time given the bothersome conversation that Aunt Lyddie was insisting on having yet again.

"Aunt Lyddie, I know you mean well, but we've been over this so many times now. Must we go through it again? It really is becoming quite tiresome."

"As Gavin's father, Kyle has every right to know," Aunt Lyddie persisted even knowing there would be no changing Lara's mind. She could tell by the crease upon her niece's brow that she was pushing Lara to the limits of her patience.

"No," Lara replied firmly, keeping her voice down so as not to disturb her son. "He gave up that right when he made me choose. Why, Aunt Lyddie, are you so insistent on my telling him when he was the one forcing me to turn away from you? I have given this serious thought time and time again. There is nothing good that could come of him knowing."

"Your son needs a father. Kyle can provide for Gavin and for you."

"We'll be fine on our own."

"Lara, you barely have time to tutor the few students you have. Even with that, you're not making enough to support the two of you. You can't keep this up. You'll wear yourself ragged."

"We'll manage," Lara responded stubbornly.

"Write Kyle a letter," Aunt Lyddie suggested. "I will personally deliver it into his hands when I return to Charleston."

Lara shook her head in refusal. "Why would he want anything to do with me now? If status and connections were so important to him nine months ago, don't you think they would be even more so now that he has become Manager of one of the largest banks in the Carolinas?"

"Lara, you have given him a son. That's not anything a responsible man would take lightly."

"You're right," Lara declared. "He's bound to take such matters seriously. Think of what would happen to his career once it becomes known that he has fathered a bastard child with the niece of Charleston's best known madame. Do you think he would let anything jeopardize his career and good reputation? No, Aunt Lyddie, you would be wrong to think that he would open his heart and take us in. Just as I was wrong in believing he would come to accept you for what you are."

"You don't know that for certain. Kyle Harrison is an honorable man."

"I have my pride," Lara's voice faltered under the emotions churning inside. "I refuse to go begging on his doorstep with our son in my arms."

"I would never suggest such a thing. All I'm saying is that Kyle has a right to know that he has fathered a child. Tell him about Gavin. Give Kyle a chance, Lara. I know you still love him. Perhaps—"

"Please, Aunt Lyddie," Lara begged, her eyes glistening with tears. "Don't give me false hope!"

"I beg you to think of Gavin."

"And I beg you to think of both of us! If Kyle were to find out he has a son, he may want to claim Gavin as his own and he would have every legal right to. If I didn't have Gavin in my life, I would have nothing. He dulls the ache inside and comforts my soul. He brings purpose to my life and fills my anxious heart. I love him more than anything else in this world and I couldn't bear it if he was taken from me."

Aunt Lyddie reached for Lara's hand. Softly she spoke, "That could still happen should Kyle ever find out on his own."

Lara looked into her aunt's dark brown eyes. "Then he must never find out. Please Aunt Lyddie, promise me you won't ever tell Kyle."

~ . ~

With her father's violin nestled comfortably under her chin, Lara ran the bow across the stringed instrument. The notes to a normally lively waltz, the one she and Kyle had first danced to, had been purposely slowed to a softer melody. Like many times before, the soothing tones were enough to lull Gavin into a deep slumber, and to ease some of Lara's own frustrations after that last heated discussion with Aunt Lyddie.

Lara was ten years old when Linette Kendrick decided it was time to introduce her daughter to music. With a violin in William Kendrick's possession, the stringed instrument was the most economical choice. After several months of informal study and practice, the Kendricks found their daughter a more knowledgeable teacher. Immediately the young child showed improvement within a more formal setting and rigid structure. Although Lara had never proven herself to possess great musical talent, she was able to give an acceptable representation of many of the more familiar violin sonatas. After the death of her parents, Lara would often spend hours alone playing her father's violin. It mattered not how well she performed her renditions, for more important was the comfort in hearing the music for it took her back to the happier times spent with her parents.

This particular piece of music, though, held memories of a different time and of a different kind of love. What a romantic gesture for Kyle to have purchased the sheet music for her shortly after Irina's wedding. Lara had learned the piece, each and every note taken to memory just as with each moment of that first dance with Kyle. Lately though, these once sweet notes no longer seemed to hold the same soul and essence as they did before. The naïve innocence of a young love had been erased with the somber responsibilities of raising a child without his father.

Lara set aside the stringed instrument. At Gavin's crib, Lara placed a blanket over her sleeping son. She bent down to place a tender kiss upon Gavin's forehead and brushed her hand over his tiny head, barely touching him for fear of waking the child. His hair was fine and soft. Like down. Blonde. Like Kyle's. Her eyes started to fill with tears and her heart ached with regret as she thought of how things might have been and what kind of future she and Gavin might have had with Kyle. Be strong, she encouraged herself. Be strong!

With half-hearted determination, Lara brushed the tears away before they could roll down her face. She picked up her music only to crumple the sheet into a ball and toss it into the wastebasket. Never would she play those notes again!

Chapter 3

∞

The Last Breath

Charleston, South Carolina
April, 1841

Kyle Harrison sat on the edge of the four-poster bed. He held firmly onto Lydia Randall's hand. It was warm, but limp. By means of this small gesture he was hoping that she was aware of his being there and that she would find some comfort in his presence. She continued to lie unceasingly still, her face ashen. The only sign of life came from her breathing and that had become more labored over these last few hours. *Any time now.* The prognosis from Dr. Daniels ran through Kyle's head as he waited for that tragic moment. These, he realized, would be Lyddie's last moments here in this world.

There came a gentle rap upon the bedroom door, then a low creak as it slowly opened wide. Kyle acknowledged Captain Dane Haley's presence with a silent nod.

"Any change?" The sea captain's footsteps sounded overly loud as he walked to the other side of the bed. A glance at Lyddie and the sound of her troubled breath was enough to tell him that her condition had deteriorated in the few short hours since he had left her side.

"It's not good, Dane," Kyle answered, shaking his head.

"Did she wake at all?"

"Not once. The doctor was here three-quarters of an hour ago. He tried rousing her, but she only opened her eyes for a few seconds."

Lyddie's glazed and hollow look would remain with Kyle forever. It seemed she didn't even notice Dr. Daniels. Her eyes had rolled upwards to the heavens for the few moments before she closed them again. It was as though she was already in the other world. Only her body lingered, not yet ready to let her spirit move on.

"Have all the arrangements been made?" Kyle asked the captain.

"The ship and crew are ready to sail upon a day's notice. We'll leave for Savannah immediately after the funeral. It will surely be a hard task telling Lara. My letter only mentioned that Lyddie was ill. I never thought to prepare her for this."

"You couldn't have known her condition would turn so harsh and so quickly. It even surprised Dr. Daniels."

"There is the very good chance that Lara will decide not to come," Dane contemplated aloud so as to prepare Kyle for the possibility of disappointment.

"She will," Kyle responded, but only to reassure himself before discarding the dismal thought altogether.

Over the years Kyle had been able to build a solid, trusting friendship with both Lyddie and Dane, and yet neither one had shared Lara's whereabouts with him despite his many pleas. In those first six months since his return to Charleston, Kyle had painstakingly scripted three letters to Lara. Each had been a heartfelt attempt to solicit some response, but none came. It was through Adam and Irina that Kyle eventually discovered that Lara had abandoned Brooklyn City within weeks of his own departure. Where Lara had disappeared to had remained a mystery and it was only Irina's best guess that her friend might have returned to Savannah. With that slight possibility Kyle had initiated a search, but over a span of several months his contacts reported no signs of anyone by the name of Lara Kendrick.

Yes, thought Kyle, Lyddie's death will shatter Lara's world. Lyddie is the last of Lara's family and he would never forget how much she loved her aunt.

Kyle left Lyddie's bedside to reclaim the armchair by the window. From this corner he watched as the sea captain fussed over Lyddie. It was an odd sight to see such a tall, muscular man perform the loving task of smoothing out the bed linens and tucking the blankets in around her. There was a pained expression on the captain's face. It was proof of how difficult it was for him to bear witness to her death. Kyle watched as Dane brushed back a long strand of Lyddie's auburn hair before taking a gentle hold of her hand. How helpless he must feel, hopelessly waiting and watching his beloved slip away. Realizing there was nothing more he could do for her, Dane allowed himself to settle into the chair beside the bed.

Kyle, too, followed Dane's lead and relaxed into the comfort of his own chair. Once again his thoughts turned to Lyddie's finances. Methodically he accounted for each of her assets in his head. Since the fall of 1837 he had been able to slowly rebuild her portfolio of stocks and bonds. It had astonished him when she had approached him a few years ago to ask his help in saving her investments. He had thought to refuse her at first, but realized that a relationship with Lyddie might, sooner or later, provide him with the opportunity of seeing Lara again. To secure such good fortune was more than he could hope for, but never had he thought nor wanted it to be Lyddie's death that might bring his lost love back to him. He had grown immensely fond of Lyddie these last four years and he would miss her dearly. He will surely feel Lara's loss.

Kyle had worked with Duncan Whitelock, Lyddie's solicitor, to prepare everything as Lyddie had directed. But what of the terms? Without any doubt he knew Lara would not be pleased, but would she abide by her aunt's last wishes or defy them and give up everything that Lyddie worked so hard for?

Although Kyle was not privy to all that was in Lyddie's will, he did have a good idea of how her financial assets were to be distributed. There would be monetary gifts to the orphanage and to the hospital, but the bulk of the estate would surely go to Lara. The construction of a new home on Wentworth Street had been completed a few weeks before Lyddie's death. In addition to her investment portfolio, there was a sizeable amount of money held with the Planters Bank of South Carolina, and an overly impressive collection of flowing gowns and sparkling jewels. Then there was the brothel. Lord, what would Lara do with the brothel!

Kyle's eyes were drawn, like many times during his vigil, to the portrait of aunt and niece hung above the fireplace mantle. The likeness of Lyddie was remarkably true. The artist had captured her natural beauty and revealed her wondrous spirit in her expression. The younger Lara too, he thought. Even though she couldn't have been more than fifteen when the portrait was painted, there were features captured in the image that were distinctly Lara: the curve of the girl's smile; the tilt of her head; and those beautiful, round chestnut eyes which hinted at some mischievous play. Perhaps aunt and niece had shared a private joke while posing for the artist. In coming to know Lyddie, he had learned that the two women were, in many ways, much like mother and daughter; and in others, more like sisters. There was an unbreakable bond between aunt and niece. He had learned that first hand. That, too, he would never forget.

Kyle closed his eyes to rest. The sound of Lyddie's breathing invaded his thoughts. Each breath was heavy and erratic. Then abruptly, a loud silence filled the room and Kyle was forced to open his eyes. Immediately, Kyle knew. The feeling of dread cut deeper when he saw Dane leaning over the lifeless body to place one last tender kiss upon her forehead. Lydia Randall was gone.

Chapter 4

Charleston Again

Charleston, South Carolina! Mrs. Lara Mackenzie Quinn took in a deep breath of cool sea air. She was thankful that the journey from Savannah was finally at an end. Dressed in black silk grenadine, Lara stood out among the bustling crowd. She stepped forward and turned toward the water in an effort to ignore the curious looks cast her way by the strangers rushing about their business along the quay. Her dark mourning garb reflected her somber mood. She was weary and emotionally spent and wanted nothing more than the comfort of a hot meal taken in some quiet, cozy corner.

In part her fatigue could be explained by her sea journey. She had boarded the *Southern Belle* at an uncivilized early morning hour. For the entire voyage, Lara was restricted, by the rough seas and the wet and windy weather, to the cheerless confines of a cabin, cramped and cold. With only her rambling thoughts to keep her company, Lara found herself growing increasingly restless as they sailed ever closer to Charleston. Nagging anxieties continued to torment her as she fretted over what was awaiting her. She had left so much behind in Savannah. Only time will prove as to whether or not her decision to return to Charleston to claim her inheritance was a wise one. No matter, she told herself, the choice had been made and the voyage was now over. She would have to make the best of it!

A rumbling drowned out her thoughts and within seconds a carriage pulled up beside her. Captain Dane Haley jumped down. Family friend and overseer of the Warren Enterprises merchant ships and storehouses, he had captained the *Southern Belle* to Savannah to deliver the sudden and unexpected news of the death of her Aunt Lyddie. As he finalized the shipment of goods to be transported back to Charleston, Lara struggled to make her decision as to whether or not to return with the captain. Dane had been patient. With the cargo loaded and the ship and crew ready to sail, it was to be another three days before Lara forced herself to make her decision. In the end, she found herself rushing to make the necessary arrangements.

"Here we are again." Lara gave her aunt's long time friend and confidant a faint smile. "It seems the task keeps falling upon you to bring me back to Charleston."

"Perhaps this is where you belong," Dane braved. He knew of the countless times Lyddie had tried to convince Lara to return and that those same discussions often ended in anger and frustration for both women. He was never told why it was such a contentious issue between the aunt and niece. He only knew that it had been Lyddie's endless wish to have Lara with her.

"You know I have other responsibilities," Lara replied, her fatigue evident in her voice.

"You do," Dane acknowledged, wisely choosing not to say another word. "I think a room at The Charlestown Hotel would do well enough for you."

"I'd like to go by the cemetery."

"You must be tired. A rest would do you good," Dane suggested.

"I'll rest more easily after the cemetery."

With that, Dane gave the driver instructions before loading Lara's luggage onto the carriage.

"I'm sorry I can't come along," Dane apologized. "I have the ship and the cargo to tend to. Captain's duties, I'm afraid."

"Of course," Lara acknowledged, her voice confident and filled with understanding. "I'll be fine on my own."

"I should be finished by midday tomorrow. Why don't you come by the warehouses and we can have lunch together?"

The frenzy of activity on the wharves prevented nothing more than a slow walk of the horses. Nor was their pace much faster as the carriage rolled down Church Street and through the business district to the Baptist Church located at the far end of the city. During the long ride Lara's thoughts came to settle upon her aunt.

Lara had learned of her aunt's profession shortly before coming to live in Charleston. Lara was eleven years old when dengue fever erupted in Savannah. Wide spreading of the disease and panic drove Linette Kendrick to send her daughter to live temporarily with her twin sister in Charleston. Lara remembered the heated discussions between her parents for William Kendrick could not bear the thought of having his only child in the care of a Madame and living in a whorehouse. But Linette knew of the extreme circumstances that had forced her twin sister to make the decisions she did. Fate had not been kind to Lydia Randall. First came the sudden death of a loving husband after four short years of marriage. Left penniless, she fell mistress to an unscrupulous gambler. That same black Irish rogue would later abandon her and his own son in the unfamiliar port city of Charleston. She didn't have the heart to turn her back on the boy and soon became desperate to find some means for the two of them to survive.

As the fever raged on, William gave in to his wife's pleas, but only after he himself fell ill. With the city under the threat of quarantine, Linette Kendrick pleaded with a sea captain to escort their daughter out of Savannah. Captain Dane Haley had relented and the frightened young child was sent off to her aunt in Charleston. Afterwards Lara had received only two letters from her mother, but never saw or heard from her parents again.

It was soon after that Lara came to realize that her parents were two among the hundreds that died from the outbreak.

Lara and Lyddie had provided each other with the comfort and support each needed upon the deaths of Lara's parents. Lyddie had lost a cherished sister with whom she shared a bond that only twins could comprehend. She found in Lara someone to care for, to watch grow, to love. She had showered the young Lara with as much love and attention as any mother would her own beloved child. No expense was spared in the raising of her only surviving relation. Lessons in dance, violin and etiquette were arranged easily enough. And when the proper time came, Lyddie sent Lara off to the Brooklyn Female Seminary in New York state for the best education her money could buy. Lara's visits home to Charleston were made as often as possible and these were always filled with fun-filled days of shopping, dances, concerts and theatre.

During these times Lara would learn valuable people skills from her aunt as the older woman interacted daily with all classes of Charleston society. The brothel gave Lyddie the opportunity of honing her social skills, and she was able to deal with even the most boorish and narrow-minded of individuals with great tact and diplomacy. This setting also allowed her to make important contacts with influential men from the economic and political spheres. Lara knew the brothel had paid for her lifestyle and education, and had provided her with many opportunities and experiences that would not otherwise have been afforded. Thus aunt and niece came to rely on each other in more ways than one, and certainly in every way that mattered most as family.

Lara's thoughts were interrupted when the carriage came to a full stop after pulling in front of the church. Now wandering through the graveyard in search of her Aunt Lyddie, an eerie feeling settled in. Her eyes were drawn to the death's head tombstones that marked the graves dating back to the Revolutionary War. She found these carved depictions difficult to ignore for it seemed as if the skeletal skull images were watching her every move. As a young child Lara had been struck with fear the first time she saw such a morbid pictograph. To calm her daughter, Linette Kendrick had pointed out the angel wings and explained that they carried the righteous soul of the deceased into heaven above. Lara's fears were appeased somewhat by her mother's tale, but the skull and cross bones still left her with a feeling of dread that never completely disappeared.

Lara found her beloved Aunt Lyddie buried under the protective cover of a sprawling magnolia tree. Her grave was impressively marked with a large granite gravestone. Lara felt the heavy weight of the precisely carved words and it took several moments filled with calming breaths before she could bring herself to read them: *Lydia Auclair Randall. Born 1792. Died 1841. A woman of love, life and laughter.* Until now, it seemed she had been living a nightmare, but kneeling before Aunt Lyddie's grave and staring down at the crystalline rock, Lara came to feel the hard truth, to know finally that she was living in a world without her precious Aunt Lyddie. Her heart ached with her loss. Lara dropped her head and, for the first time since hearing of her aunt's death, tears began to stream down her face.

~ · ~

Lara shivered. She had not been able to warm herself after her graveside visit and now the air seemed much cooler under the sprawling canopy of the live oaks. She peered out the coach window. Her eyes, still red from crying, became fixed upon the plantation house as it came into view at the far end of the lane. Haven Manor. After six years, Lara was finally home! But what little anticipation or excitement she felt faded quickly as the carriage emerged from the cover of the trees and out into the open expanse of the homesite.

Lara's heart sank even more as she took in the scene before her. The large dwelling stood cold and unwelcoming with no heart and no soul. Dried leaves, broken branches and twigs lay scattered about the neglected yard. Weeds grew amidst the camellia and rosebushes that were once highly prized by her aunt. The plantation white paint on the house had dulled, beaten by a long, harsh winter. A film of dirt clouded the glass panes of the picture windows. Their heavy drapes had been drawn together to hide all that was inside from spying eyes.

The carriage had barely come to a full stop before Lara threw open the carriage door. Immediately her eyes were drawn to a notice posted on the front entrance. The starch white of the paper was a brilliant contrast to the mahogany wood. Even before reaching the top of the porch steps, she was able to make out the large bolded print at the top of the poster. She came closer to glare at the words: *By Order of the Planters Bank of South Carolina.* Lara stood aghast. Haven Manor had been repossessed!

Lara gasped upon reading the date upon the notice. Her disbelief was immediately replaced with a furious rage as she realized that Haven Manor had been seized the day after her aunt's death. Why? Who? Lara stormed up to the entrance and clawed at the notice. She broke a fingernail as she stripped the poster from the door. The tearing sounds seemed overly loud as she tore the paper apart. Her hands worked the pieces into a crumpled ball before she threw it hard against the portico floor.

~ · ~

The ornately carved clock in the lobby of The Charlestown Hotel struck eight as Lara strolled down the sweeping staircase. There was not much activity in the reception area, but she could hear the faint drone of the music emanating from the hotel dining room. It was long past the dinner hour and Lara was looking forward to a hearty meal to satisfy the hunger inside her.

"Good evening," the Maitre d'Hotel greeted her as she entered the dining room. "My name is Michael. I am your host this evening."

Lara responded with a sweet smile. "Thank you, Michael. I'm Mrs. Quinn."

"We're pleased to have you join us. Have you dined with us before?"

"Yes, many times. Your restaurant was a favorite of my aunt's, Mrs. Lydia Randall."

"Ah, yes, Mrs. Randall. I'm sorry for your loss," the man offered with sincerity. "Mrs. Randall came often and we enjoyed having her."

"She enjoyed dining at a particular table overlooking the dance floor."

"Yes, she did. Let me see if it's available."

Seated comfortably at her aunt's favorite table after placing her food order, Lara sat back to observe the crowd. Like her aunt, Lara had always enjoyed watching people. She would observe their movements, expressions and mannerisms. She would often try to guess their occupations and where they hailed from. Lara's table was strategically positioned for doing just that. From her seat, she could see the whole of the dance floor, the tables along the side, and at the other end of the room. Tonight, however, she was in no mood to sit and watch. Instead she concentrated on her meal, allowing the fruity wine and the flavorful cuisine to energize her body and lift her sullen spirits.

As Lara struggled with the last bite of her meal, she noticed a couple that had strolled out onto the dance floor. The woman was petite and beautiful. Her hair shone a deep, honey gold against her ivory-toned skin. Even from this distance her eyes sparkled with life as her partner offered his hand to lead her into a waltz. Tall and proud, the gentleman swept her across the dance floor. They stepped in unison to the swaying rhythm of the melodic waltz. A shadow of a smile grew on Lara's face as she continued to watch the charming pair. How romantic!

Another couple swept into Lara's view. The woman's expression immediately touched Lara's heart. The twinkle in her pretty eyes and the adoration in her smile declared her affections for her partner. The young woman was vibrant and beautiful. The pair stepped into a turn and Lara found herself looking directly into the face of Kyle Garrett Harrison. Lara sat frozen, stunned as her eyes met his over his partner's shoulder. Paralyzed by those piercing blue eyes, Lara's pulse raced while she waited long seconds not knowing if Kyle would recognize her. Suddenly his eyes grew wide with recognition and he stumbled, having lost his concentration and timing with the music.

Barely regaining her senses, Lara fumbled through her purse in search of the coins to pay for her dinner. Hurriedly, she dropped the money on the table and she rose quickly to abandon the room.

"Mack!"

Lara's heart jumped and she stopped. Kyle's voice was unexpectedly recognizable. Frantic, her thoughts were a jumbled mess. With nowhere to run, Lara turned to see him rushing towards her, his strides long, quick, purposeful.

Lara had forgotten how intense Kyle's blue eyes could be as he stared at her in disbelief. His wavy, ash-blonde hair had been cut to a more fashionable, shorter length and swept neatly back. His face had grown leaner, but that only seemed to accentuate its fine, chiseled lines. Indeed, his features were now more pronounced, giving him a more rugged look than the few years before. He was still roguishly handsome! No doubt he could still make a woman's heart flutter wildly and send her into a dither with only a casual glance her way. And not just any woman, but her as well!

"Welcome home, Mack," came Kyle's greeting.

Her middle name sounded foreign for it had been a terribly long time since anyone had so endearingly called her "Mack". At a loss for words, she needed another moment or two to collect her thoughts and regain control of her emotions. She had spent the last five years and seven months trying to forget everything about Kyle Harrison: his deep, smooth voice; his tall, muscular form; his searching blue eyes; and that dimpled smile that had a way of melting her heart. Now, standing before him, she realized how futile her efforts had been. Unforgettable! Everything about Kyle Garrett Harrison was unforgettable.

"Good evening, Kyle," Lara surprised herself by managing a simple greeting, her voice calm and controlled.

"When did you arrive in Charleston?" Kyle placed his hands upon her shoulders to draw her into his embrace.

Lara stiffened; his touch too sudden and too intimate.

Surprised by her reaction, Kyle quickly released her. "How have you been, Lara?" he asked, hoping he didn't upset her.

"Is everything alright, Mrs. Quinn?" Michael came forward upon witnessing Lara's hurried exit. Concerned that her meal or their service had not been to her satisfaction, he felt compelled to make sure nothing had gone wrong.

Instantly, the smile disappeared from Kyle's face. A knife pierced into his heart could not have been more agonizing for him than to hear Lara so formally addressed as the wife of another man.

"It was a fine meal, Michael. Thank you." Lara then turned towards Kyle. "I've been well." She answered most politely. "I see that Charleston has been good to you."

"Mrs. Quinn?" Kyle asked, barely able to utter her name.

Lara surrendered her weakest smile. She had no intention of offering any more information and an awkward silence followed.

Kyle forced himself to discard the heartbreaking notions running through his head and to concentrate on the moment at hand. "Lara, I'm… I'm having dinner with friends. Will you allow me to introduce you? And your husband, of course."

Lara glanced across the dining room to the other side where Kyle's companions sat watching the two of them with great interest. She recognized the first dancing couple, both with curious looks upon their faces while the delicate blonde wore a more troubled expression.

"I'm here alone," Lara confirmed. "I'm sorry, Kyle. I've had a very long and exhausting trip. I would make a better first impression if I were to meet your friends another time." There was another brief period of awkward silence while Lara waited for Kyle to say something, anything. "How are things at the State Bank?" Lara finally asked.

Kyle smiled broadly, pleased that she had remembered the posting that had brought him home. "Actually, I'm with the Planters Bank now."

"The Planters Bank of South Carolina?"

"Yes, going on two—"

"You couldn't have waited until Aunt Lyddie was buried before taking Haven Manor! How could you be so heartless?"

Lara turned and took steps to leave, but Kyle reached out to catch her by the arm.

"Lara, wait." He couldn't let her go. Not like this.

"Money and profit come first! Is that the kind of reputation you've made for yourself?" Lara glared down at his hand firm around her arm. "Let go of me!" she demanded, and she wrenched her arm free. Her voice was loud enough to turn heads from across the room.

Kyle became aware of all the eyes suddenly watching them. Standing helplessly, he could only watch as Lara fled the room.

~ · ~

Lara lay huddled beneath the bed covers as she watched the flames in the fireplace that warmed her hotel room. Oh, how she loved the way the flames danced! She glanced up to the pewter picture frame placed on the bedside table. The portrait was enough to bring a smile to her face and ease her frustrations. She had been away from her son for less than twenty-four hours and already she was missing him dearly. As she stared at Gavin's image, she realized again how naïve and foolishly hopeless it had been for her to try to forget Kyle. Gavin has those very same blue eyes. And the soft, ash-blonde hair. Gavin had inherited that too. As a baby, as a toddler, and even more so now as a young boy, his image was growing more like that of his father each day. Gavin, she thought, her son and Kyle's son. Would she be able to find the courage to finally tell Kyle the truth about Gavin?

Lara felt tired in body and weak in spirit. Yet as drained as she was, Lara could not fall asleep. There were too many vivid images and restless thoughts running rampant through her head. She felt fretful and anxious over the day's events. These left her with the same jumbled mix of emotions as did those disturbing thoughts upon the *Southern Belle*.

Seeing Kyle for the first time since Brooklyn City had evoked such a bizarre rush of emotions. These emotions raged war against reason and logic. She had not expected her heart to begin racing when she caught sight of him, or to lose her ability to think rationally when he called out her name. Even after all these years he was still able to hold her captive by casting a glance her way. Such tendencies were reserved for sweethearts, were they not? Such feelings for him should have faded away long ago. If there was anything left, it could only be regret and disappointment in herself for allowing him into her heart. Still though, Lara was not able to close her mind to their last night together in Brooklyn City. Those memories and emotions had taken years to banish to the darkest corners of her heart and mind. Now they all came flooding back, the plagues of her own Pandora's box released. From these there would be no sanctuary, no place to hide.

And then she had overreacted in the dining room downstairs. She should have had better control of herself when she discovered Kyle was with the Planters Bank. Could it be that there was little left of Aunt Lyddie's estate? She had to have defaulted on more than one payment for Kyle to have had the legal right to repossess Haven Manor.

Lara lay exhausted, surrounded by the solitude of yet another unfamiliar room. She remembered childhood nights like this when sleep had been difficult. Aunt Lyddie would cuddle up with her on a long chaise and the two would whittle away the time with endless chatter until Lara finally drifted off into a restful slumber. Long gone were those innocent days. Now there was no one here to listen to her ramblings, to calm her doubts and fears, and no one to share her dreams with. Sleep might come if she could somehow shut out her unrelenting thoughts of Gavin, Kyle and Aunt Lyddie. But they were never-ending. Gavin, Kyle, Aunt Lyddie. Ceaseless. Gavin, Kyle and Aunt Lyddie. Suddenly Lara's strength and courage crumbled. Tears flooded her eyes again and her mournful crying broke the silence of the room.

~ · ~

It seemed a long carriage ride back to the Landrey plantation. Morgan Landrey sat fiddling with the strings of her handbag. She had been waiting ever so patiently for Kyle to volunteer an explanation of the events at dinner. However, he seemed lost in his thoughts and unwilling to offer any sort of explanation. After a few unsuccessful attempts at conversation, Morgan finally forced the topic upon him.

"Lara is a friend from Brooklyn City," Kyle offered.

"From that scene I would think otherwise," Morgan suggested. "Indeed one might get the impression that the two of you shared much more than friendship."

There was a thoughtful pause from Kyle. It was late and he was not in the mood to have to explain anything to Morgan, but he owed her at least that and perhaps it would be best to take advantage of the opportunity.

Kyle held her gaze as he formulated his thoughts with good intentions to tell her everything. "Adam and Irina Toews introduced me to Lara at their wedding. That was almost six years ago. Lara and I discovered that we had much in common and, yes, our friendship did grow into something more."

"In what way?" Morgan asked, wanting to know everything about him and Lara.

"I had asked her to marry me."

Morgan sat back. The shock of his declaration showed clearly on her face. She had not dared to think it had been as serious as an engagement.

"You were in love with her," Morgan realized. She couldn't bring herself to ask what next came to mind for fear of hearing the answer she would not be able to accept. Later though, she would regret letting the opportunity pass for she would be wondering incessantly if he was still in love with Lara Quinn, even if the woman was now married.

"But you didn't marry. Why not?"

"Lara Quinn is Lydia Randall's niece. I was making preparations to come home to accept the manager's position at the State Bank of South Carolina. My banking career was just starting and I didn't think I could jeopardize it by having a wife with such a connection."

"Naturally," Morgan responded, able to understand his reasoning. "So you broke off your engagement."

"I was selfish. I asked Lara to sever all ties with her aunt and she refused. She was the one who rejected me."

"She didn't love you enough. She's a fool," Morgan scoffed. "She didn't deserve you."

Having enough of the conversation, Kyle turned away from Morgan. He pondered her last words as he stared out into the night, but he knew better. He was the fool! It wasn't Lara who didn't deserve him, but he who didn't deserve Lara!

~ · ~

Back at home in the solitude of his own bedroom, Kyle opened the top drawer of his tall chest and pulled out a velvet pouch. From amongst the jewelry items inside, he withdrew his mother's wedding ring, the same band which he had once offered Lara. The solitaire twinkled in the soft light as he turned to see the engraved initials, now LMH, on the inside.

The day after he had proposed, the day after their wicked quarrel, Kyle had taken the ring to a jeweler to have Lara's first initial placed in front of his mother's. He was quite persistent, almost rude to the craftsman, insisting that the work be completed immediately while he waited. Kyle's intention had been to win Lara back by presenting the band to her again. She would not have refused him once he apologized, and not after seeing her own initials inscribed on his mother's ring. She would have realized how remorseful he was and all would have been made right again. As bad luck would have it, he had never been granted the opportunity.

Kyle walked back to his chair and placed the ring on the side table. He picked up his glass carefully so as not to spill a drop of the scotch whiskey that had been poured almost to the rim. He took a long hard swallow before sinking into the chair. There he sat brooding, the ring a constant reminder of what could have been. He had waited years for Lara to come home to Charleston. Waiting for the chance to make amends with the hope of rekindling that lost love. How surreal it was to turn and find Lara seated at a dinner table. If that had not been enough of a shock, it was when he discovered she now belonged to another. "Mrs. Lara Mackenzie Quinn," he muttered aloud. He scowled. The thought of Lara in love with another man, and the thought of her making love to someone else - both were unbearable.

Of course, he realized, that's why his contacts couldn't find Lara in Savannah! They were looking for "Lara Kendrick" and not "Lara Quinn." All this time, she was no more than a hundred miles away. Why hadn't Lyddie told him Lara had married? Lyddie knew he was still madly in love with Lara and he would have done anything to win her back. Why did she let him keep on hoping?

Money and profit come first. The sting of Lara's words drove deep into Kyle's conscience. He had worried that, upon returning to Charleston, Lara would venture out to Haven Manor. There she would have seen the notice posted on all the doors. As he had predicted, she would have felt as betrayed and angry as that last night they spent together in Brooklyn City. All through these last few years he had dared to hope that her anger would have dissipated enough to allow for reconciliation as friends if nothing more. Had this deed eliminated the chance for even that? If only he had been given the chance to deliver the unwelcome news himself.

To make matters worse, Lara would soon discover that he was to have a controlling interest in all her financial affairs. She will think he's invaded her life and will come to despise him for this, too. No doubt her husband would also have a few harsh words to say about it. Suddenly Lyddie's final instructions made no logical sense. What had she been thinking? What could have possessed her? Kyle had made Lyddie a promise and now there was no way of getting out of what would surely be the most awkward of situations. Why had she chosen him instead of Lara's husband? Confused and filled with new doubts, Kyle shook his head and took another swallow of scotch.

What had Lara told her husband, if anything, about the times they shared in Brooklyn City? How would he ever be able to look the man in the eyes and shake his hand? Kyle stared down at his mother's ring and thought again of the initials engraved inside.

"Lord," Kyle muttered to himself, "what a bloody mess!"

Chapter 5

Duncan's Advice

$\mathcal{I}$t was six-ten in the morning when Lara woke to the sound of rain. She extended her arms and legs into an arched stretch as a deep yawn escaped her. Before rising, Lara reached for the picture frame on the bedside table to give her son a silent good morning greeting.

Wrapping herself in a blanket, Lara went to the window. She opened it wide and immediately nature's own distinct fresh and clean scent filled her nostrils as the lightest breeze caressed her cheeks. High above, grey powder-puff clouds rolled out towards the sea and a patch of light blue sky could be seen on the horizon. Even at this early morning hour, the streets below were busy as farmers' wagons rolled down the cobblestone streets. All were loaded and ready to supply the local merchants with fresh produce and dairy products. Shiny coaches carried well-to-do planters through the business district. More wagons followed, each heavily laden with supplies, tools and slaves as they rumbled through the streets. Slowly the people of Charleston – black and white, free and bonded – emerged from their homes to begin another day.

Now rested and in much better spirits than the night before, Lara puttered about her room at a leisurely pace. She took extra care with her attire for she intended to make a strong first impression with the people she was planning to see. She positioned her bonnet and veil carefully before donning the black lace gloves. Giving her cheeks a good pinch, Lara took one last critical look in the tall mirror. She wrinkled her nose at her reflection. She had come to despise the color black and it was only out of deep respect for her aunt that she continued to wear the drab mourning garb.

"It won't be for much longer," she told herself.

Lara entered the lobby when a large mantle clock chimed once for half past seven. The manager greeted her with a broad, infectious smile when she approached the front desk. His eyes gleamed through the lenses of his small, wire-framed eyeglasses. Even the most serious or discontented patron would not be able to ignore such a cheerful welcome.

"Did you have a pleasant night, Mrs. Quinn?"

"Yes, thank you, Mr. Gilmore. I have several errands about town planned for today and I was hoping there might be a carriage available."

"In fact there is. Mr. Harrison has reserved one for you. He thought it might be stuffy in a coach and had arranged for a small landau instead."

"Mr. Harrison was by this morning?" Lara stopped, unsure of what to make of Kyle's initiative on her behalf.

"Yes, Ma'am, he came by bright and early for a breakfast meeting and stopped to make the arrangements. Shall I have the shay brought around for you?"

Lara's first stop was at the legal offices of Whitelock and Lane. Although Dane had traveled to Savannah to inform Lara personally of her aunt's death, he had also carried with him a letter from Duncan Whitelock, Aunt Lyddie's solicitor. Along with the formal condolences, the letter stated matter-of-factly that Lara had been named as one of the heirs to Lydia Randall's estate. Lara had been advised to make an immediate trip to Charleston to claim her inheritance and initiate the transfer of holdings.

Lara had expected a quick stop with the intention of only making an appointment with Duncan Whitelock. Instead she was surprised when his clerk announced her arrival and then ushered her into the lawyer's office. The introductions and preliminary chitchat lasted longer than necessary for Duncan took a bit of extra time to get to know his new client.

Lara guessed that Duncan was nearing his sixties. His relaxed attitude and good humor seemed to contradict his meticulously formal appearance, as well as his tidy and comfortable surroundings. He seemed to possess a keen sense of awareness and Lara soon became aware of his sharp, inquisitive mind. With a bit of levity and tact, he was able to delve past Lara's general comments for more specific information without making her feel ill at ease. Lara knew that Duncan was one of Aunt Lyddie's most trusted friends and soon there was no doubt in Lara's mind that her aunt's interests, and now her own, would be well served by this man.

"Where are you staying, Lara?" Duncan asked.

"I'm at The Charlestown Hotel. I had hoped to be at Haven Manor, but I stopped by yesterday only to find it boarded up."

The hint of disappointment in her voice was not lost on Duncan. "Yes, the bank has taken possession," Duncan confirmed.

"I was hoping I could start packing away Aunt Lyddie's things. There were also a few personal items and some bits of furniture I would like to retrieve. Mostly sentimental. Do you think the bank will allow that?"

"The Planters Bank should have no objections to you taking clothing, personal papers and such, although the furniture might be a different matter. Leave it with me. I'll see what I can arrange for you."

Duncan's offer came with a sense of relief. She was grateful that he had offered to deal with Kyle and the bank on her behalf. "What will happen to Haven Manor now?"

"The Planters Bank will put the land and buildings up for auction."

"Is it too late to make good on the overdue payments?" Lara asked.

"I'm sure the bank would allow it, but you would be required to pay the interest and the arrears before taking over the mortgage debt. It's a considerable sum," Duncan forewarned, as if advising against it. "But, depending on your plans for the future, it would be wise to consider all options. Mr. Quinn and your son, Gavin, did not accompany you?"

"No, as a horse-breeder it's a busy time for Aidan on the ranch, and I didn't think it necessary to bring Gavin. Should they be here?"

Duncan answered only with a silent tilt of his head.

"Aidan would have no claim over any of Aunt Lyddie's estate, but your letter mentioned that I'm only one of Aunt Lyddie's heirs. Did she remember Gavin?"

"Gavin William Kendrick is mentioned in your aunt's will. As is his father, Kyle Harrison."

Lara was taken aback that Duncan knew of her secret. "In what way?" she asked cautiously, wondering exactly how much Aunt Lyddie had revealed to Duncan.

"That will be made clear during the reading of your aunt's will." Duncan placed a firm hand over Lara's. "My dear, if there is anything you need to have settled with Kyle Harrison, I advise you do so before we execute Lyddie's will."

Lara's silence gave away her fears as she gazed into Duncan's cool, green eyes. "I believe Aunt Lyddie has told you quite a bit about my circumstances."

"Your private matters, as they pertain to your aunt's requests, were discussed in sacred trust. They have been safe with me, but I cannot guarantee my silence for much longer. Lyddie's last wishes will seem quite illogical if you choose to leave things as they are. Questions will be asked and Lyddie had left specific instructions as to how to answer them."

Lara knew exactly what Duncan meant. He did not need to clarify further.

"When will the reading take place?" Lara asked.

"It can be at your convenience." There was a thoughtful pause before Duncan advised further, "But know there will be repercussions should you wait too long."

"Then it would be best to have it over with as soon as possible. I'm anxious to get home. Perhaps within the week?"

Duncan agreed, recognizing in Lara the same strength and determination that Lyddie had often shown. Like her aunt, Lara did not seem like one who would put off an unpleasant task. "I will have my clerk make the arrangements and will let you know the date and time."

Lara nodded. She knew enough to not ignore Duncan's advice. She would have some serious thinking to do over the next few days.

~ · ~

The morning clouds had all disappeared by the time Lara emerged from the offices of Whitelock and Lane. Directly overhead the April sky was now painted powder blue and Lara could feel the warmth of the sun's rays as they shone down upon the port city. However, the sunny day did nothing to help her forget her worries and lift her spirits. And dressed all in black with long sleeves, a snug collar and cuffs, and then the gloves. All did nothing to keep her cool and comfortable on this unusually hot spring morning.

Lara stopped in front of the Planters Bank of South Carolina. She stared at the sign painted on the window while debating as to whether or not she should go in to apologize to Kyle for the scene the night before.

"Miss Lara! Lara Kendrick, is that you?"

Lara turned toward the vaguely familiar voice to see a woman running towards her. Immediately she recognized the pretty face of one of Aunt Lyddie's girls.

"It's good to see you again!" Beth Winthrop exclaimed. The woman's arms were open wide to surprise Lara with a hug. "Wait 'til the girls find out you're home."

"How are you, Beth?" Lara responded in a reserved manner.

Beth frowned. "We're having a terrible time after being thrown out of Haven Manor. Some of the girls have moved on, but there's still a few of us left in Charleston."

"You were evicted?"

"Tossed out like garbage. All of us and with no warning whatsoever! They gave us half an hour to pack and then herded us out like cattle. The house was locked up and boarded shut. I didn't think they could do that, but they did. That Kyle Harrison and the Planters Bank, they have no heart," Beth rambled on without any concern for who might be listening. "We were hoping you'd come home and claim Haven Manor. You'll be staying on in Charleston, won't you?"

If Lara had been in a better mood, she would have laughed at the thought. Now it only sounded like a crude joke. "I'm afraid not, Beth."

"It would take very little to start Haven Manor up again. With your fine figure and pretty looks, we could easily build on Lyddie's success, I know we could!"

Lara felt awkward. This was not the appropriate time and the middle of the street was certainly not the place for such a discussion. "I don't have any plans for Haven Manor, nor do I intend to stay on in Charleston for any longer than is necessary."

"But you must. We're all depending on you."

The two women had become the center of attention and strangers started to gather around them, all eager to catch more of their conversation.

"I'm married now, Beth. I have responsibilities of my own and Charleston is not where I belong. I'm sorry, but I'm late for an appointment." With that, Lara tried to break through the crowd towards her landau, but Beth followed close to her heals in pursuit.

"Is that all you have to say? You can't just abandon us. We need you!"

"I'm afraid she must. She has an appointment," came Kyle's familiar voice. "Come, Lara, we're late."

Lara felt Kyle's hand firm at her elbow as he turned her about to guide her into the Planters Bank.

"You watch out for him, Miss Lara," Beth shouted after them. "He'll turn on you the first chance he gets! He can't be trusted!"

"You needn't have come to my rescue," Lara declared as she let Kyle lead her through the crowd.

"You should be glad I did," Kyle replied. "I know first hand how determined Beth Winthrop can be."

"Did you learn that through banking business or through more intimate personal transactions?" Lara asked without thinking. Almost immediately she regretted her words.

Kyle returned a blank stare. Her sarcasm had taken him completely by surprise.

Ushered into the bank and then into Kyle's office, Lara's attention was immediately drawn to the small pile of papers on his desk. Her gloved hand went to the sheet at the top of a pile on which "Haven Manor" had been written in Kyle's own cursive scrawl. The slightest crease to her brow would not normally have been detected by anyone else, but Kyle caught her reaction and was reminded of how angry she was over the repossession of Haven Manor.

Lara looked up to find him watching her. "What else, Mr. Harrison, have you absconded with?" she dared to ask.

"I haven't absconded with anything," Kyle replied innocently.

"Isn't that what you've done with Haven Manor?"

"The bank had every right to call the mortgage."

"It's always business first with you, isn't it, Kyle? How could you have the heart to throw those women out? Couldn't you even have given them some sort of notice?"

"Two or three are still in town if you're of a mind to start your own brothel," Kyle mocked with a sarcastic grin for he was able to give as good as she. "With your womanly ways and seductive charms, I've no doubt you would do very well. I might even pay a coin or two to have you warm my bed."

Lara was not in any sort of mood to take his smutty remarks. Her hand went up to strike, but Kyle was ready and caught hold of her wrist before she could follow through. He pulled her closer to him. She felt her anger and frustration mounting. Her pulse raced with the sudden nearness of him.

"Control yourself," Kyle directed in a stern voice. He brought her arm down to her side. Convinced she wasn't going to lash out again, he let her go. He reached behind her to close his office door then motioned to the chair beside her. "Please, sit down."

Lara refused to be seated.

"When Lyddie died, there were two mortgage payments in arrears with a third soon coming due," Kyle explained. "You should be grateful we took possession of Haven Manor. We saved you from having to deal with those money hungry whores. Yes, Lara. That's exactly what they are. Each and every one was waiting for Lyddie to pass on, each having some plot in their pretty little head as to how to take over the business. Lyddie was ready to give up the brothel and they all knew it. That's why she built the house on Wentworth Street. She was tired of that life and wanted something quiet, more fulfilling."

Lara remained silent. Kyle hadn't said anything that Aunt Lyddie, herself, had not written to tell her. If asked, Lara would have admitted that she had not been looking forward to dealing with those ladies. She, too, had many times witnessed how aggressive they could be. Kyle had done her a favor and saved her from a difficult and unpleasant task. Lara was suddenly plagued with guilt and she felt awkward being there with him. This was her second encounter with Kyle in as many days and both times she had accused and insulted him. Never before had she been so thoughtless and she despised herself for it. She had always been respectful of other people's feelings, but being with Kyle seemed to make her forget herself. What was wrong with her?

"Lara, are you alright?"

"Kyle, I'm sorry. I apologize for the scene at dinner last night, and for being so rude just now. I don't know what's come over me."

"I know how much Lyddie meant to you. I'd bring her back for you if I could."

Even if Lara had been able to manage a smile it would have been overshadowed by the sadness in her eyes.

Kyle reached over his desk to pull open a drawer from which he withdrew a small trinket box. "I have something for you."

Lara waited and watched as Kyle came to her side to open the box.

"This is something to remember Lyddie by. I hope you like it."

Lara picked up the mourning brooch. Made of jet, the black opaque stone had been beautifully carved and polished to a high sheen. With her thumb, Lara gently brush over the single forget-me-not. "In memory of Lydia Randall" was scripted on the reverse along with her date of death. Lara opened the locket. A miniature likeness of Aunt Lyddie had been painted on enamel on the inside cover. A lock of her aunt's auburn hair had been carefully coiled inside.

"It's beautiful," Lara whispered.

"May I?" he asked, taking the brooch from her.

He stepped closer to pin the piece to her bodice. His tall figure, lean and muscular, commanded her attention. Lara trembled at the feel of Kyle's nimble fingers upon her chest. Profoundly touched by his sentiment and generosity, Lara could only stare, mesmerized by those soulful eyes warm with empathy. She was lost in his presence and, before she realized it, his arms had encircled her waist and she was being drawn gently to him. Her heart raced. His head bent down so close to hers that she could feel the warmth of his breath upon her lips.

From somewhere deep within, Lara summoned her self-control and she turned her head to deny him her kiss. "You forget yourself, Mr. Harrison," she whispered softly.

Kyle stared over her shoulder for the few moments it took to regain his composure. He stepped back, releasing her from his embrace. "I did. My apologies, Mrs. Quinn."

~ · ~

Lara had finished her midday meal with Dane. She sat across from him with her cup of tea while he nursed a shot of bourbon.

"Did you get to the cemetery yesterday?" Dane asked.

Lara nodded. "A woman of love, life and laughter," she recited from memory. "Did you pen that?"

"Lyddie would have liked that, don't you think?"

Another nod. "She would have."

"Kyle arranged for the gravestone," Dane revealed. "In fact, he took care of all those details. A fine job he did."

Lara was too shocked to respond. She sat quiet, staring into her tea as she puzzled over what sort of relationship her aunt might have shared with Kyle. He seemed to have taken a keen interest in all of Aunt Lyddie's affairs, and now he was expending effort with regards to her own needs. Lara didn't know what to think.

"I went by Haven Manor," Lara revealed. "Did you know the Planters Bank has taken possession?"

"It was done the day after Lyddie passed away."

"Was it true that Aunt Lyddie had defaulted on the payments?"

"There were a few overdue on the day of her death. Lyddie was fully aware of the situation. I'm surprised the auction notices haven't been put up yet."

"What do you think I should do about it?"

"Are you thinking of keeping the plantation?" Dane asked as though the thought had never occurred to him before.

"It's a possibility. I ran into Beth Winthrop earlier today. She wants me to keep Haven Manor and reopen the brothel. What do you think, Dane? Would I make a good madame?"

Dane choked on his swallow of bourbon. His face turned a deep red as he sputtered and coughed to regain his breath. His adverse reaction prompted a hearty laugh from Lara. Only then did Dane realize she was joking.

"Seriously now, should I try to save it?" Lara asked again.

"Let it go," Dane advised. "It's too large a place for one woman and a child. You have neither the servants nor the income to support it. You can't afford to keep both the house in town and the plantation, now can you? And I doubt Aidan would want to leave Savannah."

"No, his daughter, Abi, the ranch, and the horses are his life," Lara admitted. "He would never leave them and certainly not for Charleston. There are too many painful memories here for him, but perhaps it's time Gavin and I left."

"Leave Aidan and Abi and come here?" Dane asked. "You surprise me, Lara, by even thinking of it, especially after all the times Lyddie had begged you to come home."

Lara couldn't count the number of times her aunt had suggested moving back to Charleston. The topic was raised at least once during each of Aunt Lyddie's visits to Savannah. There was always that topic and the one suggesting that Kyle be told of his son. Aidan always ended up playing referee and trying to keep discussions civil between her and Aunt Lyddie. It got so tiresome that Aidan eventually laid down the law and both topics were forbidden under his roof.

"It is an option, but I'll have to wait until the will is read before making any plans. From the little that Duncan has told me, Aunt Lyddie may have a surprise or two left for me. He recommended that I settle any concerns I may have with Kyle and Aidan. Do you think Aunt Lyddie would have named Kyle as Gavin's father in her will?"

"She might have, although she has done well to keep your secret for so long. She said naught a word to me."

"You certainly were surprised," Lara recalled.

"In shock was more like it! Lara, Kyle should be told," Dane advised boldly. He remembered back to that day when he had called upon Lara shortly after arriving in Savannah. How stunned he was, only to learn of the boy's existence when the child came running, calling out to his mother! In Dane's mind, the resemblance between the boy and Kyle was indisputable. It was only at that particular moment that Dane was able to make sense of so many of Lyddie's ramblings. He could only imagine how stupefied Kyle would be if he were to learn of his son in a similar manner. "The man should be told," Dane pressed again.

Lara frowned. How could she possibly find the courage to tell Kyle Harrison about his bastard son? "He wanted nothing to do with me and he'll want even less from Gavin. It's better this way."

"Even if you're right, it should be Kyle's decision."

"He made it five years ago," Lara responded tersely.

"You know that's not fair. You said yourself that you didn't know you were pregnant until several weeks after Kyle had left Brooklyn City." There were a few moments of silence before Dane pushed on. "He would be a good father to Gavin."

"And if you are right, if Kyle becomes the loving father that Gavin wants and needs, what do you suppose will happen then? Do you think Kyle would allow his son to remain with me? I think not."

Lara had voiced her greatest fear and Dane finally came to understand why Lara had left Gavin behind in Savannah. Even if Kyle did somehow discover the secret of his son, the boy was safely far away and beyond his reach.

"There is still much to be resolved between you and Kyle. Whatever your differences, you should know that Lyddie was fond of him, and he of her. He did everything possible to see that she was well cared for and got everything she needed. He was there by her side, right up until she took her last breath."

Again, Lara didn't know what to think. Did Kyle truly care about Aunt Lyddie or did he only want to gain control over her estate?

"Tell me, Lara. What kind of man is Aidan Quinn?" Dane asked.

"He's a good, honest man."

"Is he a good husband?"

Lara stared at Dane, surprised by his question. What had Aunt Lyddie told him?

"No wonder you were in such a rush to get through the inventory." A deep voice interrupted their conversation. "I'd rush off too if I was lucky enough to have such fine company waiting for me."

"Bryce, Jenna." Dane rose to greet the handsome couple standing before them. The next few minutes passed with Dane introducing Lara to his employers, Jenna and Bryce Landon, the owners of Warren Enterprises, and the other couple from last night whom Lara had seen on the dance floor.

"How long will you be staying in Charleston?" Jenna asked Lara.

"I'm not altogether sure," Lara replied. "I'm here to settle my aunt's estate."

"Lara is Lydia Randall's niece," Dane offered.

"Of course! There was something awfully familiar about you, but I couldn't put my finger on it. I see the resemblance now," Jenna responded without a second thought. "Lyddie and I had worked together on a few charity events for the orphanage and the hospital. I shall miss working with her."

That was far from the response Lara had expected for she feared of being snubbed upon revealing her ties to her aunt.

"Quinn from Savannah," Bryce Landon joined in. "You must know Aidan Quinn."

"He's my husband," Lara responded and like so many times before, a niggling twinge rose from inside to haunt her conscience. "How do you know Aidan? Have you purchased horses from him?"

"Three in fact," Bryce revealed. "That was six, almost seven years ago. Just after the death of his first wife. It was an awful time for him and I'm afraid I got the horses at more than bargain price."

Lara's memories took her back to when she first arrived at the Quinn ranch outside Savannah. It had been almost two years after Aidan's wife, Chelsea, had passed away. It was immediately clear that Aidan had been devastated by the loss of his beloved. His despair had brought a shadow over the entire household and a distance between himself and his daughter, Abigail. Lara remembered how difficult the first months were with having to settle herself and Gavin into a new household, and to try to console and support Abi while doing what she could to bring Aidan out of his depression. Such a long and difficult time it was!

~ • ~

"I'll take care of it," Kyle promised.

"Good. I'll leave you to it then," Duncan responded, confident that Kyle would keep his word and do all he could to assist Lara with sorting through Lyddie's possessions. "And you will be reasonable with Lara's living allowance."

"Of course," Kyle confirmed.

The two men exchanged handshakes before Duncan went along his way.

Kyle tossed the handful of papers onto his desk. His heart jumped as he watched the documents brush up against the inkwell. The force was enough to shift the blue-black vessel along its base, but not enough to tip the bottle onto its side. He breathed a sigh of relief before settling into the comfort of his high-backed chair. He glanced at the mantle clock. 3:40 p.m. He had lacked the motivation to tackle his work after returning from his midday meal with Morgan. He had been in an odd mood the entire day. Morgan had sensed it and he was grateful that she did not bring Lara up in conversation again. Then again there wasn't much more he could add to their discussion from the other night.

There was a lot on his mind today. It had started early in the morning when it was brought to his attention that the amount of the Bank's notes being returned for deposit over the last week had been much smaller than normal. The possibility that someone was hoarding bank notes for some ill-conceived purpose was now raised and this prompted Kyle to review the more recent deposit and withdrawal records. He poured over them for an hour or so, unable to uncover anything of serious note. He had to admit, though, that he was having difficulty concentrating. The numbers were like a blur. Several times he had stopped to reread entries he had reviewed only seconds before. He stared at the journals, his mind preoccupied with endless thoughts of Lara.

Kyle knew his mood had changed that night after seeing Lara for the first time after Brooklyn City. He had forgotten his manners when he abandoned Morgan to chase after Lara. He couldn't help himself. He had to know that the vision he saw was real, that he wasn't hallucinating, that Lara had finally come home. He had lost his senses when he tried to give her a hug. It was such an idiotic thing to do!

Lara's voice sang like a long time favorite melody, sweet and familiar. The soft floral scent of her perfume was intoxicating. He hadn't had time to come to his senses before being jolted by the discovery of her marriage. He had made a concerted effort to maintain a cheerful front when he rejoined his friends, but he knew his companions had sensed an abrupt change in his frame of mind. No doubt Jenna and Bryce were more than curious as to his connection to Lara, but were much too polite to persist past the initial inquiry. Even if they had, he wasn't sure how he would have answered. What is his relationship with Lara Mackenzie Kendrick after losing touch with her for more than five years? Could he call her "friend" or would he be more correct to consider her a mere acquaintance? Mrs. Lara Quinn, he corrected himself. He couldn't help but wonder what would she have to say on the matter.

A crease lined his brow as his attention was caught by a shadow floating onto his frosted office door window. He shifted in his chair, sitting upright as he half expected a knock upon his door. The shadow remained frozen for a few seconds then drifted away. Pleased to be left undisturbed, his thoughts immediately went back to Lara.

She has changed, thought Kyle. Still strikingly beautiful, but more now than five years ago, everything about Lara reflected a more self-assured and self-reliant woman. Not only in the way she carried herself, but also in her forthright actions. Is that what marriage does to a woman? It gives her strength and confidence? Such changes in one's personality do not come easily nor quickly, and it made Kyle wonder all the more as to what sort of man Lara had married, and what kind of life she had been living since she ran from him that last night together.

Many times before Kyle had wished Morgan possessed such confidence and independence. No, that wasn't fair, he told himself. Morgan was four years Lara's junior and Morgan had led a sheltered and privileged life. She had yet to experience the loss of a beloved family member. Neither had she known a trying time that commanded the strength and determination of being on one's own. Thus she had never been forced to experience the hardships and to make the kind of decisions like those demanded of Lara. As an only child of a wealthy banker and tobacco planter,

Morgan's whims and wishes had always been granted to her by over indulgent parents. She had never had to go without. Lara and Morgan were two women with little in common by way of interests or upbringing. Two distinctly different personalities: Morgan, patiently waiting, nay, expecting him to ask for her hand in marriage; and Lara, who had years earlier fallen passionately, head over heels in love with him.

So it was years ago. Now, it seemed, Lara had put that all behind her. She's made another life for herself. A life without you, Kyle told himself. Perhaps, he thought, he should do the same. He shook his head, then ran his hands through his hair. He had done himself a disservice with pining over Lara all these years. He had given himself false hope, and all for naught!

"Enough," he chided himself. Kyle sat upright and pulled his chair closer to his desk. Determined to get back to work, he reached for the pile of papers he had tossed aside minutes before. His hand brushed up against the inkwell and the vessel tipped onto its side. He jumped out of his chair only to watch helplessly as the blue-black liquid spilled onto his desk. "Damn!"

Chapter 6

∞

A Scuffle

Lara had found two notes waiting for her at the hotel reception desk that morning. The first was from Duncan, informing her that he had been able to schedule the reading of her aunt's will to take place in five days' time. He had also spoken to Kyle who would be in touch shortly to discuss her request to retrieve some items from Haven Manor. The second card was Kyle's in further reference to Duncan's letter. Kyle's schedule was open for the morning, and he had suggested that she go by the bank any time before the noon hour to discuss matters further.

At the Planters Bank of South Carolina, Kyle's manner was cool and distant throughout their entire conversation. There was no social chitchat, not even the usual trite comment about the weather. It seemed he was being overly careful to keep their discussions to topics of business, all of which were completed quickly, almost hurriedly. He had arranged for Addison Kent, a young bank teller, to accompany Lara out to Haven Manor. Kyle had excused himself from personally escorting Lara for he had appointments scheduled that could not be postponed.

Lara had been surprised to learn that the bank had drafted a list of her aunt's possessions. Kyle offered no explanation for the inventory and Lara was left to assume that the more valuable pieces would be auctioned off with the land and buildings. Together, she reviewed the list with Kyle, noting the particular items she knew she wanted to claim. Kyle marked each off on the list without any objection or comment. In the end, Kyle handed the list over to Addison who was to accompany Lara out to Haven Manor. Kyle gave him specific instructions to mark the furniture pieces Lara wanted for easy identification. After that, arrangements would then be made to transport them to storage or to the Wentworth manor house, whichever Lara preferred.

Addison was a strapping, young fellow of nineteen years. Standing over six feet in height, his muscular, broad-shouldered form would make any fellow second guess his chances of winning a fist fight against the teller. He was smitten with Lara immediately upon their introduction. As they started out for the plantation, he initiated a long-winded monologue of all that Charleston had to offer. He was trying his utmost best to impress his new companion with his knowledge, all the while not knowing that the port city had once been her home.

Upon reaching Haven Manor, Lara knew she would not have the patience to put up with him following behind her or with his incessant babble. With a sweet smile and a fair bit of coaxing, she was able to convince him to return to Charleston and come back for her a few hours later, thus giving her ample quiet time to review her decisions regarding which items to keep and which to let go.

A layer of dust several months thick had settled on every object in the house. Sunlight poured through the glass panes when Lara threw back the curtains and opened the windows to fresh air. The long shafts of light turned into a soft haze as dust particles floated through the sunbeams. The brothel parlor and bedrooms in the west wing were empty. The smaller furnishings and knickknacks had left with the ladies. Lara had never been permitted in this part of the household for these were the rooms for the intimate entertaining of Aunt Lyddie's wealthy clientele.

The east side of the second floor was forbidden to all except Aunt Lyddie, Lara and the servants. These were private quarters where Aunt Lyddie would retreat from the world. It was the family sanctuary only for herself and Lara.

Lara's bedroom was as she had left it almost seven years ago. Bed linens of pure white Venetian lace decorated her high-poster bed of white oak. Bottles of scented bath oils were clustered together on her small dressing table and her hairbrushes lay waiting. Two favorite wooden dolls, a few toys and many books adorned a high bookshelf. The lamps were all filled with oil, the wicks waiting to be lit. It was a bedroom for an eleven-year-old girl. As Lara grew, neither she nor her aunt had had the heart to pack away the little girl dreams and memories.

Like her own room, Aunt Lyddie's was neat and orderly. None of her aunt's things had been touched. All the ornaments and curios had been left in full display, ready to be appreciated or used. Lara sat on the bed. She smoothed the linen covers with her hand and immediately her thoughts went to Aunt Lyddie. Questions filled her head as she wondered what her aunt's last days had been like. Did she suffer much or did the pneumonia take her quickly? Lara looked up to the large portrait hung above the mantle. She remembered sitting with Aunt Lyddie for countless hours under the pink magnolia while they posed for the painting. How hot it was! Lara laughed, remembering how Aunt Lyddie would dip her hand into a pitcher and playfully flick the water onto her face to cool her off. Their antics had annoyed the artist and several times they had to endure the man's scolding as the two struggled to sit still. Lara had never been able to appreciate the sentimental value of the portrait as much as her aunt—at least not until now.

Lydia Randall was a beautiful woman with a curvaceous figure that turned men's heads and made other women jealous. The deep red hues of her hair set off the fire in her vibrant green eyes. High cheekbones accentuated an oval face that was warmed by an engaging smile. She had an elegant quality about her, most evident in the graceful way in which she carried herself. She possessed a generous nature, capable of profound understanding and forgiveness towards others. Lara had always admired her for her strength and her compassion. However Lyddie had her weaknesses too, for always present in her mind were fears of being abandoned and left penniless as had happened to her after the death of her husband many years before. Lyddie had known hunger and cold, heartache and despair. Expressed many times in many ways, these were fears that she had hoped her niece would never have to face.

After her initial tour walking through the rooms and reminiscing, Lara settled down to work. She started in her old bedroom by removing from the drawers and shelves anything she wanted to keep. She sifted through the contents, grouping the "wanteds" neatly against the wall and out of the way. Afterwards she began the task of packing and cleaning. She rummaged through the kitchen and the dusty cellar and found several sturdy boxes and sweetgrass baskets. As each was filled, she carried them down to the foyer where they would remain until ready to be transported to Charleston.

With all her boxes filled, there wasn't much left she could do and there was still a good hour before Addison's expected return. In Aunt Lyddie's bathing room, Lara found herself a towelette. After filling a pitcher with water, she stripped down to her chemise and the last of her petticoats to wash away the sweat and dirt from the packing. She closed her eyes, splashing water on her face. How refreshing it felt!

"I was starting to think the house had been abandoned."

Lara jumped upon hearing the voice. She turned to see a tall, lean gentleman standing in the doorway. Refined and well-dressed, one might have mistaken him to be the perfect gentleman. The smirk on his face was indication that he was expecting to share more than a cup of afternoon tea. His eyes swept over Lara's scantily clad body. By the expression on his face it would have seemed Lara was standing before him naked. Thus there was no doubt in Lara's mind as to the purpose of this intrusion. She glanced about the room in search of something to cover herself, but there was nothing within reach.

"Are you the only one here?" he asked.

Horrified by his presence, Lara was at a loss for words. She could only feel the rushing beat of her heart.

The man stepped into the room. Lara heard the door shut tight behind him.

"No matter. I'm sure your company will prove quite delightful." The stranger reached out, his leer clear evidence of what he had in mind for her.

Panic began to set in. Lara made the mistake of stepping away as his fingers toyed with the drawstrings of her chemise. The man did not miss his opportunity and with a quick tug, the knot slipped away to expose the cleft of Lara's bosom. Pleased with what he saw, his grin broadened.

"Sir, you're making a grave mistake."

"Don't worry about the coin, my sweet, you'll find I can be quite generous." He stepped forward and suddenly his iron arms were locked around her waist, squeezing her tight. His mouth covered hers in a hot, demanding kiss. Lara's effort to break free seemed nothing more than a timorous attempt against his physical strength. She barely caught her breath before his second kiss.

Lara fought, slipping out of his hold. He advanced, forcing her to retreat backwards. She used the wall to support herself while trying to push him away, but she was easily overpowered. She felt the weight of his body hard against hers and the cold wall against her back. Pinned against the corner, she pummeled his back with her fists, but her efforts were futile. He pressed harder against her body, eventually grabbing hold of one of her hands to twist her arm behind her back. He applied pressure. Lara winced, feeling enough pain to stop struggling. With no further resistance, he immediately eased his hold, but held her arm there should she start to struggle again. With his free hand he worked at her petticoat. She felt the buttons pop and heard the cotton tear. Her skirt fell limp from her waist to leave only the token armor of her cotton chemise. Then came another smothering kiss while his large hand cupped her breast.

"No!" Lara screamed.

Then his kisses stopped. His breath was hot and heavy in her ears. "I do enjoy a good scuffle, my dear. It gets my blood going."

"Please," Lara begged. The first tear started to roll down her face while she tried once again to gather enough strength and courage to gain even the slightest advantage. "I'm not one of the girls!"

Lara's fear and frustration deepened. She knew he had no intentions of letting her go. The man felt Lara squirming. He was relishing the feel of her body struggling against his. His eyes were full of laughter. He was mocking her, purposely taunting her, and fueling her anger.

The man tugged at her chemise in an effort to free the folds of her undergarment from between them. Successful, he slipped his hand underneath to feel the curve of her hip, then upwards. Lara screamed with his next bold touch. Would there be no one to save her?

Lara's silent prayer was answered when the door crashed open. The intruder had not yet turned about when strong hands grabbed onto his upper arms and yanked him back. Free, Lara shrank into the far corner of the room.

~ · ~

Kyle's patience wore thin while he waited in Lyddie's bedroom for the time it took for Lara to come out of the bathing room. When she finally emerged, it seemed she had regained control over her emotions, on the surface at least. Still, Kyle couldn't stop worrying. Silently he debated if she was in a sound enough state of mind to be left alone for the night. Whether his judgment was sober or clouded, he decided to take Lara home with him. She voiced little resistance and it took no effort for Kyle to convince her that it was for her own good.

At the Harrison residence, Casey O'Leary, Kyle's loyal housekeeper of fourteen years, had settled Lara into the guest room across from Kyle's own bedroom.

Filled with grave concern, Kyle sat in his favorite library chair as he attacked what was left of his second glass of whiskey. At Haven Manor, Lara's screams had chilled his bones and the look of horror on her face would be etched in his memory for eternity. Unforgettable, her eyes were dark and wide with fear. Nor would he be able to dismiss the feeling of uncontrollable rage that swept over him when he pulled the molester away.

Kyle had startled Lara when he had returned after throwing her attacker out. It must have taken all her strength to have been able to accept his touch when he placed a blanket over her trembling body. There was nothing else he could do for her. No other comfort could he offer and it was torture for him to see her huddled in the corner and sobbing uncontrollably, barely able to stand being in the same room with a man.

Kyle had immediately become concerned when he discovered that Addison Kent had returned to the bank and Lara had been left alone at Haven Manor. The blame was his for he should have cancelled his afternoon appointments and accompanied Lara to the plantation house himself. If he had then surely none of this would have happened. Kyle took his last swallow of whiskey and rose to fetch a third dose when his housekeeper entered the room.

"How is she?" Kyle asked. "Should we fetch a doctor?"

"Her nerves are frayed, but I think she'll be fine," Casey O'Leary reported. "She's asleep now. That's the best thing for her."

Kyle nodded in agreement.

"Who is she?" Casey asked. "What happened to the poor thing?"

"Her name is Lara Quinn. She is Lydia Randall's niece. She was out at Haven Manor packing some things when she was attacked by one of Lyddie's patrons. I got there in time to throw the bastard out."

"Was he someone from these parts?"

Kyle trusted the woman and knew she would understand the implications of what he was about to tell her. "It was Cameron."

"Senator Palmer?"

Kyle nodded.

"Oh my." There was a long pause, then Casey asked, "Mr. Harrison, sir, what are you going to do?"

"I don't know, but right now I need another drink." His eyes glazed from the strong drink, he handed Casey his empty glass.

Kyle fell back into his chair. He closed his eyes as he tried hard to sort through all that had taken place. Yes, he asked himself, what was he going to do?

∽ · ∼

Lara could not see beyond the midnight blackness that filled the room yet instinct told her she was not alone. She could feel a presence lurking in the shadows, an ominous spirit that sent her heart pumping with fear.

"I do enjoy a good scuffle, my dear. It gets my blood going."

The sinister voice had barely finished speaking those chilling words when she felt a hand take hold of her breast. Suddenly the lean face appeared before her, the menace bearing a grimacing, self-satisfied smile.

Lara screamed as she bolted upright in bed. Filled with panic, she was too distraught to remember where she was. She wasn't sure if she was awake or still dreaming for her surroundings were as dark and unfamiliar as the prison room in the nightmare from which she had just escaped.

The door to the room suddenly swung open and she could see the silhouette of a tall figure rush through the doorway. Her fear rose, then struck again as she felt ironclad hands firm upon her shoulders. She shrieked as primeval instinct commanded her to fend off her attacker. She lashed out, swinging her arms wildly about.

"Lara! It's Kyle!"

Hands caught hold of her wrists and she was pulled forward until she felt the warmth of another body next to hers. She continued struggling, trying to free herself from the strong arms that encircled her.

"It's me, Kyle! You're safe, Lara!"

Lara finally heard the familiar voice in her ears and she immediately stopped her struggling. She fell into his arms, sobbing.

"You're safe with me," Kyle reassured her again as he hugged her close. "I won't let anything happen to you."

The unfamiliar room now felt warm and secure as he joined her on the bed. Slowly, the fear and panic began to subside as Kyle rocked her in his arms.

"Ssshh, it was nothing but a bad dream. No one's going to hurt you," his voice was calm and soothing. "You're safe with me."

Lara felt his gentle touch as he brushed back the stray locks of hair that had fallen over her face. She let go of her doubts and fears and, for a brief time, Lara forgot their troubled past to find both comfort and sleep in Kyle's protective arms.

~ · ~

Morning had come much too quickly. Lara rolled onto her side to look at the same clock that she had glanced at several times already. The hands pointed to seven o'clock. As a guest in the Harrison home, she would not have the luxury of staying in bed and hiding from the world. She sat up for a better look at the timepiece. She had hoped that she had misread the time, but its hands still pointed to seven. She reached out to touch one of the gilded icons that adorned the clock face. A light rapping on the bedroom door was enough to startle her and Lara withdrew quickly.

"Kyle?" she asked aloud.

"It's Casey O'Leary, dear. I've brought your clothes. May I come in?"

Lara closed her eyes and drew in a calming breath. Be strong, she told herself. "Come in."

The door opened and a small plump woman swept into the room. She wore a bright smile upon her expressive Irish face. "Good morning, Mrs. Quinn, I've got your clothes. I'll leave them here on the bed for you."

The housekeeper laid the dress and petticoats down before her. Her clothes had been pressed and folded with care. Lara quickly went through the layers of the neat bundle to find that one of her petticoats was missing.

"Shall I prepare your bath?" Casey asked.

Lara did not expect to be so graciously pampered. "Thank you, Mrs. O'Leary, but I'm able to manage. I'm sure you have other duties to attend to."

"You can call me Casey, dear. There isn't anything that can't wait. Except Mr. Harrison," the housekeeper hinted. She was subtly polite for Kyle had risen early, anxious to find out for himself how well Lara had come through the rest of the night.

Lara reflected back on her crazed state the afternoon before and how this woman had helped calm her disposition. She'd had Lara change into one of Kyle's nightshirts then coaxed her into taking a dose of scotch whiskey to settle her nerves. She then ushered Lara into bed. What had Kyle told her? How much did the woman know?

Casey read the expression on Lara's face. "You need not worry, dear. I'm best at keeping secrets and Mr. Harrison is the perfect gentleman. Though he can become quite the lion if kept waiting too long." Her face became rounder with her smile. "Let's see to that bath, shall we?"

～ · ～

Kyle jumped from his chair when he heard Lara's footsteps approaching. He wanted to wrap his arms around her and tell her everything was all right, but her expression and movements clearly communicated her desire to maintain a physical distance.

"Good morning, Lara. How are you feeling?"

"I'm fine," she lied, still tense and jittery.

Kyle held out a chair for her. He couldn't help but notice how stiff she was as she took her place at the table. "You must be hungry," he said, remembering the few sips of scotch she took the previous night.

The morning meal was filled with a string of attempts by Kyle to initiate light conversation. He was determined to alleviate Lara's downtrodden spirits despite her abbreviated answers and her refusal to meet his gaze. He could only watch as she played with the food on her plate. She poked at the tidbits with her fork only to take a morsel now and again even though she had no appetite, and despite the fact that Casey had prepared a most delicious meal.

"I'm taking the day off from work," he announced cheerfully. "I thought we would do some shopping and get you properly settled in at the new house. You'll be much more comfortable there than at The Charlestown."

Lara poked a bite-size piece of potato. "Kyle, you needn't fuss over me. I'm fine. Really, I am."

She's strong, Kyle thought, but she's not fine. "I'm looking forward to it. You'll need to open accounts with one or two merchants at least and it'll be much easier if I'm along. Afterwards we can go by the hotel to fetch your things."

"And take them to the house? I didn't think it could be made ready so soon. I'm not even sure we should bother. I don't even know yet what I want to do with the house. And shouldn't we wait for the will to be read?"

"A formality," Kyle acknowledged. "And yes, it will take a day or two to move the furniture. In the meantime, I think it would be best if you stayed here."

Lara put her fork down and lifted her eyes for the first time. "Kyle, you've been most kind to take me in, and I'm grateful for you coming to my rescue at Haven Manor, and again last night after that nightmare. I'm sure I wouldn't have been able to cope if left on my own, but it is quite improper for me to be staying here with you. My presence is bound to start the gossips nattering and nothing good can come of it. What happened at Haven Manor was the most horrifying experience. I realize now how foolish it was of me to have sent Addison away. It never occurred to me that…that such a thing could happen, but I'm not afraid. I know I'll be safe at the hotel."

~ · ~

After breakfast, Lara sat down and, with Casey's help, concentrated on a list of the essential items to be purchased for the new house while Kyle tackled some work in his study. It seemed odd to be thinking of such things when she, herself, wasn't sure she wanted to stay.

It was nearly an hour later before the three set out on the town. Lara was overly conscious of the curious looks and prying questions from the townsfolk as Kyle escorted her from one store to another. He avoided introductions whenever possible and those that could not be evaded were kept short. At every place of business, the merchants hovered near them. Were they hoping to catch some tidbit of information about Lara or did they only want to be near at hand to render assistance if needed? Regardless,

Kyle did not seem in any way disturbed by their overly zealous and watchful service.

Lara was also keenly aware of Kyle's attentiveness towards her. To anyone looking on, one might have thought the pair to be more than friends. Kyle showered her with thoughtful consideration, not like a banker would his client, but rather like a man would his sweetheart. He's only being kind, she reasoned, nothing more! However even with Casey along as chaperone, Lara wondered what sort of ill-conceived tattle would be following them around Charleston.

The two ladies were pouring over the selection of ironstone when Kyle went to seek out the store manager to arrange credit. He was negotiating payment terms when Cameron Palmer's voice called out to him.

"Kyle, weren't we scheduled to meet this morning?" the man asked shamelessly. "I waited for an hour at the bank. Look, I hope our little scrimmage yesterday didn't affect your decision about the loan. I thought she was one of Lyddie's girls. It was a harmless misunderstanding. No grudges?" The man offered Kyle his hand.

From a few feet away, Lara shuddered upon recognizing the distinct tones of the stranger's voice. Without hesitation, she set down a bowl and bravely approached him from behind. Her voice was sardonically sweet when she spoke. "Kyle, won't you introduce me to this *fine* gentleman?"

Cameron Palmer turned upon hearing Lara's sweet voice. It took only a second for his smile to vanish and the color to drain from his face. Before he could recover from the shock of seeing her, he felt the sharp sting of her palm hard upon his cheek.

Even with such a blow, the man seemed unaffected. "You little slut! Do you know who I am?"

Kyle caught hold of the Senator's wrist as he raised his arm to strike. Forcefully, Kyle held Cameron back to stop his advance on Lara. Kyle turned the man about. Now face to face with Lara's assailant, Kyle threw his fist.

Hit hard across the jaw, Senator Palmer fell against the store counter behind him. The pyramid display of soap bars toppled to the floor. Slowly, the man rose to his feet. The Senator shook his head. He wiped the corner of his mouth with his hand. Anger flashed in his eyes when he saw his palm tainted with his own blood. "Damn you, Kyle. Have you gone mad?"

~ . ~

Back at the Harrison home, Kyle had to put up with Lara's interrogation.

"Are you going to tell me who that man is?"

"He's Cameron Palmer—Senator Cameron Palmer."

Lara sat back in her chair, stunned that a member of Congress would act in such an ignoble manner. "I assume he was a patron of Aunt Lyddie's?"

"He was a frequent visitor to Haven Manor. His exploits with women are well known, much to his family's embarrassment. He has taken a townhouse in Columbia for the term of his senate seat, but his home is in Georgetown. He has a rice plantation there. Like all the other planters, he's an absentee landlord during most of the growing season so as to avoid the country fever. When not in Columbia or Georgetown, he's here enjoying our society."

Lara fixed her eyes on his. "You didn't forget about your meeting with him, did you?"

"No," Kyle admitted. "I didn't want to face him. Not after what he did to you."

"He's a state senator. He brings business to your bank. You can't afford to offend him."

"Our meeting this morning was to discuss a loan to last him through to harvest. The fever took too many of his slaves last year. A small harvest of marginal quality was the result. He lives extravagantly, beyond what any good crop can fetch these days. Financially, he's not in a sound position and the bank has turned down his request for a loan once before. So you see, there's no reason why I should cater to the man."

"But he proposes legislation to govern how banks do business."

Kyle gave her a reassuring smile. "I doubt Cameron would be bold enough to let a personal matter interfere with state business."

"Please, promise me you won't do anything to jeopardize your position with the bank."

"There's no need to concern yourself, Lara. You concentrate on getting yourself settled into your new home." Kyle paused, wondering if Lara was emotionally prepared for another trip to the plantation. "I'll make arrangements to have everything brought into town tomorrow. We'll need for you to tell the men what pieces you want. Lara, if you're not ready to go back to Haven Manor then we can put it off for a few days."

"I'll have to go back sometime. The sooner the better, I suppose. I would feel better if you came along."

She felt comfortable enough to have asked and that pleased Kyle. "Of course I will! Finish your tea. I'll take you back to the hotel and you can have a rest before dinner. Shall we dine at The Charlestown or would you prefer to go elsewhere? Or we can have Casey prepare something if you'd rather stay in."

"Kyle, you've been most generous with your time and with opening your home to me, but I'd prefer a quiet evening alone."

Lara did look tired. It had been a long day and perhaps dinner was a bit much to ask so soon after the assault. Yet she had handled the day about Charleston rather well and she couldn't be blamed for the confrontation with Cameron Palmer. Still Kyle did not like the idea of leaving her alone.

"I'll be fine," Lara reassured him.

"Then at least let me take you back to the hotel."

"Aren't you being a bit over-protective?"

The corners of Kyle's mouth lifted to barely a smile and Lara knew he was quite serious and was not to be swayed.

The night was unusually warm and stuffy. A far cry from the cold evening of only a few nights ago when Lara needed the warmth of a small fire to keep from shivering. She looked to the open door of her balcony where the floor length drapes lay still against the wall. There was no indication of even the slightest breeze to dull the night's heat and humidity. Was this discomfort meant to further test her emotional strength? Had she not yet endured enough? Lara lay in bed with Gavin's portrait propped up against the pillow beside her. She ran her fingers along the side of the pewter frame. In the dark, her son's image was nothing more than shadows of grey, but nonetheless the picture of his sweet face was sharp and clear in her own mind. That in itself was all she needed.

From her discussion with Duncan Whitelock, Lara was almost certain that Aunt Lyddie had meant for Kyle to be told of his son. But her aunt had given her solemn promise and she could always be trusted to keep her word. What should she do? Should she say nothing to Kyle on the chance that Aunt Lyddie had kept her pledge from years ago? Or should she reveal the truth and risk the consequences, whatever they may be? If the truth was to come out in their next meeting with Duncan, it would be best for Kyle to have been told beforehand, and of course she was the best one to tell him. Back and forth Lara debated until she came to the realization that this particular decision could not be made based upon reason alone. This dilemma demanded more than logic and common sense and Lara could no longer suppress the whispers growing louder from her conscience.

Chapter 7

A Revelation

Kyle stood flabbergasted as he stared back in disbelief at the hotel clerk. "She what?"

"Mrs. Quinn left this morning," the man repeated.

"Where did she go?"

"I believe she went home."

"That can't be! Are you sure she checked out?" Kyle asked a third time.

"Yes sir, Mr. Harrison, just before ten this morning."

"You're absolutely sure? Check again," Kyle insisted.

The clerk turned the register around for Kyle and pointed to Lara's record. "It's right there. Four dollars and fifty cents for six nights," the clerk confirmed, slightly miffed for being doubted.

"Did she say anything about where she was going?"

"Like I told you before, she said something about going home," the clerk reiterated, the emphasis on the last word was another sign that he was losing his patience.

Kyle stood aghast, dumbfounded by the thought of Lara running off before settling her aunt's estate. She hadn't left any word, nor had she even hinted that she was thinking of returning to Savannah. It made no sense, none whatsoever! Perhaps the incident with Cameron caused more emotional damage than he thought.

The mix of confusion and dismay remained with Kyle as he rushed to the bank to cancel his appointments for the day so he could seek Lara out. He would go by the docks, and check out the train and the stage with the hopes of catching her. Dane or Duncan! Yes, thought Kyle. Lara would have gone by to see both of them before leaving Charleston. He was sure of it!

~ · ~

Duncan Whitelock steered the shay onto the lane. Lara drew in a deep breath at the sight of the three-storey Italianate house. Full of quaint charm, the residence was set off by rows of arched, two-paned windows. A decorative crown topped each casement and large eave brackets adorned the underside of the low-pitched roof. Tall columns flanked each side of the small entry porch and together they framed an arched double door.

"124 Wentworth Street," Lara whispered to herself, thankful that Duncan had granted her possession of the house so soon.

"This is it," Duncan confirmed. "The frame and exterior finishes were completed at the end of last fall, but the interior wasn't completed until March. Lyddie had walked through the house twice to inspect all that was done. She was quite pleased with the results."

Their voices and footsteps echoed lightly as Lara let Duncan lead her through the building. The quality of the workmanship was evident in even the smallest details. Most rooms were still empty, but there was the odd piece of new furniture lying about. Even still, there was a heart-felt warmth within the rooms and a feeling of calm with the tall windows and high ceilings. Lara fell in love with the size of the master's quarters. There, the bedroom had been newly furnished with only the basic pieces, but enough to keep her comfortable, at least until Kyle made good his promise to have her chosen items brought in from Haven Manor.

Down the hall, Lara could imagine the second room painted in Gavin's favorite shade of blue. Ideas of how to furnish and decorate filled Lara's head, and by the end of the tour Lara knew she would enjoy the task of turning this dwelling into a new home for herself and her son should she decide to stay. That would be impossible, Lara reminded herself, for Aidan would never call Charleston home, not after being abandoned here by his father.

"It's wonderful," Lara declared.

"It would make a good home for you and Gavin," Duncan hinted. "You think you might stay on in Charleston?"

"That sounds a little like Aunt Lyddie talking."

"In that regard, she made her wishes well known," Duncan responded. "She wanted nothing more than to have you and Gavin here with her."

It was a cautious smile that came to Lara's lips. There was still much uncertainty and she had not dared to let herself form any firm plans for their future. To live "happily ever after" was a sentiment found only in fairy tales. Seldom do things turn out the way they're supposed to, and no one knew that better than she.

~ • ~

The last few hours had been the most trying for Kyle. He had had no success in tracking down Dane or Duncan, nor had he been able to confirm as to whether or not Lara had indeed run off and left Charleston. Tired and disillusioned, Kyle decided to return home. As he came up to the newest Italianate-style house on Wentworth Street, he caught sight of the curtains fluttering behind the open windows of the second floor. Immediately his pulse began to race. Kyle ran up the lane and took in a deep, calming breath before knocking on the door. He waited impatiently, his heart pounding for all his hopes hinged on the slight possibility of finding Lara inside.

Relief for Kyle was immediate, almost overwhelming when Lara came to the door, and it took a good deal of restraint on Kyle's part to refrain from sweeping her into his arms.

"Kyle," Lara greeted happily. "I'm so glad you got my note."

"Your note?" Kyle asked, his own smile broad and infectious.

"I left you a note at the Bank. You hadn't arrived yet when I came in to tell you that Duncan was giving me possession of the house. But how did you know I was here if you hadn't read it yet?"

"I was on my way home and saw the windows open. I thought I had better come check things out. May I come in?"

"Yes, of course," Lara opened the door wide. "I'm sorry, but I can't even offer you a chair."

Like many times before, Kyle was bewitched by the sparkle in her eyes and the warmth of her smile. It didn't matter that she had nothing to offer for finding her here was all that he had hoped for.

"Is there something wrong?" Lara asked as she started to feel uncomfortable under his constant gaze. "Is my dress out of fashion or my rouge too bright?"

Kyle chuckled. "Nothing of the kind. You are as captivating today as the first time I laid eyes upon you. Do you remember that day?"

Lara turned away, her mirthful smile suddenly gone. Of course she did. The memories of that entire day were still alive in her heart, but she was not prepared to relive those moments. Not now and not with him. "Would you like to see the house?" she asked, desperately needing to change the topic.

Entering the master bedroom, it was clear that Kyle had caught Lara in the middle of unpacking her belongings. Immediately she caught sight of a few undergarments that were tossed carelessly onto her bed. Quickly she picked them up and tucked them into a nearby dresser. Gavin's picture lay flat on top of the bureau and his image worked to remind her of the decision she had made last night. Determined, Lara picked up the picture frame.

"I'll try to arrange to have the furniture from Haven Manor brought in over the next day or two," Kyle decided. "Then you might offer me a chair the next time I visit."

"It would be good to get settled in," Lara responded. "I'd like perhaps to spend the summers here," she turned to face Kyle. "I would like my son to come to know Charleston."

It was clear by Kyle's expression that her disclosure had caught him completely by surprise. For some reason it had never dawned on him that she would have given Aidan Quinn any children. Perhaps it was because he couldn't bear the thought of Lara being intimate with any man other than himself that he could afford such an absurd assumption. "I wasn't aware you had had a child. These last years have been good to you," Kyle offered with as much sincerity as he could muster, all the while trying to suppress the jumble of emotions churning inside him.

Lara held out Gavin's picture as she came to stand before Kyle. "He's a wonderful boy," her voice was filled with pride.

Kyle held Lara's gaze for a few seconds before forcing himself to glance down at the miniature likeness. In those next moments, confusion and disbelief reigned as he became hard struck by the innocent face staring back at him. He hesitated for a moment as he reached for the portrait. Dumbfounded he stood, mesmerized by the boy's blue eyes and the hint of a dimpled smile, but most of all by the striking resemblance for it was he, himself, whom he saw in the child's image. It was as though he was looking at his own childhood portrait. It couldn't be, he told himself. It was impossible! Inconceivable!

"Your son," Kyle could barely get the words out.

"Yes," Lara answered without hesitation.

Kyle looked at her with cold, piercing eyes. "By Aidan?" he finally braved, but from deep within he already knew her answer.

"By you," Lara replied softly. "It's a good likeness. You can see Gavin has your eyes and your dimples. He has a playful manner and loves to laugh. He is very much your son in looks and in temperament." So many times Lara had imagined Kyle's reaction, but nothing could have prepared her for the anger that filled his eyes and the dismay on his face. She was stunned by his reaction and guilt quickly invaded her conscience. "Please, Kyle, don't look at me like that."

"Like what? Like the conniving witch that you are! Curse you, Woman, what have you done!"

The harsh bite to his words alarmed Lara even more, but she was not going to let him make her feel small or guilty. "I'm telling you the truth and I've done nothing for which to be ashamed. Years ago you chastised me for not revealing my connection to Aunt Lyddie. Now you're doing the same when I have willingly told you of our son. Would it have been better to have kept this from you and chance you finding out from someone else?" Lara stopped herself. She could feel the tension mounting with the rising of her voice. Suddenly she was afraid she might say something she would regret later. To allow such talk would do nothing but drive them further apart and there were already enough irreconcilable differences between them. "I fell in love with you, Kyle," Lara confessed. "I honestly thought you felt the same for me. I never would have given myself to you if I had even the slightest doubt."

Kyle shook his head, then ran his fingers through his hair. "When did you discover you were with child?" he asked, still dazed by all she had to say. "Did you know that last evening we spent together?"

Lara shook her head. "I found out a few weeks after you left Brooklyn City."

"Five, almost six years. All this time. Why didn't you come to me or write to tell me?"

"So many times I wanted to pack my bags and follow you to Charleston. And just as many times I had started to put pen to paper, but I was too stubborn and too proud," Lara answered honestly, trying to remain calm and composed. "You weren't able to accept me for who I was then, and I was certain you wouldn't accept my child either."

Her words were sharp, though softly spoken. It was unfair of him to have forced her to choose between him and Lyddie, but only now did Kyle come to know the extent of the damage that had been done that night. "When was he born?" Kyle asked after an uncomfortably lengthy silence.

"His birthday is August fifteenth."

"He'll be five in a couple of months?" It was more a statement than a question. "You named the boy Gavin?"

"Gavin William," she answered, her voice trembling.

"Kendrick or has he taken the Quinn name?"

"Kendrick," Lara replied.

Kyle repeated the boy's name to himself. "I would have done right by you, Lara."

"How? By marrying me? Why is it so difficult for everyone to understand? I didn't want you on those terms. You would only come to feel trapped in a marriage with a wife you didn't want, with a babe you didn't want. You were already concerned with my connections and how they might have affected your career. Marrying me under those conditions would only have done more damage and made it that much harder for you to succeed. You would have grown to resent me and Gavin. I—" Lara's voice cracked. She forced herself to pause, to take a breath. "I wouldn't have been able to bear that; to watch our love disintegrate into hate and resentment. I'm not that strong."

"Then tell me what we have now. What's left of the love we had for one another?" Kyle held her gaze as he waited for her answer. His own eyes were moist, filling with tears and emotions after coming to realize what he had lost. "I did love you. With all my heart, I swear I did." With Gavin's portrait still in hand, Kyle turned to leave. He paused at the door, his back still towards her. "I've never stopped loving you, Lara. Not for a second."

Kyle's declaration left Lara stunned. She was jolted back to reality with the slamming of the front door a few moments later. Only then did she realize that tears had fallen and were streaming down her face. Lara ran to her window to watch Kyle's back as he took long, quick strides away from the house and away from her.

~ · ~

Lara had not seen nor heard from Kyle since she told him of Gavin several days ago. She had even begun to wonder if he would show up for the reading of Aunt Lyddie's will. Thus she was somewhat relieved to find Kyle already seated in Duncan's office when she arrived. However, his curt and formal greeting was enough of an indication that he meant to keep a cool distance. Clearly this was to be nothing more than a business meeting to him and that suited Lara quite well.

There was little chitchat before Duncan settled down with Lyddie's will in front of him. Lara sat quiet and still as she listened to his every word.

"I believe you're aware that all of Lyddie's finances were managed by Kyle through the Planters Bank of South Carolina."

Lara nodded.

"It's because of this relationship that Lyddie has named Kyle as Executor of her estate. The task now falls on him to ensure that all endowments will be distributed as Lyddie had intended."

Lara exchanged a quick glance with Kyle. "Does Kyle have any other obligations or responsibilities?"

"He does," Duncan confirmed. "We'll get to that shortly."

Lara shifted in her seat, unsettled by Duncan's reply. There was more to come and the thought of the unknown made her more anxious and uncomfortable in Kyle's presence.

Duncan began to read from the Will. To the city's hospital and to the Charleston Foundling Home, Lyddie had bequeathed a sum of a thousand dollars each. Duncan confirmed that Lara had inherited the remainder of the estate. Lyddie's investments, Haven Manor, the property on Wentworth Street, and all other possessions had been gifted to her as the one person whom Lyddie had loved and cherished more than anyone else in the world. In Lara's mind, the fortune her aunt had built was staggering, and her generosity was overwhelming. Lara was speechless.

Lyddie had made considerable investments in stocks and bonds over the years. Duncan surmised that at one time the portfolio would have been worth a good fortune, but the fallout from the panic of 1837 had had its adverse effects. Although Kyle had estimated the current value of the holdings at almost twenty four thousand dollars, it now stood at only a third of its worth as compared to four years ago. Economically the country was beginning to recover, but the Presidency had been passed on from Van Burren to Harrison to Tyler; three presidents all in a span of a few short months. Now the nation waited to see which direction President Tyler would take.

"Lyddie's portfolio had declined considerably before she came to us," Kyle joined in to explain. "We worked hard to restructure it. It had been doing conservatively well until last year. This slump is temporary. With patience, it should regain a good portion of its original value within the next year or two. It's a matter of time."

Despite Kyle's comments, Lara still believed twenty four thousand to be a fortune and the thought of selling the stocks and bonds to save Haven Manor flashed through her mind.

Duncan read on to reveal the sum of cash left in a bank account with the Planters Bank of South Carolina.

"Four thousand and some dollars is a sizeable amount of money," Lara stated. "I don't understand how Aunt Lyddie could have retained such an amount after purchasing the land and building her new home. And why would the bank—" She broke off abruptly, looking at Kyle.

"Why would the bank repossess Haven Manor when there was money in the account?" Kyle finished her thought for her. Lara nodded.

"Lyddie made a conscious decision to default on the mortgage."

"I thought the plantation was free and clear."

"Only up until a year ago," Kyle revealed. "When she decided on the Wentworth Street property, she took out a mortgage on the plantation to buy the land and build her house. Once settled into her new home, she had planned to sell the plantation to pay off the debt. With a good sale price, there would have been a tidy sum left over and Lyddie would have been able to live comfortably for many years without having to delve into any of her other assets."

Now it was Duncan's turn to add to the discussion. "After your Aunt's death we had no way of contacting you to find out what you wanted to do with Haven Manor. We only knew Lyddie didn't want you involved in the business - in any way. On the day of her death, the mortgage was in arrears. She had purposefully defaulted on two payments and there was another coming due a week after her passing. Kyle and I had discussed the matter at great length. We had no rights to sell the property on your behalf; neither could we foresee you being able to make up the overdue payments and keep the mortgage current. Thus we thought it best to let it go to the bank. If it were any institution other than the Planters Bank of South Carolina, Lyddie's bank account would already have been seized and the plantation sold to cover the balance due."

"So why haven't these deeds been done?" Lara directed her question to Kyle.

"There was the chance you might prefer the plantation to the new house," Kyle started to explain. "If that should be your wish, it would only be a simple matter of selling the house to cover the mortgage. I thought the choice should be yours. If you choose to let the plantation go, you might want to make arrangements with the bank to auction it off on your behalf. The bank will recover its losses and walk away ahead with the interest payment. Any monies left over will go back to the estate."

Kyle was cunning, Lara reminded herself. Yes, he did intervene on her behalf, but he would take advantage of every opportunity to flaunt his abilities to ensure that the bank would see a healthy profit.

"I didn't realize she wanted to sell Haven Manor," Lara thought aloud. "She had never mentioned such in her letters."

"Lyddie was ready to shut down the brothel," Duncan continued. "There was still much she wanted to see and do." His voice trailed off as he thought silently how tragic it was for Lyddie's life to have ended so early. "She even thought of keeping Haven Manor and turning it into an orphanage. Her work in support of the orphans was very important to her as evidenced by her donation to the foundling home. Lara, there is one other thing you need to know," Duncan forewarned. "Lyddie's estate could quickly be free from debt. To do so, Kyle and I recommend that you forfeit Haven Manor and keep the Wentworth property, but you, yourself, must make that decision. Whatever you decide, you will inherit a good piece of property and some investments, but you must fulfill one condition before you can claim it all as yours."

Lara sat upright in her chair. "And what would that be?"

"You must remain here in Charleston for at least the next twelve months."

"I can't possibly! A month or two at most, but not for a full year."

"I must admit it is an unusual request. One which Lyddie never fully explained, but it is little to ask, Lara, for what you would receive in return."

Lara didn't need to think hard about her aunt's reasoning. Aunt Lyddie would have known that Lara couldn't leave Gavin. This was Aunt Lyddie's last effort to have Lara move to Charleston. Even temporarily, it would give Kyle the opportunity of getting to know his son and a chance, if he wanted it, to try to win Lara back.

"I have family and responsibilities in Savannah. I can't abandon them," Lara tried desperately to explain.

"The house is valued at more than twelve thousand dollars. That alone is worth staying for, wouldn't you agree?" Kyle asked.

"How can you ask that of me?" Lara demanded, unable to contain her frustrations. She had told herself repeatedly that her stay in Charleston would last no more than a few weeks. Now it would be no less than a year. All this would warrant serious thought.

"You have been named heir to Lyddie's estate. As such, you have the right to sell or convey any of the assets, provided you have consent from both myself and Kyle."

"I don't understand, what does Kyle have to do with all this?"

Duncan paused long enough to cast a glance at Kyle before continuing. "Lara, Kyle won't be overseeing only your aunt's final wishes. He'll be overseeing your financial affairs as well."

Lara sat back in her chair. Dazed by Duncan's news, she could only ask him to repeat himself. "Did I hear you correctly? Kyle is to govern my activities?"

Kyle's voice was firm when he spoke again. "Lyddie had requested that Duncan handle any legal concerns. In addition, I'm to advise you on financial matters and all assets in the estate will continue to be managed under my direction. Together, Duncan and I have been entrusted to oversee your well being."

"That's ridiculous!" Lara refused the thought. She stared hard at Kyle. "How can you even consider such an obligation? You can't possibly make any sort of objective decision on my behalf!"

Kyle frowned. "This is not of my doing," he reminded her, his own patience tested. "Do you think I would have agreed to such arrangements if I had been aware of all the circumstances? Of your marriage, and of Gavin? I assure you, things would be quite different had I known what Lyddie was up to."

"No, I should have realized you wouldn't want any responsibility where Gavin is concerned," Lara confronted.

"You know that's not what I mean! Confound it, Lara, you know me better than that!"

The room fell silent with Lara mulling over her predicament. She was nothing less than totally perplexed by the turn of events. How could she be expected to deal with Kyle on any simple business matter let alone her own personal concerns? Aunt Lyddie knew how she felt about Kyle. How could her aunt even have considered such an arrangement, and then to have carried through with it! However, Lara knew Kyle was right. It was obvious Aunt Lyddie had thought all this through, and very carefully at that. She meant to force Kyle back into Lara's life and for as long as possible. What better way than this?

"All of Aunt Lyddie's possessions are now mine to do with as I please, so long as I have your permission." Lara locked gazes with Kyle before continuing on. "These assets, as you put it, which you have declared to be mine are, in truth, not mine at all. My whims and wishes, my plans for my own future, all these are subject to your approval. What if I were to refuse these terms?"

"Lara, it would be irresponsible of you to forfeit," Kyle responded quickly. "Lyddie wanted you to be happy and to know you would never be without."

"What would happen?" Lara asked again as she held Kyle's gaze.

"It was Lyddie's wish that Gavin would inherit it all," Duncan surrendered. "The estate would be held in trust to be managed on Gavin's behalf until the boy turns twenty-five years of age."

"To be managed by Kyle?" Lara assumed.

"Yes, by Kyle Garrett Harrison," Duncan recited from the will, "the boy's father."

Kyle's gaze shot up. Anger flashed in his eyes. "How long have you known?" he demanded.

"Lyddie drafted her will two years ago," Duncan answered, unruffled by Kyle's indignation.

The crease across Kyle's brow deepened. It was only days ago that Lara had told him of his son, and yet Lyddie, Duncan, and Aidan Quinn, a complete stranger, had been aware of the fact for years.

Lara, too, sat confused and angry. Kyle had suddenly been forced back into her life and yet she could only feel remorseful and sympathetic as she watched him. Like her, he had his own doubts and feelings to try to come to terms with. The two sat quietly, their gaze locked upon each other. Neither knew what to say or do to help ease the tension building between them.

"Don't be hasty, Lara," Duncan turned to advise her. "These provisions are quite reasonable. Some would even say generous. Give it serious thought and don't let your feelings push you into making a decision you will surely regret later."

"Duncan, is there anything else we should be aware of?" Kyle interrupted, his tone of voice betraying his own dissatisfaction with the turn of events.

Lara's heart jumped. She could feel the blood rushing through her veins as she waited for Duncan to speak. She sat up straight and stiff on the edge of her seat. What other instructions did Aunt Lyddie leave for Duncan? Would he now reveal the true relationship between her and Aidan? Lara held her breath. She prayed silently, hoping that Aunt Lyddie had not told Duncan all her secrets.

"You know all the relevant facts," Duncan confirmed.

Kyle shook his head. "I don't understand. Why would Lyddie choose me instead of Aidan Quinn as Executor of her estate? As Lara's husband, he would have been the most logical person to manage Lara's inheritance."

"Aidan raises horses. He knows little about finances," Duncan answered.

Lara breathed a deep sigh of relief. Duncan couldn't have given a more logical or simpler explanation. Pleased, she held Duncan's gaze. In those brief moments, Lara knew by the man's expression that Aunt Lyddie had also told him everything about Aidan Quinn.

"Duncan, I need a few minutes alone with Lara," Kyle demanded.

~ . ~

Kyle and Lara had both been hit hard by Lyddie's scheming and a heavy silence filled the room while each gathered their thoughts.

"I'm sorry you're so angry," Lara finally surrendered.

"I'm angry, I'm disappointed and most definitely confused! Damn it, Lara! You had no right not to tell me about the boy." Kyle took a deep breath.

Lara was not going to apologize and there was nothing else she could think of to say. She could feel her own anger rising as she continued to think through the mess at hand.

"I'm sorry too, Lara," Kyle started again, trying his best to put aside his own feelings to try to ease Lara's. "I imagine all this is as much a shock for you as it is for me. I know how displeased you are, but Lyddie only wanted what was best for you. Your Aunt was a charming lady —"

"Despite her profession? I can't believe you agreed to this?" Lara demanded.

"I'm fulfilling a commitment made to a friend."

"Yes, a commitment to meddle in matters which don't concern you. You have no right interfering in my life, none at all."

"Your Aunt granted me the privilege. As does my rights as... as a father," Kyle sputtered.

Lara bolted from her chair. "You stay away from Gavin! You have no rights as far as he's concerned!" She could feel herself losing control with each word spoken.

"Lara, I can't take back what happened between us in Brooklyn City. I was insensitive and selfish. I can't tell you how sorry I am. When I came back to Charleston, —"

Lara turned away from him. Kyle reached out and took her by the arm, refusing to let her go.

"No, Lara, listen to me. When I came back to Charleston, I met your Aunt and I found out what a decent and generous woman she was. We did become good friends even if we didn't share the same social circles. I understand the decisions she made and I respect her for having the courage to make them. She trusted me to oversee her business affairs and I promise you now, as I did your aunt, that I will do everything within my power to carry out her wishes as she had wanted. I will work to serve you the very best I can."

Lara's eyes glistened in the light as she met his gaze. "What could you possibly know about Aunt Lyddie's wishes or mine? I can't believe she would even consider you for this position, not after knowing —"

"About us? You're wrong, Lara, if you think Lyddie didn't give serious thought to her decision. I had to prove myself to her. Our first business dealings were simple matters, but they were a test; a test of my character as well as my business prowess. You see, Lara, your Aunt didn't believe me to be the ogre you painted."

"So she discovered for herself what kind of a man you are. It is most unfortunate you were not as generous to have given her the same courtesy years ago. Well I know your character, and that too was learned through my own experience. I was a fool to have given you my heart, Kyle Harrison. Years I have tried to free my soul of you and now you stand here only to have me endure more. Have you no conscience?"

Her words cut deep. He had hurt her profoundly that last night together and he knew her anger had raged on long past his leave of Brooklyn City. He had often wondered how well she fared. Now he knew those stinging feelings still hounded her even after all this time. "I made a mistake, Lara. Only now have I come to know how grave a mistake it was. I am truly and deeply sorry. I can only ask that you not make the same one and give me a chance to prove myself, to earn your trust again and to make amends."

"Then you have a hard task before you. I can't forget and I'm not sure I'm so generous as to be able to forgive. And what of Gavin? Are you willing to call him your own or do you intend to cast aside all responsibilities as his father?"

Kyle released Lara from his hold and turned away. When he came back to her, his doubts were written on his face. "I need time," he answered, not knowing what else to say. "We both do. Will you at least give us that?"

"You have no more than twelve months. Less if my strength and determination should fail me."

~ • ~

Lara stood alone. The air was delicately scented with the rose essence from her bridal bouquet. She could hear the organ music calling her from the other side of the narthex doors. As they opened wide, her eyes were drawn to the stained-glass mosaic wall at the far end of the nave. The brightest of lights shone down to illuminate the church and the colorful patchwork windows faded into the haze. Intrigued by its power, Lara was instantly drawn to the light. She felt its warmth and she wanted to be immersed within it.

Lara heard her name. She knew the man at the altar was waiting for her. He wanted her there beside him. He called out to her again with his deep, smooth voice. As she took her first steps towards him, the light began to dim, fading lighter and lighter with each step that took her closer to the one waiting. The skirt of her long silk satin gown flowed like a sinuous white wave behind her. Now only steps away, a strong masculine hand reached out for hers. She felt his firm and gentle strength as he brought her forward to join him at the altar. Lara's heart was overflowing as she looked up, eager to gaze into the loving eyes of the man who had won her heart.

Lara's dream faded. She fought to reclaim the vision, but her efforts worked only to bring her further into the conscious world. Like the last flicker of a candle flame desperately searching for fuel, the feeling of elation subsided. Her eyes opened slowly to find herself surrounded by the dark shadows of her new bedroom. She had dreamt this same fantasy several times and, as each time before, she woke before seeing the groom's face smile down upon her. It was no less frustrating this time.

Lara was tired, but her mind, now roused, refused to let her find sleep again. It had been such a long time since she last had that dream. Now she had to lie and endure its haunting effect. What hidden message did Morpheus have for her? Who was this elusive man who was to claim her as his bride? And when, oh when, would her heart be so filled with passion and love? Lara couldn't even wager a guess for she had long since lost faith that she would one day find her soul mate.

In some ways, her aunt had been very fortunate! She had found a loving partner in Kenneth Randall. Together they shared four years of a blissful marriage before it came to a tragic end when Kenneth was thrown from a horse. Then again years after his death, Lyddie found a second love with Captain Dane Haley. Dane had been more than a friend to her aunt. He had been a husband of sorts, with all the emotional and physical love, but without the blessing from Church and God. Even so, the two had nurtured a profound, unconditional love which many married couples had yet to discover. It was this kind of love Lara had mistakenly believed she had found with an ambitious assistant bank manager half a decade ago.

Aunt Lyddie and Dane had both been gloriously happy whenever they were together. Her aunt would have given up running the brothel out of Haven Manor if Dane had asked her. Lara was sure of it. However, Dane was also in love with the sea. He needed to command the power of a ship, to charter the mysterious oceans, and to experience different lands and cultures. The sailor's life called to him and he could never stay away for any great length of time. He, himself, had admitted several times that he would have left Aunt Lyddie too often and for too long. She would have been left to sit at home alone watching the harbor entrance, not knowing when or if he would ever come back to her. Dane was not so selfish as to ask that of the woman he loved. And he did love her aunt. There was no doubt about that.

Lara had often compared her relationship with Kyle to that of her aunt and Dane. She was baffled more often than not. Dane had not been able to ask Aunt Lyddie to give up the brothel, but Kyle, on the other hand, had felt he had the right to demand that Lara sever her own ties with Aunt Lyddie because of what went on at Haven Manor. Lara had never been able to make sense of that all.

Chapter 8

The Senator's Gift

*K*yle had everyone organized at Haven Manor. The furniture that Lara had selected had been moved down to take up space in the foyer or on the portico. Six strong men had been hired and were busy loading the pieces onto wagons. Kyle had persuaded Lara to take a few more items in addition to the ones she had tagged more than a week ago. His argument was sound enough for these were free for her taking and she would settle in more comfortably by having them. From his persuasive comments, it seemed he was expecting her to stay in Charleston—permanently.

Casey and two other maidservants from the Harrison household had accompanied them out to the Randall house. The three had started in the kitchen busy packing dishes, pots and other kitchen items. With everyone working on their assigned tasks, Lara wandered through the house perhaps for the very last time.

The mantle in her aunt's bedroom was overly large and stark without the portrait of aunt and niece. Most of the furniture had been removed and only boxes and piles of Lyddie's personal belongings remained. There would be another full day or two of sorting and packing before the house was emptied of its possessions. However Kyle had made arrangements for that as well, calling upon an auctioneer to appraise whatever was of value and disposing of that which was to be left behind.

Lara rummaged through the contents of a wooden crate for worry that she might have missed something of sentimental value. She went through the last of the large wardrobes as well. Like many times before she was awestruck by the many gowns, all richly colored and finely trimmed. Here, hung on iron hooks, was a small fortune in silks and satins, cottons and velvets, wools and muslins. Lara had chosen a select few of the finest with hopes that a skilled seamstress might be able to alter them to fit her own figure. Such a waste, she thought. Would anyone be able to make use of the gowns that remained?

The thought was still on her mind when she stopped cold, realizing she had entered the bathing room. Suddenly engulfed by sharp images of Cameron Palmer, her eyes darted to where he had her cornered. She remembered the feel of his body pressed hard against hers; his hands free upon her breast. Clearer still were the feelings of oppression. Lara closed her eyes to quell the feelings of panic.

Held prisoner by the memories of that harrowing event, she did not hear the oncoming footsteps. Lara screamed, woken abruptly from her nightmarish trance by the weight of a hand upon her shoulder. She heard her name then felt a firm grip upon her arm as she was turned about.

"Lara!" the commanding voice rang out again.

The instant of panic and fear passed. Lara looked deep into worried, blue eyes as Kyle wrapped his comforting arms around her.

~ · ~

In all her musings of returning to Charleston, the idea of having to purchase slaves had never entered Lara's mind. Then again she never believed she would be staying for more than a month or two. Discouragement turned into frustration as she spent the last week interviewing for a housemaid and a manservant. There had been only a few good candidates for the positions, even a husband and wife team, but each declined when she explained that twelve months of employment was all she could guarantee. Overly generous salaries, even free meals with separate and private accommodations were not enough to sway anyone into accepting employment with her. Whether local residents or newly arrived immigrants, those most capable were discriminating enough to hold out for a more secure and permanent posting.

Kyle had discussed with Lara the option of purchasing slaves, but she had refused, quick to recite the usual moral and ethical issues to support her stance. Without hesitation, Kyle reminded her that, like Georgia, the anti-slavery movement in South Carolina had achieved little success. Slavery was still very much a deep-rooted, integral part of the economic and social structure. Nowhere was this more prevalent than in Charleston where, by law, every negro was presumed to be a slave. There were an endless number of people who adamantly opposed her views, an extreme few who shared them, and rarer still were those brave or bold enough to openly support or voice the same beliefs as she.

"As much as I agree with you, you don't have much choice," Kyle stated. He had read her mind again.

"I suppose not. It's such a lot of money."

"Think of it as an investment in your future." Kyle pulled on the reins. The horse and buggy came to a complete stop in front of the auction house.

Lara stared up at the sign. Large black letters were painted against a blood red background: *Blackley's - Daily Auction of Choice Slaves*. Lara couldn't help but wonder how many men, women and children were bought and sold each day through the city's slave traders.

"I'll go in and see what they have. It's best you stay here," Kyle instructed.

Lara nodded her agreement for she needed no convincing to remain behind in the shay. She had heard many horror stories about traders and the wretched hovels in which they kept the slaves. Much like pigs in a pen, she imagined.

Lara could hear the gallop of horses slow to a trot behind her buggy. The two riders came alongside. A cold shiver went through her body as she recognized the finer dressed gentleman.

"Good morning, Mrs. Quinn. Needing a slave?"

She would never forget that voice. He had somehow discovered who she was. She glared back at Cameron Palmer with the silent hope that her fear would be masked by her contempt for the man. Lara gave a quick glance to Palmer's companion only to be greeted with a devilish leer before the man dismounted.

Her inhospitable silence provoked a chuckle from the Senator before he, too, dismounted. "Many men would consider such impertinent behavior from a comely maiden to be a challenge to overcome. Wouldn't you think so, Jackson?" he asked of his companion.

"Yes, sir," the man replied quickly, his eyes hard on Lara.

How arrogant of Palmer to accuse her of being rude. "My impertinent behavior, Senator Palmer, could only be described as exemplary when compared to your own actions."

The man raised a brow. "You know who I am."

"Mr. Harrison was kind enough to enlighten me."

"I'm sure Kyle had nothing other than words of praise for me," Palmer chuckled at his own sarcastic wit.

"I must admit I was shocked to learn of the prominent position which you hold within the community. Tell me, sir, do the powers of the Senate give you the authority to accost any woman you please? From your behavior, it would seem the laws you draft are meant for every citizen, but yourself."

"I can assure you that the law applies equally to each and every man. I admit I deserve every offensive, defamatory thought running through your pretty head. I know you are too gentle a woman to express such views," his voice became deeply somber, hinting of his shame and regret, "but if you did I'm sure they would not come close to my vulgar attack upon your person. I will not apologize for my misdeeds as that would only sound insincere and patronizing. I can only hope for the opportunity to make amends." Cameron Palmer swept off his hat and bowed before her. With that, he strolled into the auction house with his companion following close behind.

Lara didn't trust what she had just heard. The man's egotism and self-confidence vexed her even more, ruling out the possibility of any rational thinking. She sat in the buggy confused and furious, and feeling somewhat lost without Kyle.

~ • ~

Kyle committed himself to one thousand, four hundred dollars for the two house slaves. The husband and wife were an older couple and Kyle was convinced the pair had the experience to serve Lara well. The two stood together on the platform holding hands, but standing proud. The woman's oval face was flawless, healthy. Her tall frame was well proportioned to her husband's muscular stature. Based upon his physique, it seemed that he would have been better suited as a field hand and not a domestic servant. The two looked over the crowd, both keenly aware that their immediate future would be determined over this round of bidding.

"One thousand, four hundred is the bid. Do I hear five?" bellowed the auctioneer.

"One thousand, five!" boomed Jackson's voice. It was then that Lara realized the man was employed by Palmer as his overseer.

"One thousand, six!" was Kyle's next bid.

"Seven," Jackson countered.

"One thousand, seven hundred! Will you go one thousand, eight for the pair, Mr. Harrison? It's still a good buy for two healthy, well-trained and well-disciplined house slaves. They won't give you any trouble."

"I'll go eight." A new bidder joined in.

"One thousand, nine!" Jackson came back again.

"Two thousand," bid the newcomer. The offer was abnormally high and evoked a series of oh's and ah's from the disbelieving crowd.

"Two thousand, fifty!"

The crowd was abuzz.

Kyle stood up and motioned to Lara. He had had enough of this madness. "Come, Lara. They've overbid. For some reason Palmer's man, Jackson, seems determined to have them. Let's leave them to battle it out. We'll try another trader."

However the sale of house slaves had ended for the day by the time Kyle and Lara arrived at the second auction house.

"Shall we try again tomorrow?" Kyle asked, showing not even the slightest sign of disappointment.

"Can you spare any more time for this? I've kept you from your work so much already."

"You know I've never been one to shirk my responsibilities. Besides, there isn't anything at the bank that can't wait or can't be delegated."

"I could perhaps ask Duncan or Dane to help me."

"You forget that you, too, are my responsibility; one which I intend to take seriously."

"Is that all that I am to you, a responsibility?" Lara challenged.

Kyle steered the horse and buggy into the lane. "What are they doing here?"

Cameron's man, Jackson, sat leaning against the carriage house with the two house slaves standing beside him. All stood at attention when Lara and Kyle approached.

"Mrs. Quinn," Jackson greeted after remembering to remove his hat.

"What are you doing here?" Kyle demanded roughly.

Jackson ignored Kyle altogether and took a step closer to gain Lara's attention. "Mr. Palmer would like you to have these slaves, Ma'am."

"I don't understand."

"This should explain everything." Jackson handed her a folded paper then walked to his horse. He had already mounted and was galloping off before Lara was able to comprehend what had just happened.

Lara read the record then handed it to Kyle. She waited for Kyle's own disbelieving reaction.

"This is a chattel paper totaling two thousand, three hundred dollars," he confirmed. "It acknowledges full payment for Shani and Avram Hayes." Kyle looked up to the negro male. "You're Avram Hayes?"

"Yes, sir. This is my woman, Shani."

The negress took a small step forward.

Kyle glanced again at the paper then looked up at Lara. "These name you as their mistress, Lara. Legally, they are your property."

"Why would Palmer buy slaves for me?" she asked, confused by such an overly generous offering. "Could this be his way of apologizing? He did say he wanted to make amends."

"When was this?" Kyle demanded, uncomfortable with the thought of Lara being anywhere near the blackguard.

"Palmer and Jackson rode up after you went into the auction house. He said an apology would only sound insincere and patronizing and that he wanted somehow to make amends."

"Well, there's no disputing the receipt, but Palmer's motives are highly suspicious. His extravagant tastes and expenditures are usually reserved for himself. He's not known for his generosity towards others."

"What other reason could there be?" Lara asked the very question that would weigh heavily on both their minds.

Inside the house, Lara found some boxes for Avram and Shani to unpack while she and Kyle continued their conversation. A short while later, unable to come to any sort of logical conclusion,

Kyle had to leave to return to the bank. Lara took advantage of the situation and sat Avram and Shani down to discuss their duties. Afterwards the three settled down to unpacking more of the boxes that had arrived from the plantation, and to organizing the kitchen.

It was early evening when Lara showed the couple to their room above the carriage house. The large one room flat was bare except for a feather tick on the floor, a small stove in the middle of the room and a series of coat hooks along one wall. The couple beamed with gratitude, overjoyed with the luxury of having their own private quarters. If they had been living on a plantation, they would have been forced to share such a room with three or four other slave families.

By the end of the day, Lara was convinced that Kyle was right: Shani and Avram would serve her well. In a few short hours the two slaves had quickly proven themselves experienced with running a household. Each seemed to know the required domestic chores and completed them with little prompting from Lara. When assisting their mistress, their comments and suggestions were offered with caution, timidity and respect. Such were the thoughts running through Lara's head as she stood in the window to watch Avram who was busy at the woodpile in the far corner of the lot. He swung the axe in a smooth, circular motion. The blade hit its mark and split the stump with ease. As she looked on, Lara caught the scent of Shani's cooking as the teasing aromas wafted through the house. Lara smiled. Was this the feeling of security she was looking for? Could this be home? Perhaps, she told herself, but only if she had Gavin there with her!

~ . ~

Kyle had again stopped by after his work. He and Lara were seated in the parlor amidst the boxes and furniture piled against the walls. Once again, Cameron Palmer was their topic of conversation.

"Lara, I grew up with the man and I've years of business dealings with him. He's a manipulator with barely any morals or ethics. Everything he does is for his own personal gain."

"This has nothing to do with business. Don't you think you could be wrong this one time?"

Kyle shook his head. "I don't like it! And I'm not just speaking about business. Cameron Palmer is not one to be trusted! His infamous reputation with the ladies and in business dealings is well-known throughout the Carolinas."

"How could he possibly benefit by gifting me with two slaves?"

"I don't believe you, Lara! Listen to yourself! You're defending the man who assaulted you only days ago. That's the man the world sees and knows. You must realize what would have happened if I hadn't come along when I did!"

Lara rose from the settee. She didn't need to be reminded of the misdeed nor did she appreciate Kyle's tone of voice. However, he was right, of course. Palmer's extravagant gesture did nothing to erase her memory. Rather it only made her feel beholden towards the man who molested her.

Kyle came to face her. "I'm sorry, Lara. I didn't mean to be so brazenly harsh."

"It's obvious you have no respect for the man, and I must admit I'm not comfortable with having Shani and Avram presented to me in such a manner. Can I afford to repay him?"

"I think that would be best. I'll arrange for payment in state bonds first thing tomorrow."

"I should pay Mr. Palmer a visit myself."

"I can call for you in the morning. Would ten o'clock be convenient?"

"You needn't come. I'll take Avram and Shani with me." Lara met his questioning gaze with a confident smile. "Come now, Kyle. The man's not likely to assault me again."

"I wouldn't put it passed him!"

But Lara didn't need nor want anyone to keep guard over her. "This is something between the Senator and myself. I'm sure we can work it out."

Kyle did not expect any less from her. "Keep your stay short," he instructed. "Make sure you come by the bank afterwards. I will want to know all that happened."

Lara would have laughed if not for the serious tone of his voice and the solemn expression on his face. "Aren't you taking this all too seriously?"

His eyes bore into hers. "I'd say you're not taking this seriously enough." Then unexpectedly there was a gentle caress of his hand against her cheek. "I don't want anything to happen to you. I would never forgive myself." He cupped her face in his hands as his mouth came down upon hers. There was a shy touch of the lips, then another before he declared his affections for her with a longer, lingering kiss.

Lost in the passion of the moment, Lara was enveloped by his presence. For that one moment she forgot all the unpleasantness that had happened between them. Her eyes opened slowly to Kyle's handsome face.

Kyle hovered over her, searching those brown eyes for some hint as to her feelings for him. "I'm sorry."

In the next instant Kyle was gone and Lara was left standing alone to wonder what exactly his apology was for.

~ . ~

In a long letter to Aidan, Lara had scribed a recounting of events since her arrival in Charleston: her chance meeting with Kyle on her first night, the repossession of Haven Manor, the conditions of her inheritance, her encounter with Palmer, and the newly built home. And all financial concerns to be managed by Kyle Garrett Harrison. Yes, the same man whom she had met and fallen in love with in Brooklyn City. The same man whom Gavin, under different circumstances, might have come to call "Papa." Then there was her obligation to remain in Charleston for a year, and most recently Senator Palmer and his gift of two slaves.

Pen to paper, Lara had managed to relive the string of recent events on seven pages. Even after reading it over, it still seemed somewhat surreal that all this could have taken place in such a short period of time. Aidan too, she knew, would think the same. She folded the pages of her letter then tucked them into the crisp, white envelope. One last time she dipped her quill pen into the inkwell to address the front of the packet: *Mr. Aidan Quinn of Horseplay Stables, White Oaks Road, Savannah Georgia.* The letter was left on her bureau to be posted first thing the next morning.

Yes, rather bizarre it all was and today was no different. Lara continued to mull over the events of the last three weeks as she lay in bed. She had tried unsuccessfully to hire free labor only to have Kyle talk her into buying slaves to help keep the house and grounds. At first she regarded the idea with abhorrence, but quickly came to realize there was no other option available to her. Then the disappointment of not being able to win an auction bid for a slave was eliminated with Shani and Avram presented to her upon her own doorstep. Yet that only raised new doubts and stronger suspicions for how could she possibly accept such an endowment from anyone let alone the blackguard who had tried to rape her.

If Cameron Palmer truly was the scoundrel Kyle made him out to be, then the purchase of Shani and Avram could be nothing more than a villainous scheme to win her over. However after their first encounter, it would take more than a bribe of slaves. Still, what could Cameron Palmer possibly gain from that? Was he after her inheritance? Then the surprise would be his when he discovers that she has no control over her own financial affairs. As a lawmaker, Cameron would know better than any man how limited a woman's choices would be. He could only gain access to her money and property by marriage. Kyle had to be mistaken about the man's motives. Cameron's offering must have been meant as a sincere apology with only good intentions in mind. Regardless, she would know better tomorrow morning after paying the Senator a visit.

The cool air breezed through the tall windows and into her bedroom. The light weight of the cotton curtains billowed off the floor as they yielded to the night wind. Lara watched the darker shadows dance to the fluttering of the fabric. Only when the room turned uncomfortably cold did she rise from the snug warmth of her bed to close tight the glass panes, but not before peering out to see if the Harrison house was within view of her bedroom window.

Weeks ago she had convinced herself that she would see very little, if any, of Kyle Harrison while in Charleston. The last few days had proven her wrong. He had involved himself in every aspect of her settling into her new home and, in so doing, had once again become a part of her life. At first she found his presence most uncomfortable, but Lara now had to admit that she felt secure in knowing he was there to oversee her interests.

The memory of Kyle's tender kiss played sweetly upon her lips. His touch had come as a complete surprise to her. There was little doubt that he still cared for her. He had declared his feelings willingly and confidently, without expecting anything from her in return. How long would that last, she wondered. Would he soon be wanting more from her? She felt it in his kiss and heard it in his apology and that frightened her. As did her own reaction. She had done nothing to push him away or reprimand him for his bold behavior. She would have forgotten herself completely if there had been a second kiss. Could she fall for him again? Lara scolded herself for even having that thought. She could never forget how powerful and blinding a force his love could be, and how swiftly and completely it could crush her heart.

~ · ~

"Please tell Senator Palmer that Mrs. Quinn, the woman he met at Haven Manor, is here to see him."

The house servant cast Lara a seriously suspicious look for any woman coming from *that* place could only mean trouble for the master. Without doubt, *that* kind of trouble could damage the Senator's career.

Lara waited in the foyer for the maid to return. She stood, clutching onto an envelope. Did she look as nervous as she felt?

To alleviate her anxieties she concentrated on her surroundings. The regal staircase stood before her with its curved lines and wide stairs. The focal point within the tall walls and high ceiling of the open foyer was worthy of the stately grandeur of the large Georgian mansion. Various sized portraits decorated the walls, grouped together, evenly spaced in proportion to one another and in size with the other objects in the room. The furnishings were of polished burled walnut. Imported from England, Lara assumed. Stunning pieces of fine Chinese porcelain adorned the shelves and tabletops. A thick wool pile rug lay at the center of the room. Its emerald border encircled a floral pattern. Lara likened it to an English rose garden surrounded by a lush green hedge. The hand woven carpet brought a splash of vibrant color into the room. Everything here was tastefully put together, and it all bespoke the wealth of the household. There was nothing pretentious, only a warmth within this butter yellow room that, odd as it seemed, eased some of the jitters she felt only moments before.

"Master Palmer will see you now."

Lara followed the petite housemaid down the corridor. The quietude faded and she could hear strange noises coming from down the hall. The sounds grew louder as they approached a pair of doors. A dog? No, not one, Lara determined.

The study doors opened and Lara was surprised to find Cameron Palmer seated on the floor and surrounded by a litter of golden retriever puppies. Six energetic and playful pups!

Cameron looked up to greet Lara with a broad smile. "Good morning, Mrs. Quinn. I hope you don't mind the dogs."

"Not at all. They're darling." Lara commented as she knelt down to pet the first of the litter that came up to greet her. Then came another to sniff at her skirts and quickly she too was drawn into the raucous. "How old are they?" she asked before getting her hand licked by one of the puppies.

"Fourteen weeks," the Senator replied. "Jane, it's time to take them back to the stables." Cameron leashed the pups. He gave one last rough and playful pat to each before handing the reins over to the servant. He and Lara both watched as Jane tried to maintain control of the six pups without getting herself and them tangled in their leashes. Cameron chuckled after them as he rose from the floor.

Senator Cameron Palmer posed a formidable figure standing tall in front of Lara. His long limbs and broad shoulders were signs of his physical strength while his poised stance gave evidence of a man confident in his own powers and abilities.

Immediately Lara felt a peculiar attraction towards him, a familiarity and yet she wasn't able to define any specific quality that drew him to her. She could only sense that there was something about the man that she found appealing. It was somewhat unsettling and Lara had to force herself to put aside her distracting thoughts. "Thank you for seeing me, Senator Palmer."

"I'm both surprised and honored by your visit." His broad smile was matched by the twinkle in his blue eyes. "You have some business, I presume, for I think a social call would be too much to hope for. Please join me." He motioned to the settee. "I must admit. I had worried that the next time we meet it would be in the company of your husband who, I am sure, would be ready to do me serious harm."

"You needn't worry. Besides, I think Kyle Harrison did well enough on my behalf." Lara replied, remembering the hard blow Kyle had delivered to Cameron's jaw.

"That he did," Cameron agreed.

Lara sat on the edge of the couch. She did not want to get comfortable, but neither did she want to risk offending her host. She waited for Cameron to take a seat and was relieved that he opted for a tall, high-back chair for himself rather than taking the place beside her.

"I came to thank you for sending Shani and Avram to me."

Cameron sat back. "With a home here and another in Columbia, I know how difficult it can be to find good house slaves. I hope they will serve you well."

"They shall, but I cannot accept them as a gift. You must allow me to repay you." Lara handed Cameron the large envelope and waited as he pulled out the bond papers.

"What if I were to refuse repayment?"

"If you decline then you leave me no choice but to refuse your gift entirely. I would return Shani and Avram to you and have come prepared to do so. They are waiting outside in the carriage."

Cameron Palmer fanned the debentures. Silently, he debated accepting Lara's offer.

"We thought you would prefer bonds instead of bank notes," Lara explained.

"We?"

"Mr. Harrison had the market value confirmed this morning."

"I'm sure he did, although Planters banknotes would have been acceptable. I know they would be honored for their full value and not be discounted. Tell me, what is your association with Kyle?"

Lara hesitated, surprised by his sudden interest in her relationship with Kyle. "I inherited a small estate from my Aunt Lyddie. Kyle has been entrusted with overseeing my financial affairs."

"Lydia Randall was your aunt and that's how I came to find you at Haven Manor," Cameron contemplated aloud.

Lara nodded. "I had been packing some things and thought to wash up before returning to town. May we return to the business at hand?"

"Yes, of course," Cameron agreed. Like Lara, he had no desire to rehash those moments. "I will accept repayment, but twenty-three hundred is not a fair price."

"I don't understand. Two thousand, three hundred is the sum on the chattel papers."

Lara watched him handle the bonds. He placed each of the debentures on the table in front of him as he counted them out. He had not gone through all the certificates when he stopped. Those left in his hand were returned to the envelope and the package handed back to Lara.

"I'll accept your offer of repayment, but will only take nineteen hundred. I had overbid and my gentleman's pride will not allow you to bear the penalty for my folly."

"Please, I insist. It wouldn't be right if you were to take anything less."

"Mrs. Quinn, you run the risk of offending me."

"My intentions are just, Mr. Palmer. I mean no offence. I want only—"

"To free yourself from any perceivable obligation towards the man who accosted you. Please, Mrs. Quinn. I know we would be on much better terms had I not jumped to the wrong conclusion at Haven Manor. There are no excuses for my actions. I whole-heartedly regret the incident and must take some responsibility. I want nothing other than to reconcile myself to your favor. Until then my conscience will not grant me peace. How can these gnawing feelings be eased if you will not accept at least a token gift of my good faith?" Once again he offered her the bonds. "Nineteen hundred and all is forgiven?"

Lara looked into his blue eyes and laughed when he charmed her with a flirting grin. "One thousand, nine hundred. All is forgiven, but not forgotten."

"Fair enough."

With her goal accomplished, Lara rose, ready to give her excuse to leave.

"Before I let you go, I have two requests of you. I know I will find pleasure in both."

"Pleasure, Mr. Cameron? Of the most innocent kind, I hope."

The man chuckled, reconciling her comment as a good-humored tease. "Harmless, I assure you. My first request is that you refrain from calling me Mr. Palmer or Senator Palmer. You may reserve such formal titles for my father should he ever have the good fortune to make your acquaintance. For myself, I'd prefer you call me Cameron."

Lara paused. The man had somehow erased the anxieties that had accompanied her here. Upon knocking on his front door, she felt like she was walking into the lion's den. But the lion's den turned out to be a bright, clean and organized library belonging to a man who loved dogs. Now she was surprised at how comfortable she felt in his presence. "Cameron it shall be. And your second request?"

"There is to be a formal gathering on Friday, the twenty-fifth of June. All of Charleston will be in attendance. I would be honored if you would accompany me. That is unless you think your husband would object. It's an annual event held in the Great Hall of the Exchange Building to raise money for the orphanage. A cause dear to your aunt, I believe."

"Yes, it was." Lara hesitated, her mind not quick enough to come up with an excuse.

"It promises to be a grand evening," he coaxed, sensing her apprehensions. "It is still weeks away. You needn't answer me now, but promise me you will give it some thought."

~ · ~

Lara had taken both Shani and Avram with her to the Palmer plantation. As she had told Cameron, she had come ready to return them to their true master if he had not accepted her offer. Secretly she was relieved the need did not arise. How immoral it seemed to even consider treating individuals as property to be bought and sold, gifted or willed away without needing their consent, knowledge, or good opinion. "But this is the South," Lara reminded herself, "and that's how it is here."

Avram kept the horses at a gentle trot as the three traveled back into the city. Lara could see nothing but endless rows of cotton plants under a cloudless, powder blue sky. They passed teams of slaves who were hard at work in the fields, their bodies toiling to the hard pace set by a drummer. Their song rang out long and loud. Lara listened to Shani's sweet voice as it rose above the harmony. Coupled with Avram's own deep soulful sound, the two joined in to sing the tale of woe:

> *Go down, Moses*
> *Way down in Egyptland*
> *Tell old Pharaoh*
> *Let my people go.*

The sorrow song was one that Lara had heard many times before as she traversed these same roads as a young girl. This time, though, the words caught her ears and she listened carefully to their profound message of hope and freedom. For Lara, music had always been a favorite pastime whether through song or through an instrument. Only now did she become fully aware that lyrics and melody held a much different purpose for her than for the hundreds of enslaved working the land around her. Yes, this was the South!

Back in Charleston's business district, Lara had the two servants wait for her inside the Planters Bank. She would have sent Shani and Avram home, but was quickly reminded that slaves were not permitted to walk alone or be out of sight from their master, mistress or overseer. Lara was greeted by Addison as soon as she entered the bank. Once again the young man bombarded her with the usual pleasantries and insignificant chatter. Too kind to be rude, Lara waited for that opportune moment to seek Kyle out. When she did break free, she found Kyle in his office. His door was slightly ajar and she could overhear his conversation with Miss Morgan Landrey.

~ • ~

"Darling, I've hardly seen you at all this past week and never more than a few minutes at a time," Morgan declared in her usual sweet, sugarcoated voice. "Let's go out for dinner tonight," she cajoled. "Just the two of us. We have so much to catch up on!"

"Morgan, you know I have a meeting with your father and the other partners on the second Thursday of every month," Kyle reminded her.

"Of course, Father even mentioned it at breakfast this morning. How silly of me to forget."

There was a moment of silence before Morgan was brave enough to broach the next subject. "Casey tells me Lara Quinn has settled into her aunt's home on Wentworth Street. Isn't that just a few houses down from where you are?"

It hadn't taken Morgan long before she brought Lara up in conversation. "Most of the furniture has been brought in, but there's still some unpacking and settling in to be done."

"Will you be seeing her again soon?"

"Likely so."

"She is earning herself quite a reputation. Charleston is abuzz with the scene at The Charlestown her first night back and then the other day at the mercantile with Senator Palmer."

Morgan waited, but Kyle remained quiet and unmoved by anything she had to say.

"You've been seeing a lot of her since she's come to Charleston," Morgan continued on. "I must admit I'm a little jealous. She's taking away from the time we could be spending together."

"It's true that Lara and I have met on a few occasions and I'm sure we'll being seeing much more of each other." Kyle was trying his best to be truthful without hurting Morgan's feelings unnecessarily.

"What more do you have to do for that woman? Tell me again what she is to you."

"Lara is a good friend."

"Are you certain there is nothing more between you? One would think she was more than that," Morgan accused. "You've been seen all over Charleston with her. Rumors have even begun circulating."

Their conversation was becoming stilted. Morgan's usual sweet demeanor was fading quickly and Kyle could read the telltale signs of impatience on her face and in her voice. Still he remained calm. "I can't control what people think or say. It's up to you as to whether or not you want to believe the gossip. But that's all it is, Morgan, nothing but idle talk."

~ • ~

Upon his insistence, Kyle had made Lara promise to come by the bank immediately after her meeting with Cameron Palmer. Early afternoon turned into early evening and still Lara had made no appearance. Kyle grew increasingly concerned. His day had been busier than usual and he had not been able to get away for even a short while to search Lara out.

In the evening's meeting with Owen Landrey, Granger Wilkes and Matt Stevens, Kyle had cautiously tabled his worrisome news. He had informed the three owners of the Planters Bank of South Carolina that the quantity of their banknotes being returned for deposit was significantly lower than usual. The alarm had been raised once before during Kyle's term with the bank. The last time resulted in the same intense discussion as to what to do to alleviate the problem and how to eliminate the concern altogether.

Without any sort of central governing system, American banks were permitted to print their own paper money. Each note represented an equivalent value in specie—gold or silver coin—and the bearer could exchange the paper note at any time for the precious metals. As was always the case, banks would print more credit notes than the specie reserve on hand. Thus the banks knowingly put themselves at the risk of not being able to honor the exchange should a customer present an overly large amount of banknotes to be cashed in for coin. To protect the depositors, legislation required bank owners to take out state bonds equal to the total amount of bank notes printed. Although this helped to reduce the number of bank runs over the last few years, it did not eliminate the problem for even the value of state bonds fluctuated over time. As bond prices rose, the banks would print more paper money. When the market value of the debentures fell, the banks would often do nothing to offset the difference, thereby ignoring the increased risk and liability.

Kyle reported to the three partners that there did not seem to be any noticeable change in the amount of other banknotes being taken in, nor had there been an increase in the demand for gold or silver coin. Thus it was extremely difficult to determine if this was an abnormal fluctuation or if someone was purposely hoarding Planters' banknotes for some ill-conceived purpose. Regardless, there was now the greater, disquieting risk that the bank might be caught short.

A heavy silence filled the room. Kyle sat thinking of the banks that had been forced to close their doors in recent years. A flashback to 1837 brought to mind the New England bank that had been caught short with more than five hundred thousand dollars in notes outstanding and a specie reserve of less than nine hundred dollars. Terrible business, that was. Then there was the closure by the State of the Farmer's Bank of South Carolina when it failed to redeem its notes in coin. Kyle glanced at the faces of the three partners and he knew they were deep in similar thoughts.

Granger Wilkes looked overly concerned. The creases in his brow seemed permanently etched upon his forehead. A widower, he was getting on in age. His luck with investments had run out a couple of years ago and with it went his savings for retirement. Whatever he had was tied up in the bank and this left him strapped for cash. Such a poor state of affairs!

"What are our numbers?" Matt Stevens asked.

"Our specie to note ratio is one to twelve. We have just over nine hundred thousand in notes." Kyle had learned to be prepared when attending any meeting in which Matt Stevens was expected. Matt was a numbers man. He could easily work through the most complicated set of financial statements to determine the true worth of any enterprise.

"Seventy-five thousand in specie reserve," Matt stated, completing the simple math in a blink.

"Better than most," Owen Landrey commented.

The discussion went around the table with each partner expressing their own worries. In the end, it was decided that they could not sit idly by. Gold and silver were in limited supply so there was no fast or simple way of increasing the bank's specie reserve. Obtaining loan certificates from a private clearinghouse was discussed and quickly rejected. There could be dire consequences if the public discovered that the bank suddenly needed to increase its holdings by a large sum. At best, their notes would be highly discounted by local merchants and other banks. At worst, the talk could start a run should depositors panic over the gossip. This same risk would hold true if the bank decided to prematurely call in some loans. Thus after a long drawn out discussion, the only logical alternative was to protect the bank by increasing their holdings of state bonds under the guise of wanting to print more notes. With hopes that this would reduce some risk, Kyle was directed to complete the necessary transaction before close of the next business day.

The monthly board meeting had gone on longer than Kyle had anticipated. He had become impatient and restless as the discussion progressed into the evening for he had not been able to put aside his growing concern for Lara. Anxiety quickly turned to anger when he arrived at the Quinn home to discover from Avram that Lara's visit with Palmer had gone without incident. It seemed Lara had purposefully not sought Kyle out after stopping by the bank immediately after her meeting. In Kyle's mind, she had not kept her promise and had made him worry needlessly throughout the larger part of the day.

"Where is she?" Kyle demanded of Avram.

"Miss Lara is indisposed."

"Where is she?" Kyle repeated, his raised voice warned of his increasing ire for he had little patience left.

"Miss Lara is in her bedroom. She's just—"

Kyle ignored Avram's verbal attempts to stop him. He charged up the stairs, his long legs taking several steps at a time.

Lara was seated at her dressing table. She was clothed in her chemise and robe after a bath. The air softly scented with lavender. Shani was brushing out Lara's brown tresses when they heard footsteps advancing. The bedroom door burst open to give both ladies a fright.

Lara felt the rushing beat of her heart. "Kyle! What's the matter?"

"Leave us!" Kyle commanded the two servants, his icy stare fixed on Lara.

Avram had followed Kyle upstairs and stood outside Lara's bedroom door. The servant was not certain as to what he should do, but he was not about to leave without hearing his mistress's consent to do so. Shani, too, stood wide-eyed and waiting, frightened by Kyle's aggressive demands and fretting over what was going to happen next. Their lingering served only to erase what was left of Kyle's patience and fuel his rage.

Kyle knew it wouldn't take much effort on Avram's part to physically remove him from the house if that was to be Lara's directive. He stood firm knowing that any negro would be smart enough to think twice before laying a hand on a white man. His eyes darkened, his voice was low and stern when he uttered his command to Lara. "Dismiss them."

"It's alright," Lara calmly reassured the servants. "You may leave us."

Kyle's eyes followed Shani out of the room and waited until the door was firmly shut. Finally alone with Lara, Kyle did not change his antagonistic behavior. His eyes were hard upon her as he watched her work the buttons of her robe into their holes. "Where have you been?"

"I've been home all evening."

"You know what I mean. I expected you to come by the bank after seeing Palmer."

"Is that what this is all about? You're upset because you didn't see me this afternoon?"

"I'm upset because you didn't keep your promise. You had me worry needlessly."

"I'm sorry, Kyle, I didn't think that—"

"That's right. You didn't think!"

Lara might have found humor in the situation if his intolerant manner had not provoked her resentment. "That's not fair!"

"No? After pulling Cameron off of you the other day and knowing you were foolish enough to venture out to his plantation alone, how could I not think the worst?"

Lara rose from her seat to confront him. "I'm not a child, Kyle! You may have some say in my finances, but your obligations stop there. I am not required to report to you my every movement and you have no right to demand that of me!"

"Cameron Palmer is a scoundrel! I was there when he attacked you. Your face reflected the horror of your first encounter with the blackguard. I will never forget it. Given all that, did you really expect me to not worry over your safety?"

The room fell quiet.

"Kyle," Lara responded in a calmer tone, "I understand and appreciate your concern, but I'm a grown woman and I can take care of myself. Cameron was polite and sincere. He feels remorse over the entire incident. He even refused to accept full payment for Shani and Avram."

"Did he? Polite and sincere, you say?"

"Yes, he was."

"Imagine that," scoffed Kyle. "I suppose you gave in to his guileful charms?"

Again, Lara could feel her impatience growing with his unrelenting manner. She tried to remain passive to his insults, but found it increasingly difficult. "Rest assured, I kept my senses."

"Yes, your actions have proven that to be true."

Lara threw her hands in the air. She had had enough of his sarcastic words and had finally lost her patience and her composure. "Enough! Cameron was every bit the gentleman, unlike the shameless man who stands before me now! You besmirch another based upon your own prejudices. How just and honorable is that?"

"You dare compare me to that scoundrel?"

"Perhaps you should worry less about Cameron for surely your time would be better spent examining your own words and actions. Do you really think yourself that much better than he or should I assume all Charleston men are like the two of you?"

Kyle stood dumbfounded, unable to understand why Lara would have any reason to turn on him.

"When it comes to a woman, neither one of you seem to have any sense of what is decent or proper," Lara scolded. "You barge into my home and demand master's rights over my servants. You burst into my bedchamber as if it were your own and make demands which you have no right to make. Well, this is not your house and I am not your paramour! You cannot come and go as you please and I would thank you to remember that in the future!" Lara brushed passed him for her bedroom door. There she held it open wide, her intentions perfectly clear.

Kyle took long, hasty strides out of her bedroom. He stopped on the other side of the door with his back towards her to listen to her last words.

"As for going by the bank, let me inform you that I had come by to see you. Avram and Shani can attest to that as can your Mr. Addison! Upon reaching your office, I found the door ajar and came to overhear part of your discussion with Miss Landrey. Given that I was the topic of your conversation, I did not think it the most opportune time to make her acquaintance!"

The slamming of the front door could be heard throughout the house seconds later. From her bedroom window, Lara watched Kyle storm down the lane and out onto Wentworth Street towards his own home. The house was quiet once again with only the sound of Lara's footsteps as she vented her own anger by pacing her room.

~ · ~

Fuming, Kyle stomped down Wentworth Street. He stopped long enough to do damage to his hat by swatting it against a neighbor's wrought iron fence. Could he have acted any more the dimwitted fool? Of course he had no hold over Lara. He knew that.

It didn't take much more thought for him to acknowledge that his behavior was horrid and uncouth. He had called Cameron Palmer a scoundrel when he, too, had so rudely invaded Lara's privacy. *You besmirch another based upon your own prejudices. How just and honorable is that?* How insolent! How arrogant! But he knew his intentions were honorable. He had been genuinely worried about Lara and needed to know that she was alright. Why couldn't she understand that?

Neither one of you seem to have any sense of what is decent or proper. Lara's chiding words echoed through his head. It had stung to hear those words coming from her. Was she thinking of this last incident or back to Brooklyn City? Both, he told himself with certainty. What possessed him to be so impertinent?

Without having to think about it, the same answer as before came to mind. Yes, he was still in love with Lara. Insanely so. You fool, he repeated. What chance did he have of winning her back, especially now that she was married to another? He couldn't go on like this. Somehow, he had to find a way to let her go!

Chapter 9

∞

Loving Him Still

The morning sun was warm upon Lara's face as she sat out on the piazza with her tea and biscuit. There had been no word or visit from Kyle since their quarrel three nights previous. Lara had kept herself busy by unpacking boxes and cleaning and moving furniture despite Shani's discouraging pleas to leave such menial chores for herself and Avram. But Lara found these tasks to be both productive and mind settling. She needed them to keep her thoughts away from Kyle and the terrible row they had had. Throughout these last days she had been secretly hoping he would come by. They would then apologize to each other and they would put the entire incident behind them.

However, days had come and gone and still he hadn't come by. Feelings of guilt had invaded her conscience and, at times, she found herself completely distracted by her thoughts of Kyle. She should have remained composed instead of allowing his words to inflame her temper. His actions were intolerable and she had every right to reproach him, but perhaps her words were too sharp and had cut too deep. It was all such a silly little squabble!

Lara's thoughts rambled on as she spread strawberry preserve over the top half of her biscuit. Had Kyle truly been too busy to come by or was he too proud? Perhaps she should put aside her own pride and make the effort this time.

Shani's footsteps distracted Lara from her musings. "Miss Lara, this just came for you."

"Is it from Kyle?" Her voice rang out a hopeful note.

"It's from Senator Cameron. His man is at the door. He's been told to wait for your answer."

Lara removed the starch white card from its envelope. It was an impressive paper with the large scripted initials "CP" embossed upon the front. Cameron was to leave Charleston for the state capital and expressed his desire to call on her upon his return a few days before the charity ball. He also included a formal invitation to attend the fundraiser with him. Should she reject or accept his offers? The ball would be an ideal opportunity for her to meet and mingle with Charleston society. If she were to remain here for several more months then the time would pass more quickly and much more enjoyably with a few new friends. In her mind, Cameron had gone out of his way to atone for his actions. His apology seemed genuine and he deserved another chance, despite Kyle's warnings.

Unconsciously, Lara bit her bottom lip as she continued to debate her answer. Kyle would surely disapprove of her accepting any offer from Cameron, but why should his approval weigh into the matter at all? Aidan, of course, would give his consent for he was never one to hold her back on anything. A slight smile played upon her lips as she made up her mind. Yes, she would have Cameron call on her, but decided it would be best that she attend the ball on her own, if she was to go at all!

"Shani, please bring me my writing box."

Within the quarter hour, Cameron's manservant had been sent off with Lara's written reply.

～ ∙ ～

Lara approached the door to Kyle's office. It was wide open and she could see two women sitting in front of his desk with their backs to the door. Lara wasn't feeling very confident and was about to turn and leave when Kyle caught a glimpse of her.

"Lara," he stood up immediately. "Please, come in." He invited as he motioned for her to enter. The broad smile on his face evidence enough that he was pleased to see her.

"Good morning, Lara."

"Good morning, Kyle." Lara's attention went to the two women, giving them a friendly smile, then back to Kyle. "I'm sorry. I didn't want to interrupt."

"I'm glad you're here," Kyle confirmed.

"Good morning, Lara." Jenna Landon's welcome was warm and friendly.

"You two know each other?" Kyle asked with surprise.

"Dane introduced us," Lara explained simply.

"I understand you've settled into your Aunt's new house," Jenna started.

"I wouldn't call it settled. There's still quite a bit of unpacking to do," Lara replied, wondering how Jenna knew of her move.

"Lara, I'd like for you to meet Miss Morgan Landrey," Kyle started the introductions. "Morgan, this is Mrs.—"

"Mrs. Lara Quinn," Morgan interrupted. She rose from her seat, preferring to meet her adversary eye to eye. "Lydia Randall's niece. I've been hearing lots about you."

Lara looked into piercing, crystal blue eyes. Morgan's strawberry blonde curls framed an oval, bisque-smooth face. Her complexion was flawless like a fine porcelain doll. She stood perhaps an inch or two taller than Lara, tall and slender, immaculately dressed in soft yellow muslin. With Kyle by her side, the two made for a stunningly attractive couple.

"I'm pleased to meet you, Miss Landrey," Lara responded politely.

"Charleston society must seem quaint compared to that of Savannah. You must be looking forward to going home soon,"

Morgan assumed, taking care to stress those last three important words.

"Indeed, I am," Lara answered quickly for her thoughts went immediately to Gavin. For Kyle, her response came too easily and the certainty in her voice wiped away his smile.

Lara's answer prompted a confident grin from Morgan. Her eyes swept over Lara from head to toe in one slow critical inspection. "Well, Kyle, it seems you are much the sought after bachelor today. You didn't mention you had another appointment this morning. I hope you won't be canceling our lunch."

"I have no appointment," Lara admitted. "I'm intruding on Kyle's time."

"You may be an intrusion, but never an unwelcome one."

Each of the three ladies heard and understood the endearing tone in Kyle's voice. Jenna was instantly intrigued. Morgan, however, felt a disturbing pang of jealousy.

It was an uneasy moment for Lara and she hoped that her insecurities didn't show. She had come by with the intent to make right whatever had gone wrong the other evening, but that would have to wait. An apology to Kyle now would be impossible in the presence of strangers, especially when one of them was romantically involved with him.

Lara reached into her handbag and pulled out a wad of folded papers. She handed them to Kyle. "I came by to return these."

Kyle unfolded the bonds which Cameron Palmer had declined. He raised a brow, surprised by the generous amount that had been returned. "I'll take care of it."

"Well then, I should take my leave and let you all go for lunch," Lara excused herself.

"Not I," Jenna said, "I'm expected at the orphanage."

"Jenna is one of the directors of the Charleston Foundling Home," Kyle explained.

"Lara, would you like to come along?" Jenna offered. "It's not far and I don't plan on staying long. I would like the company and it would give you the opportunity of seeing some of Lyddie's work."

~ · ~

Seven children of various ages were running about the yard in play. Four older children stood by with a watchful eye while tending the flowers and shrubbery. The fervor of activity rose to an even higher level as the approaching carriage drew the children's attention. When Jenna stepped down, the children came upon her like a swarm of bees. Their welcome turned ever more boisterous when she produced a bag of lemon drops.

Jenna rattled off a series of greetings, calling each child by name. There was Blanche and Gertie, Haley and Miriam. There were the twins – Jody and Cody. Then there was a Peter and a Theodore—not Ted or Teddy, Lara was advised; and several others whose names Lara had forgotten despite her concerted efforts to remember. As Jenna revealed, there were seventeen children currently living at the foundling home. They ranged in age from two years to fourteen.

Lara toured the square, two-storey home with Jenna and Mrs. Penny Carlisle, the head mistress. Although clean and in reasonable condition, the thirty-seven year old, Federal-style residence was too small for its inhabitants, both in the size of the building and the piece of land on which it stood. Each floor had been converted to include its own bathing room while the other main rooms were used as bedrooms with three, sometimes four beds in each. The only exception was one sparsely furnished parlor and the original dining room that had been converted into the children's cramped schoolroom. Behind the main house were the smaller buildings that made up the rest of the homesite. Silently Lara wondered if it was too late to donate a few furniture pieces from Haven Manor. She would have to remember to broach the topic with Kyle.

Overall the buildings seemed to be in fair condition, but it seemed there were a number of improvements that would soon be required if all was to be kept in an acceptable state. It would take only one or two unexpected expenses for the list to become unmanageable given the home's small operating budget. Such had become a growing concern for the management committee of seven women and two men – of which Jenna and Kyle were both active and prominent members.

While waiting for tea, the three ladies sat in the small parlor discussing the current state of affairs.

"We have explored the possibility of moving or even building another home," Jenna revealed, "but there has always been one issue or another too great to overcome. Most often it's due to a lack of money. We rely mostly on charitable donations to keep the orphanage going. From that, there are the regular expenses to be paid and not much, if any, is left over."

Aunt Lyddie's gift will be a godsend, Lara told herself.

"We also plan two major fundraising events each year," Jenna continued. "The first is a ball that takes place in late spring or early summer to take advantage of the beginning of the Season. The second is usually scheduled for a few weeks before Christmas."

"What funds we raise are more often than not spent on major repairs," Penny joined in. "Overall, methinks we do quite well," she added quickly. "Thanks in large part to Mr. Harrison's talents. He watches every penny for us. I don't know what we'd do without him."

Lara observed the head mistress. Penny Carlisle was a large woman whose jolly smile seemed pasted upon her round, rosy face. Her hair was pinned up in a tight bun. With her quick wit and optimistic attitude, Penny was the kind of person who would be able to find a positive light in any situation. One could tell her work was her passion. Her love for the children was unquestionable as was her loyalty and dedication to the orphanage.

"A larger, better kept home would be grand," Penny agreed, "but the price of land, even after the panic a few years ago, has not been affordable. Land values have increased since, especially with the plantation crops yielding decent profits again."

The three women turned to the parlor door as footsteps approached. A shy, ballerina-thin girl of no more than twelve or thirteen years entered the room. Penny introduced Gemma to Lara as the young girl placed a laden tray upon the tea table. Gemma surrendered a timid smile and a quick nod of the head. Quietly and daintily the lass poured tea and offered a small plate of homemade treats to each of the ladies in turn. A kind word of praise from Penny brought a brilliant smile to Gemma's young face. Finished with the formalities, she left the room without uttering a single word.

"Lara, you've arrived just in time for our next charity social. We've been quite busy with our plans." Jenna confirmed, starting up the conversation again.

"We're putting the committee members up for auction," Penny laughed at the idea.

"There are nine of us, ten including Penny," Jenna started to explain. "Kyle came up with the idea that we would be raffled off for each dance.

"Raffled off?" Lara had never heard of such a thing.

"It is a rather odd concept and it took quite a bit of convincing to win us all over. The idea is that there would be ten containers. Each container would bear the name of a committee member. One would have Kyle's name on it, another mine, another Penny's and so on. Anyone attending the ball who wishes to win a dance with one of us would pay a dollar for each chance. Their name would be written on a piece of paper to be placed in the container belonging to the committee member they would like to dance with. Immediately before each dance, a ticket is pulled to identify the winner who would have a round on the floor with the person of their choice. We've planned for ten rounds, is that right, Penny?"

The woman nodded. "I expect Mr. Harrison will bring in the most money seeing how he is the most handsome and eligible of bachelors."

"The more you pay, the more chances of winning a dance. If you don't win, the money still goes to a worthy cause. What an original idea!" Lara responded. "With the number of people in attendance you would be sure to raise a few hundred dollars."

"We hope to! Along with other donations and with tickets to the ball being sold at five dollars per person, we'll be well on our way to meeting our goal," the pitch of Penny's voice rose to match her excitement.

"What is your goal?"

"Two thousand dollars," Jenna answered. "Will you be attending the ball, Lara? Bryce and I would love to have you in our party. His brother and sister-in-law will be coming in from Hamburg. Kyle and Morgan will be joining us as well."

"That's kind of you, Jenna, but I have already received an invitation."

"Oh, from anyone we know?"

"Senator Palmer was kind enough to invite me."

Jenna hesitated long enough to exchange a quick glance with Penny. "Cameron Palmer is quite a fellow. His reputation with the ladies is well-known around these parts."

"Yes," Lara replied knowingly, "I've already been forewarned."

~ · ~

"You've finished work early," Lara commented as she met Kyle at the bottom of the stairs.

"Only you could pull me away early." He smiled as he watched her take each poised step. He held out his hand for her. This time she took hold without hesitation and led him into the disarray that was the sitting room.

"I was pleased that you came by the bank earlier today," Kyle admitted. "Lara, I want to apologize for the other night. I had no right barging in the way I did. I hope you're not still upset with me."

"It was all rather silly, wasn't it?"

"I don't think so. It got me into your bedroom," Kyle quipped.

"You're such a rascal!" Lara laughed.

Kyle chuckled. His own spirits lifted by her lighthearted mood. His eyes sparkled with fun as he took the seat next to her on the settee. "I thought we might have dinner together then I'd like to take you to the Music Academy."

Caution ruled. "I'm sorry, Kyle. I don't think we should."

"It's not a formal event. There are a few musicians who have come together to practice for the orphans' ball. I thought you might enjoy watching them rehearse."

"Perhaps another time."

"Tell me, what other plans do you have for tonight?"

"I was hoping to get this sitting room in order. I've procrastinated long enough. The boxes must go and I'd like to give the floor and furniture a good polish before any of these things are unpacked and put away."

Kyle leaned back, feigning injury with his hands upon his chest. "Mrs. Quinn, you've rendered a hard blow to my manly pride. It's a heartless revelation to inform a man that household chores and cleaning are preferred over his company, no matter how tiresome he may be. Fie on you, for even an obvious lie would have been more merciful than the truth."

Lara laughed at his charade.

"Come with me to dinner," he coaxed. "The Music Academy, Lara, I know you'll enjoy it!"

"I would if it weren't for the fact that Shani will have dinner ready shortly."

"Then we'll dine here and then go to the Academy. What do you say to that?"

"Kyle, I…"

"I'm not asking for anything except a few hours of your time. I promise that, even with my overbearing manner, it will be more enjoyable than beeswax, dust rags and wooden crates." His hand covered his heart again. "Furthermore I promise to be on my best behavior."

Lara relented, giving in to his charming, innocent expression. "I'm not convinced that would be good enough," she teased. "I must warn you, tonight's cuisine may not be to your liking. I've asked Shani to prepare fried chicken and okra succotash. I've been craving both for days now, but we do have chocolate cake for dessert." Lara paused to wait for Kyle's reaction to her menu choices. He only raised a brow in consideration of her odd hankerings.

"Chocolate cake is my favorite," Kyle admitted.

The image of Gavin's little mouth covered in chocolate cake flashed through Lara's mind. Chocolate was Gavin's favorite as well. Like father, like son, she thought.

"I've been having my meals served out on the piazza," she continued. "With the current state of the dining room, it must be that or the kitchen. I'm certain Shani will forbid you entry into her domain. Shall I tell her to set another place?" Lara posed her question as a subtle challenge, wondering if he might be dissuaded by such simple dinner fare.

The conversation, like the meal, was casual and light with the occasional exchange of good-natured joshing and teasing. Kyle's own quick wit easily kept up with Lara's nonsensical banter. In between the bouts of silliness, they exchanged highlights of the events of their lives over the last five and half years. Both were careful not to delve too far into each other's personal affairs or to bring up any painful memories of times once shared.

Lara also broached the topic of furniture for the foundling home. Kyle took to the idea immediately, and together they decided that they would put forth an offer to Penny to go out to Haven Manor to view what was left.

"Would you like another piece of Shani's chicken?" Lara offered as Kyle relaxed into his chair.

"Another bite and I won't be able to get up from this table."

"Did you enjoy the meal?"

"I did."

"Shani was worried you might be offended by such meager offerings."

"Did you think I would take offense?"

"You have your pride. Well placed and sensible for the most part."

"Well placed and sensible, you say?" Kyle pondered, wondering how much of a compliment was enveloped in her observations.

"Would you rather I believe as Elizabeth Bennet did of Mr. Darcy?"

"Elizabeth Bennet and Mr. who?"

"Miss Elizabeth Bennet and Mr. Darcy," Lara started to explain, "are the heroine and hero of the novel entitled *Pride and Prejudice*. It's a love story in which Mr. Darcy's pride is at first mistaken by Elizabeth to be haughtiness and conceit. He acts so overly proud as to be considered vain. She, as a result, becomes prejudiced against him."

"So how does this Darcy fellow win the heart of Miss Elizabeth?"

"He proves himself through strength of character and honorable, unselfish deeds."

"Is that all? I always thought it would require a great deal more effort than that," Kyle teased.

"Oh? Is it such an arduous task to win a woman's heart?"

A long pause.

"Oh, you mustn't stop now, not when you've piqued my curiosity."

Kyle met Lara's expectant gaze while he debated with himself as to whether or not to continue. "In my experience, the winning of a woman's heart is a challenge, although a most enjoyable one.

However it's not the winning, but the keeping of it that seems to be the more difficult task."

"Tell me, Mr. Harrison, have you won and lost many?"

He released a soft chuckle. "In all honesty, I'm not sure if I have ever won a woman's heart. Have I?"

Now it was Lara's turn to decide how to answer. "A woman surrenders heart and soul to the man she truly loves. Her steadfast devotion, adoration, respect and passion are never given away freely. These treasures are bestowed only to that extraordinary man who will offer the same in return. Thus tender love once won cannot be easily lost. So when a love dies, if ever it were strong, would not die quickly or painlessly."

"Then what of true love? Could that ever die?"

"True love will never perish," Lara answered, knowing how naïve she would seem.

"You are a romantic. By your own definition, it would seem then that I have never won a woman's heart. Such affections for me faded quickly and seemingly without pain." Kyle paused, waiting long enough for Lara to refute his statements, but she chose to remain silent and quite still. "So it seems I have yet to find true love."

Lara lost herself in his words: *I never have won a woman's heart. Such affections for me faded quickly and seemingly without pain.* How wrong he was!

"May I get you anything else, Miss Lara?" Shani's inquiry interrupted Lara's thoughts.

"No, Shani, everything was delicious. My cravings have certainly been satisfied."

"That was the best chicken I have ever tasted. Cayenne pepper?" Kyle asked.

Shani beamed. "With a pinch or two of black pepper."

"The best! But don't you get me into trouble by telling Casey I said so."

"No sir, Mr. Kyle." The servant turned again to address Lara. "Shall I serve dessert, Miss Lara? Mr. Kyle might like a piece of that cake you baked this afternoon."

"I'm sure the cake is delicious, but I couldn't eat another bite at this very moment," Kyle answered Shani directly, then turned to Lara. "Perhaps Mrs. Quinn would be kind enough to invite me back for dessert after the Music Academy."

~ . ~

It was one of those comfortably warm evenings that would have convinced many that summer had arrived early. Thus it was easily decided that a walk to the Music Academy was in order for it was too pleasant a night to be confined within a carriage.

This was the first good opportunity Lara had had to venture the neighborhood. She marveled at the stately homes as they strolled down Wentworth and Meeting Streets. Each house was impressive in its own way, whether it was an older Colonial, Georgian or Federal style residence, or the more modern houses that tended to incorporate some of the Greek, Gothic or Italian architectural elements. Inspiring landscapes provided a lush foreground to the grand homes. Dazzling azalea blooms carpeted the courtyards while climbing vines cascaded over garden walls and fences to add their own splash of luscious color.

Lara stopped now and again to admire the vibrant blossoms that scented the air. Romantic clusters of soft, blue-violet wisteria; fragrant, delicate climbing roses; and the ever-present white stars of jasmine were among those vying for Lara's attention. Kyle remained close by her side and was happy to let Lara set the pace. There was no need to rush and, in truth, he wanted to make this time with her last as long as possible.

Lara released a longing sigh. How splendidly grand these homes were compared to her own wild plot of land. "I don't know when I'm ever going to get the house and landscaping in order."

"You will."

"I haven't been able to organize even one room and I'm not going to get any further along if I don't set my mind to the task."

"Then let me suggest that, since I'm the culprit monopolizing your time, I come by tomorrow to help with some moving and unpacking."

"You?" Lara didn't bother to hide her surprise.

"I take offense!" Kyle defended himself. "I can be quite useful about the house."

"Can you? I wonder what Casey would have to say about that."

"Casey is the most loyal and devoted of housekeepers."

"I suppose then that she won't be telling me any different."

"Exactly."

"Then I'll have to accept your offer so as to find out for myself," Lara declared.

At the Music Academy, there was a free spirited, almost chaotic, mood in the chamber room. Quite the opposite of what Lara was expecting. Kyle became the center of attention immediately upon their arrival. From the lively exchange of greetings Lara was able to determine that this evening's rehearsal was for the orphanage committee to review the selection of music for the upcoming ball.

Besides Kyle, Jenna Landon and her husband Bryce were in attendance. There were also two others from the foundling home's governing board. The first member was introduced to Lara as Mrs. Gwendolyn Elsey, a prominent member of Charleston society and the wife of a local indigo and tobacco planter. Her husband was most likely a very well-to-do plantation owner for she was fashionably dressed in the latest of European styles made from the finest muslin. There was the usual exchange of how-do-you-do's, but Lara found the woman's manner to be abrupt. The matron spoke in a rather irritating tone and although her comments were innocent enough, from her they sounded condescending. No doubt she could be difficult to deal with, demanding and meddlesome at times.

Lara guessed that Mrs. Faye Carin could not have been more than thirty years of age. There was nothing extraordinary about her features except for her natural luminous complexion. Her ash-brown hair was tied back with a wide cotton ribbon of the same calico cloth as her day dress. The mass of her long curls lay over her left shoulder. One could not help but admire her hair's length and healthy sheen. Her oval face lit up with a broad smile and sparkling chestnut brown eyes when she caught sight of Kyle.

"There you are, Kyle. I was starting to wonder if you were coming at all. Then again you did promise, didn't you, darling? We know you would never disappoint me." There was a hint of sarcasm, but the soft cooing timbre of the woman's voice was enough to declare her interest in Kyle.

"Good evening, Faye." Kyle responded casually. "Sorry we're late."

"We?" It was as though she hadn't noticed Lara at all. "Oh! And who is this you've brought along?"

"Lara, may I introduce Mrs. Faye Carin. Faye, this is Mrs. Lara Quinn."

"I'm pleased to meet you, Mrs. Carin." Lara responded.

"Please dearie, Faye will do quite well. Always the gentleman you are, Kyle. You know I detest the "Mrs." and have refused the title from the day Lars passed away. So! This is Lara Quinn. I've heard grumblings that Kyle had found himself a new friend."

"Lara and I have known each other for several years now," Kyle corrected.

"Oh, a sweetheart from your past. Lucky for Morgan your attractive little friend is married and spoken for," the woman cooed with keen interest.

Lara formed an immediate dislike for Faye Carin. The woman was bold to jump to the conclusion that she and Kyle had shared a "past"! How could she speak so openly when she couldn't possibly have any facts to support her assumptions? But what was even more annoying to Lara was that Faye had guessed correctly.

"What a juicy tidbit for the gossipmongers," Faye continued. "You must be careful, darling. You know even the most innocent little thing can throw Morgan into a jealous fit."

Kyle forced a shallow smile with cold blue eyes. A long moment of silence followed as if in warning. "Morgan has no claim over me. As for any gossip, I suspect you will be true to form and be the first to fuel the mindless blather. Come Lara, let us find our seats."

Lara was surprised by the coldness of Kyle's retort. It was unusual for Kyle to allow such remarks to provoke his temper. Lara let it pass and allowed Kyle to usher her towards Jenna and Bryce who were already seated in the first row of chairs facing the musicians.

In the course of the next ninety minutes, the group sat and listened to a medley of music in an effort to choose a balanced mix of the old, the new and the popular. Together, with recommendations from the musicians, a repertoire suitable for an evening of fun and dance was selected: cotillions, quadrilles, waltzes, and even a polka. The last suggestion of such a shameless dance sparked a heated discussion between Gwendolyn Elsey, who opposed the idea of such a wicked choice, and Faye Carin, who seemed more intent on provoking the elder woman than winning her over with a persuasive argument. The discussion between the two women went on much too long and slowly began to erode Kyle's patience. Finally, as talk seemed sure to digress to petty bickering, Kyle wisely called for a vote of the committee members and it was decided to have a polka. To appease Gwendolyn, it was agreed that only one polka would be played and that would be the very last song of the evening.

After the discussion, the musicians picked up their instruments for the last piece. The first few notes were enough to command Lara's attention. The melody was so familiar even though it had been years since she had last heard it. She became unsettled by the music, astonished that the memories associated with it were still strong and so difficult to cast aside. Lara became more flustered with each note. She shifted in her seat then tried smoothing out the folds of her skirt in a futile effort to distract herself. She glanced about the room hoping to find some poster or picture to concentrate on. Instead, she met Kyle's gaze. Clearly he had been watching her, waiting for her reaction. He wore a blank look on his face. Instinctively Lara knew he had remembered this music from their first dance together. Silently she wondered if he had requested this waltz especially for her? And if so, why?

~ · ~

Lara walked alongside Kyle as the two returned home after the Music Academy.

"Faye Carin is a most charming woman," Lara gibed. "Is she another who has become smitten by your handsome looks and gentlemanly ways?"

"You speak nonsense," Kyle replied with a frown.

"I think not." Lara challenged. "Her face lit up the moment she caught sight of you. Neither was she prepared to acknowledge my presence until forced to do so. I found her manner bold and brash. Is she always so direct?"

"Most times."

"Have you known her very long?" Lara asked.

"Long enough."

"You must know her quite well then?"

"Fairly."

"As well as Morgan?"

The two stopped at the corner. "Perhaps." Kyle placed his hand at her elbow and led her across the busy street.

"You're being evasive," Lara accused, wanting Kyle to respond with more than his trite, one-word answers.

"You're being silly," he countered.

"Curious, yes. Silly, never!" Lara refuted.

"Ha!" Kyle laughed. "Who was it that insisted upon, not one, but two tankards of ale for the horse?"

The memory brought a wide innocent smile to Lara's face. "It was a hot day and that was all there was at hand." She paused in front of a dressmaker's shop long enough to take a quick look at the colorful fabrics and fancy ribbons displayed in the window.

"That animal was not quite the same after that. And who was it that waded out into the river, only to end up taking an unexpected swim? Do you remember that little incident?"

"I seem to recall there was more floundering than swimming! How can I ever forget? Surely you must realize it was your fault."

"How could it be mine when it was you who lost your footing? I was nowhere near you."

Lara giggled.

The setting sun painted a deep magenta sky for the two to admire and to share. Together they relived that carefree afternoon when Kyle had persuaded Lara to remove her shoes and stockings and wade into the shallow depths of the river. In retreating from his playful splashing, Lara had slipped on the wet river rocks.

Thinking back, Kyle could almost hear Lara's high-pitched squeal and the tremendous splash that followed when she tumbled into the water.

"We must have posed quite a sight!" Lara laughed, remembering the water fight immediately afterwards, and later their lovemaking under the tall pines.

Kyle chuckled in agreement. "We never did find that lake." He turned to her and the two locked gazes.

Lara saw the gleam in his eyes and instantly she knew he was thinking of their afternoon spent making love in the woods. She had never done anything as brazenly spontaneous as that again. Her memories of their thrilling escapade brought a rosy hue to her cheeks.

"Did you enjoy the Music Academy?" Kyle asked as they turned the corner onto Wentworth Street.

"The company was interesting," Lara replied, thinking of the verbal sparring between Faye Carin and Gwendolyn Elsey.

"Did you enjoy the music?"

"For the most part," Lara answered quickly without giving further thought to the last waltz. She stopped again, this time in front of a pink magnolia tree. She reached up to cup a perfect bloom in her hand.

"Will you be attending church on Sunday?" Kyle asked, deciding it best to change the subject. "I can come by to get you."

"I'm afraid I'm not a faithful church-goer. Besides, you wouldn't want to add fuel to the gossip, now would you?"

His impish little grin told her he didn't really care. "If people are going to talk, I would prefer we give them something to talk about."

"Our attending service together would be innocent enough."

"Perhaps it would be in Savannah, but not here in Charleston."

"I think it has more to do with who *you* are than anything else. Your personal affairs seem to be of keen interest to many, especially Charleston's unmarried belles. Shouldn't you heed Faye's advice?"

"One should proceed with caution when considering any guidance from Faye Carin. As for myself, I'm sure to do better ignoring it."

There was a seriousness in Kyle's voice that made Lara even more curious about his relationship with Faye Carin. "Why is that?"

There was a long pause from Kyle.

"You were sweethearts," Lara voiced as she realized that it was Faye and Kyle who had shared a past.

"Faye and I have known each other for more than twenty-five years. Her father and mine were involved in countless business ventures and she used to come learn dance from Mother. Naturally we saw quite a bit of each other. As the years passed, we became more than friends."

"Were you ever lovers?" Lara dared to ask, but wasn't sure if she actually wanted to know.

Kyle stopped mid-stride to exchange a thoughtful look with Lara. If he were to brush aside her question then it would only pique Lara's interest more. It was over with Faye. There was nothing to hide and certainly anything concerning his relationships, past or present, would be better if disclosed by himself than by someone else. "Faye was my first love in both the emotional and physical sense of the word," Kyle confirmed. "When I went off to school, Faye promised she would wait for me. It was into the first semester of my second year when she wrote to tell me she could wait no longer. She had wanted for us to marry when I returned home that Christmas, but I refused. With each letter her requests became more demanding. I was just as uncompromising with wanting to finish my schooling and start my career." Kyle paused momentarily to formulate his next thought. "She grew restless and impatient and instead of waiting for me, she threw herself at Cameron. She made no real effort to hide their relationship and word of it came to me through one of Christopher's letters."

"Christopher?"

"Christopher Warren was Jenna's stepbrother," Kyle confirmed. "Perhaps Faye thought I would rush back home to Charleston and claim her as mine. Instead, the distance made it easy for me to ignore the whole affair."

Lara could hear the regret in his voice and she could sympathize with the hurt that he had felt. "I'm sorry, Kyle."

Kyle looked at her only to become entranced again. Her long eyelashes framed beautiful, sparkling eyes. He heard an honest sincerity in her voice and saw it on her face. That made him smile. "There's no need to be. Time and distance have a way of bringing out the truth in matters such as this. It was all for the best."

"What happened with Faye and Cameron?"

"Their relationship ended quickly after Faye met Lars Carin. Faye and Lars were married within weeks of their first meeting. He passed away a few years ago and left her Carin's General Store & Merchandise."

Lara was intrigued. "It must be difficult for her. A woman in trade, I mean. Does she have a head for business?"

"Faye has drive, vigor, and enough business sense. Altogether she does well for herself. She opened a second store in November last year over in the north end of the city. I imagine it took some doing for her to raise the capital."

"Did she approach the Planters Bank for a loan?"

Her question prompted a laugh from Kyle. "Faye would never come to me for anything, and I would give her little consideration," he admitted. "I have little regard left for her. Faye refused to honor the proper mourning period for her husband. Lars had not been in the ground two months before she approached me with a marriage proposal."

"You turned her down."

"I did, without a second thought."

"Is she still in love with you?"

"I don't think Faye knows what love is. She went to Cameron out of spite and married Lars for his money. There was no love in either of those relationships, and what fanciful feelings she might have had for me have now been replaced with ill will. She despises me for not marrying her years ago and more now for declining her offer a second time."

"And yet she stills seeks your attention," Lara commented.

"Faye enjoys her games. She looks to manipulate people into giving her what she desires most. The less inclined they are to yield, the more challenging the sport."

"You pose that challenge for her."

"For the moment, at least until someone or something else comes along."

It was hard for Lara to believe anyone could be so self-centered as to meddle in other people's lives that way. "Does she feel threatened at all by your relationship with Morgan?"

"Most likely she has become more interested with my involvement with you than with Morgan."

"Why do you say that?"

"Faye has already deduced there was once something between us. Hearing the rumors and seeing us together will intrigue her even more." Without thinking, he ran his hand down the length of Lara's arm. His long, gentle caress unsettled her and Lara stepped away from his reach.

"So my presence presents a greater challenge to her, is that what you mean?"

Kyle refused to keep the distance she had put between them and he stepped closer and back in unison with her steps. "Exactly. She knows that the chances of Morgan becoming more than a friend are slight."

Lara looked ahead to find that they were almost home. "But you must realize Morgan is looking for something more than friendship. Have the two of you discussed marriage?"

"We have on occasion, although not seriously," Kyle admitted.

"A woman can't speak of marriage without being serious," Lara advised. "With her father being one of the owners of the bank, it seems to me that Morgan has much to offer any eligible and ambitious young banker."

Kyle scowled at the thought. "If Morgan's connections were enough to entice me to marry her, I would have done so at the outset. I have my pride. I can honestly say that I have earned everything I have by honest hard work. I don't need to resort to such antics to prove my worth. If Morgan is looking for a husband in me then, like Faye, she will be disappointed. I am not willing to give anything more than friendship."

Spoken easily and with such conviction! *I am not willing to give anything more than friendship.* His words echoed through Lara's ears. "I'm sorry, Kyle. I didn't mean to offend you."

"You didn't." Kyle escorted Lara to her door. "Here we are." He turned to face her. "This would be the right time to invite me in," he instructed, a beguiling grin upon his handsome face. "Chocolate cake, remember?"

"This is not the Kyle Harrison I knew from Brooklyn City. Are you no longer concerned with appearances?"

"Appearances can be deceiving. There will always be the gossipmongers who distort the truth to embellish their stories." Kyle reached for Lara's hand and held it in his tender grasp. "It's not very late and I would like to come in. You can tell me about Gavin."

Suspicion was reflected in Lara's eyes as she pondered his possible motives.

"It's only natural that a father would want to know about his son," Kyle answered her silent question. "You won't begrudge me that, will you?"

Lara hesitated, wondering if that was an excuse to find his way into her home, or did he have a sincere interest in their son?

~ • ~

The cake was delicious! Kyle complimented as they settled on the settee, Lara with her tea and he with his glass of scotch whiskey.

"You remembered my preference for scotch." Kyle sounded content as he made himself comfortable next to Lara. "I was always asking Lyddie if she had received any word from you.

Not once did she hint of Gavin nor did she ever mention your marriage to Aidan Quinn."

Lara stared down into her tea. She ran her finger along the cup's gilded rim. "You've remained interested in me?"

"You didn't think I would?"

She looked up to meet his blue eyes. "I didn't know what to think, except perhaps that—"

"That I had put you out of my mind?"

Lara nodded.

Kyle reached for her hand and gave it a gentle squeeze. His thumb brushed the top of her hand. "Many times I had tried, but in truth you've never been too far from my thoughts. You are an extremely difficult woman to forget, Lara."

Unsettled again by his touch, Lara pulled her hand from his. So often she had wondered how their parting had affected him. Could he have suffered as much as she? Lara put the thought aside, deciding it was best to leave it be. She needed to put the past behind her and not to revisit it.

"I made Aunt Lyddie promise never to tell you of Gavin or our whereabouts," Lara confessed. "We had argued so many times over this, especially right after Gavin was born. It almost drove us apart. Yet still, she kept her promise."

"What's his favorite pastime?"

"He likes to go fishing and horseback riding. He has a pet rabbit named Bumpkin that goes almost everywhere he does, even to dinner." Lara's face lit up as she recalled the event. She remembered how difficult it had been to stay firm and not break out in laughter as she reprimanded Gavin for bringing the animal to the supper table.

Kyle chuckled as he listened to Lara's recounting. "Is he a good rider?"

"Better than most boys his age," Lara answered proudly.

"Aidan's influence, no doubt."

"Mine, actually. Gavin and I go riding every morning after our breakfast."

"Is Gavin close to his stepfather?"

"Aidan doesn't spend much time with Gavin. Aidan's a good man, but he's never shown very strong paternal instincts, not even with Abi."

"Abi?"

"Abigail is his daughter by his first wife. Chelsea died seven years ago."

"Do you love Aidan?" He went straight to the heart of the matter. Kyle was never one to waste time.

Lara hesitated. She didn't want to delve too deeply into any sort of discussion regarding her relationship with Aidan. "I'm fond of him and he has a place in my heart," Lara admitted openly to Kyle.

"You're fond of him, but do you love him?"

Lara struggled with her answer. "Like a sister would her brother," she finally answered.

"Does Aidan know about us?"

"Yes, I've told him everything."

Kyle nodded. Silently, though, he would have preferred that she had said nothing to her husband. "And Gavin, what did you tell him about his father?"

"I've told him very little. He knows I don't like to talk about you."

"But surely he's asked. You must have said something."

"He knows nothing except his father is alive and living in Charleston."

"Does he know you're here now?"

"I told him Aunt Lyddie had died and that I had to go away for a while. I didn't tell him where I was going."

"When are you expected back in Savannah?"

"I'd like to be home in time for his birthday."

"That's well short of a year."

The teacup and saucer rattled in her hands. "You'd have me miss my son's birthday?"

"You would toss aside your inheritance for a birthday cake?"

"I didn't say I wasn't going to return. Surely Aunt Lyddie didn't mean for Charleston's borders to be my prison bars for the duration of these twelve months." Lara set down her tea and rose quickly from the settee. She wasn't comfortable with how the conversation had turned so abruptly. "Is there anything of consequence to you that doesn't have a monetary value attached?"

A deep scowl crossed Kyle's brow and his long pause continued to unnerve her. "Why don't you send for him and have him brought to Charleston?"

"What for?" Lara turned to face him again. "To meet his father?"

"For a vacation while his mother settles her aunt's affairs."

"You have no plans for Gavin?"

"Should I have?"

"Stop it, Kyle, don't play games with me!" Lara demanded. "I want to know what your intentions are with regards to our son."

Kyle went to Lara's side. "I told you the other day. I need time."

"Time for what? You frighten me, Kyle. Gavin is all I have left in this world. I would die if you were to take him away from me."

He locked gazes with her. "Do you really think me that cruel? Did I hurt you so deeply that you think me completely without heart or mercy? Lara, I know I'm deserving of your anger and mistrust, but I had hoped with the lapsing of time that any misgivings you might have had towards me would have been overcome by the love we had shared."

Lara confronted him. "Countless times I have wished that I could toss aside my anger and purge myself of these haunting emotions I have for you. If only there was some voodoo magic that could wish away the pain that has wreaked havoc upon my soul for so long. Do you now expect my wounded heart to once again flutter wildly whenever you stroll within my sight? Is that what you expect from me? Then prepare to be disappointed! Such impulses ended the moment you forced me to choose between you and Aunt Lyddie."

Lara stopped, realizing how upset she had become. She breathed in a long and shaky breath to calm herself. She had waited years to speak these sorts of words to Kyle Harrison. She had even convinced herself she could recite them and chastise him with dignity and self-control. She had always expected that once spoken she would find some relief. How wrong she was! She found no satisfaction after saying those words and no reprieve from all those plaguing emotions.

Kyle lovingly brushed away the soft curls that lay over her shoulder. "I only know of a very special time when we were both so happy together, so much in love. That night you ran from me was the end of the sweetest, most beautiful dream and the beginning of my worst and longest nightmare, a living nightmare for which there seems to be no end. Everything I had ever wanted was within my grasp and I let it slip away because of my idiotic pride and confounded prejudices. If you would have given me even the slightest opportunity, I would have bared my soul and asked, nay pleaded, for you to forgive me."

Kyle's voice softened as he dared to take her hand again. "Like I'm pleading now. Please, Lara. I have waited almost six years and I'm still waiting, praying for that one chance to redeem myself. I still remember those wonderful times we shared. Each memory fills my heart with regret and it pains me to know that I may never find such happiness again. Since seeing you at The Charlestown, I have dared to hope that my nightmare might soon end. It wasn't until I was able to touch you that I let myself believe that you had finally come home. Each day I feel compelled to seek you out. Not to frighten you, but to reacquaint myself with you once more; to be with you, hoping that you might want to be with me; to try to recapture even a hint of what we once shared. That's what I want from you."

Lara turned away from him. "It's not simply a matter of wanting to be with you. I have responsibilities to Gavin and to

Aidan and Abi. No matter how much we may want or how hard we may try, our circumstances are different and it can never be as it once was."

Kyle followed to stand close before her once again. He held her attention. His eyes darkened into a deeper shade of blue. "You're right," he agreed. "It can never be as it was, but in my heart you will always be mine. I told you before that I've never stopped loving you. I can't help but hope the future will find us together and that it will be as good or better than it once was."

Kyle had spoken with faith and honesty. He knew his words had touched her heart. From somewhere deep inside he found the courage and moved slowly, cautiously, to steal a kiss from her sweet lips. He slid his arms around her waist and still she did nothing to reject him. "I would never purposefully do anything to hurt you or our son. You must believe me. If I frighten you, then it's because you still have feelings for me. Search your heart, Lara. Tell me what you find hidden inside. If you want me to leave then tell me so and I won't trouble you again. I'll leave you and Gavin in peace. I'll abide by your wish, whatever that may be, no matter how much pain it will bring me. Tell me to leave, Mack. Is that what you want?" Kyle dared to gamble. Then becoming bolder, even more confident, he stole a second kiss.

"I... I can't," she stammered, her voice trembling and weak as she searched his eyes.

His lips touched hers a third time. "Why can't you?"

"Because...." She stopped herself.

"Because why?"

Lara closed her eyes in anticipation. She felt the warmth of his breath, then the touch of his lips at the base of her neck. A tingling sensation rippled through her body and she leaned forward, allowing herself to fall into his arms.

"Why, Lara?" his whisper soft in her ear. "Tell me, I need to know."

She opened her eyes to find him hovering over her, waiting for her answer. "Because," her lips trembled, "I still love you."

The world stopped most unexpectedly. Lara stood frozen, her eyes wide as she stared into his. She couldn't believe the words that had just escaped her. That last sentence echoed through her mind a second and a third time as she struggled to reconcile the truth within her own revelation. Several moments passed before Lara gasped, her mind accepting at long last that secret unlocked deep within her heart. "I still love you," she repeated.

Kyle wrapped his arms tight around her. Now there was only each other and the stunning realization that the love they shared years ago had not died. Cautioned reigned and Kyle consciously pushed aside his own emotions of joy and revelry for worry that Lara's emotions might somehow turn against him. "Are you alright?" he asked as he stared down into Lara's chestnut eyes. His voice was as warm and tender as his gaze. With a loving touch he wiped away the tear that filled the corner of her eye.

"How could I be so blind?"

"You must believe that I love you, too," Kyle confessed. "More than anything else in this world."

Lara nodded. For the moment she needed only to believe, but she wasn't brave enough to think of the consequences that might result from this night. Lara let Kyle lead her to the settee where he brought her down beside him. She felt his arms wrapped around her in a loving, protective embrace. Cuddled together in silence, the two were content just to be in each other's presence. As the minutes ticked away, Lara's emotions subsided and she found herself with an inner peace.

"You must be tired," Lara dared to break the spell.

Kyle looked up at the mantle clock. It was almost midnight. "You make me forget the time. I should go and let you get to bed."

Lara nodded, but she remained still, nestled in Kyle's arms. She didn't want him to leave.

"Are you alright?" Kyle asked again, wanting some reassurance.

Lara's face shone with a soft, sweet smile as she met his gaze. "I'm alright. I'm just tired."

Kyle gently brushed back her long tresses and tilted her chin to receive his tender kiss. "I love you," he repeated once again, but not because he felt he had to, but because his own heart was overflowing. All because Lara Mackenzie, this beautiful woman nestled in his arms, was still in love with him!

~ . ~

I still love you. In Kyle's mind, Lara's declaration echoed like music from heaven. The memory of those four sweet words had lulled him into a deep and peaceful slumber despite knowing that Aidan Quinn stood between him and Lara. For now, there was no conflict between logic and emotion for what he knew in his mind, he felt in his heart. His lost love may belong to a stranger, but in name only. Lara didn't love her husband. She was still in love with him. Kyle was ecstatic. Somehow he had found his way back into Lara's heart. That was all that mattered, at least for now. He would be patient and bide his time. With luck and a hopeful heart, Lara's love might prove powerful enough for her to leave Aidan Quinn and forge a new life with him. What a wonderful wife Mrs. Lara Mackenzie Harrison would be!

Kyle rose early the next morning. His body and soul rejuvenated, intoxicated with the joy of living. His blithe and happy mood infected the entire Harrison household, leaving the servants to speculate as to the reason behind their master's behavior. They had witnessed such jubilation before, usually brought about by some well-deserved good fortune. Had Mr. Kyle been asked to arrange the financing for another economic project? Or maybe his investment strategy had turned another healthy profit for himself or for one of his clients? Or had he earned another promotion, possibly a position on the governing board of the bank?

"More coffee, Mr. Kyle?" the housekeeper asked.

"No, that will be all. Thank you, Casey. Is everyone ready?"

The servant grinned, sensing Kyle's eagerness to leave for the Quinn home. "Yes sir, as soon as you are. I thought we might bring Eaton along to help with the heavy moving. Between Shani, Vida and I, we should manage the rest well enough."

Kyle rose from the table while taking his last swallow of coffee. "Yes, good enough." He stopped to give the housemaid a thoughtful look.

"Not to worry, Mr. Kyle. Vida and I know our place. We will mind Mrs. Quinn and will not put Shani off."

"Ah, Casey, I have never known a wiser colleen. What would I ever do without you?" With that, he cupped Casey's round face in his hands and planted an affectionate kiss on her forehead.

Casey's cheeks turned a rosy hue. She gave Kyle a forceful nudge to push him away. "You should save your flattery and affections for someone more deserving."

"No one is more deserving than my Casey O'Leary."

"And no one mutters such silver-tongued blarney more elegantly than my Mr. Harrison."

~ · ~

The wagon had not rolled to a complete stop before Kyle jumped off. There was a dance in his steps and his pace was brisk as he walked to the front door where Avram had emerged to greet them. There was no sign of Lara.

"Good morning, Mr. Kyle."

"Good day, Avram. Where's Mrs. Quinn?"

"She's in the dining room, Mr. Harrison."

"Finishing breakfast?" Kyle asked.

"No, sir. She's been up for hours already. She and Shani have been busy putting a good, hard polish on the floors. They started last night after you brought Miss Lara home. They're almost ready for some of the boxes stored out in the coach house. I'm to start bringing them in."

A puzzled look, complete with a raised brow, came over Kyle's face. Lara was of a settled mind when he left her the night before. She seemed, on the surface at least, to have accepted her feelings for him. Could it all have been for show?

"Eaton, give Avram a hand, will you? Casey, Vida, I think we're needed inside."

Both Lara and Shani looked up on hearing the footsteps approaching. Shani was putting a good effort into the last of her hard strokes as she worked the wax into the floorboards. She beamed a smile from her scrubbing position. One look and it was obvious the two ladies had been working furiously for the glow of the deep honey polish on the oak floor extended throughout the large parlor and into the long dining room.

Lara was quick to brush back a stray lock of hair before rising to greet her helpers. "Good morning." She gave Casey and Vida a warm smile, but reserved a cool, quiet expression for Kyle. She met his gaze for only a fleeting moment.

Lara's shy and sedate salutation was not what Kyle had expected nor wanted in a greeting. After last night he had dared to expect a more potent show of passion from the woman he loved.

"You've been busy," Kyle stated.

"We've just finished the floor. Doesn't it look marvelous? Did you see Avram? He went to fetch some of the china. Casey, would you and Vida start with the polishing of the sideboard? I think Shani and I need to get away from the wax and rags for a bit. We—"

"Good idea," Kyle interrupted Lara's rambling to pull her aside. "You and Shani deserve a rest. Shani, why don't you make a cool pitcher of something to drink then sit for a bit? Lara, come tell me what you want us men to tackle." Kyle took Lara by the hand and pulled her out of the room and out of sight.

"Kyle, where are you taking me?"

He stopped, turning abruptly to catch her in his arms and bring her to him. His kiss was hard and demanding, leaving her breathless. "Good morning, my love."

"Kyle, I—"

His mouth came down to hers again. "Good morning, my love," he repeated. He was determined to not let her go until she returned his greeting.

The corners of Lara's mouth lifted into a slight smile. "Good morning," she responded.

"Is that all the greeting you feel inclined to bestow upon this heartless soul? It's true that I have no heart. One beats within this body, but it's not mine. It belongs to you; stolen from me the moment I first laid eyes upon you."

"You speak such foolishness," Lara laughed.

"I speak only the truth. You have my heart and I want to know that I have yours."

His playful manner and sly, roguish grin served only to soften his earnest request, but Lara knew how very serious he was and that frightened her. Her declaration the night before had been a stunning realization that had left her emotionally and mentally disoriented. She had not been able to sleep. Instead she rose from bed to aimlessly wander the house. Finally she decided to put her frustrations into the polishing of the floor. For a few hours she concentrated on the task while she worked through her jumbled misbeliefs and new found emotions.

"Did you sleep well?" Kyle asked with genuine concern.

"A restless sleep."

"My doing, I'm afraid."

Lara worked to choose her words carefully as her thoughts went to Gavin and Aidan. "Kyle, I can't give you what you want. My place is with—"

He placed a gentle finger over her lips. "No," he said, knowingly. "Don't say another word." The next moments passed with the two of them staring at each other. Lara didn't want to say it, nor did Kyle want to hear her speak those words. He released her from his possessive hold, but held onto her hand, giving it a reassuring squeeze. "Come," he said. "Everyone will think we've deserted them."

~ · ~

It had been a long, but productive day. The group had worked hard cleaning, polishing, organizing, arranging and rearranging furniture. Kyle had put in as much effort as anyone else and, at the end of the day, Lara had to admit that she was impressed with his ability to stay focused, and his patience and stamina in tackling domestic chores. In the end, the main rooms on the lower floor had been made ready. The group from the Harrison household had returned home after a good, hearty dinner. Shani and Avram had finished the last of their daily chores and, they too, had retired to their flat above the coach house.

Revived after a long soothing bath, Lara ventured downstairs once again. Although she was physically tired, her mind was active and she wanted to wander through the rooms another time before bed.

The music room looked like a jewelry box, Lara thought. The golden orange milk-paint covered the walls like a lining of vibrant Indian silk that enhanced the dark red tones of the rosewood furniture. A tall bookcase stood against one wall. Its scrolling pediment topped the frame of a pair of glazed doors that opened to a set of sturdy shelves. If this house were ever to become home, here is where she would spend most of her spare time: with her music, her study guides and reference books. She opened the cabinet to confirm once again that one of her two most prized and beloved possessions, her father's violin, was still inside.

Besides the sparse furnishings in the master bedroom, the dining room was the only other room in the house that her Aunt Lyddie had given thought to. She must have had large dinner parties in mind given the long length of the room. The double doors at one end opened out onto the piazza while another pair at the opposite end opened into the front parlor if the extra room was ever needed. With both these sets of doors and the front parlor windows open, a fresh breeze could flow through. Like the music room, the furniture here was made of rosewood. An extraordinarily long sideboard was placed along one wall. Its tabletop was set upon six cabriolet legs, each carved in an intricate scrollwork design. This same pattern decorated the legs of the dining table and each of the ten chairs, and the matching china cupboard. A beautiful and formal room, thought Lara. However, if the choice had been hers, she would have chosen something simpler and more intimate.

Lara strolled through the main parlor last. Here, she set her lamp down and the light spilled out from the lamp's crystal globe to fill the room with a warm cozy glow. Lara cuddled into one of two chintz chairs that now flanked the fireplace. These chairs had been Aunt Lyddie's favorites. Lara could recall many mornings and afternoons, sitting in these while she took tea with her aunt. Lara ran her hand over one of the arms to follow its curved polished lines. Her attention was drawn to the mantle after hearing the mechanical ticking of the clock. It was close to midnight.

Her eyes swept slowly across the room. Even in this dim light the mahogany furniture gleamed in deep rich tones. For this room, Lara had selected items from Haven Manor that held the most sentimental value. An oversized book rested upon its easel, the pages filled with watercolors of the northeastern countryside. Lara could remember spending lazy afternoons sprawled out on the floor as she turned page after page to admire the details of each landscape. The book had been a gift from Aunt Lyddie after she had decided to send Lara north to school. A grouping of three charcoal etchings hung on the wall, and a few fine porcelain pieces adorned the shelves. Lara surrendered a smile. Alone, she sat enjoying the space, wonderfully content in being surrounded by her happy memories and cherished possessions. Proud of what she had accomplished thus far, Lara felt that sense of pride that came with turning an empty shell of a dwelling into a home. In the short span of a few hours, everything now seemed so much more familiar and secure than it had the night before!

Lara imagined a home in Charleston. The thought was not as disagreeable as it had seemed weeks ago and she found herself wondering how well Gavin would adjust to life in Charleston. How strange for things to turn about so quickly. She had sailed into Charleston Harbor convinced that she would be returning to Savannah within a few short weeks. Any interactions with Mr. Kyle Harrison were not expected to amount to anything more than cold greetings followed by abrupt good-byes.

Perhaps there is more for her in Charleston than she ever could have imagined. Kyle had waited for her all this time. He had wished each day for her return. How hopelessly romantic! But it hadn't been so different for her. She had buried her true feelings well. She had been foolishly naïve to think Kyle Harrison would never again mean anything more to her than a faded memory. Lara sat pondering her relationship with Kyle and exploring the possibility of regaining the love they had once shared. And what of Aidan? Would she be strong enough to leave him and give up the safe haven she had come to depend upon? Could she do that to him after all he had done for her? But wasn't that what they had agreed upon those many years ago? When they were ready, she remembered Aidan saying, they would both know.

Lara snuggled into the corner of her chair with her legs tucked in close. Her eyelids felt heavy and her body longed for rest. Once again she rejected the thought of going upstairs to seek the comfort of her bed. All was calm within the walls of her new home and this rare sense of peace and tranquility was much too precious to cast aside and ignore. She would close her eyes and sit for a few seconds more. But the seconds turned into minutes and minutes turned into hours. Finally the dim glow from the hurricane lamp began to fade into the night as the wick's flame consumed the last remaining drops of oil. Lara did not stir. There was only the sound of her whispered breath for she had been lulled into a deep and peaceful sleep by her rambling thoughts, her hopeful dreams, and the hypnotic tick-tock of the mantle clock.

Chapter 10

Something To Talk About

L ara had given herself plenty of time to get ready before Kyle came to fetch her for church at seven-thirty. It would have been enough had it not been for the disheartening thoughts churning in her head as she took her morning tea and biscuits.

It had come as a sudden blow to learn of Aunt Lyddie's death. Now there was only one left in the world whom she could call family and only a select few whom she would name as friends. And still she had not yet found that one extraordinary man to love, that one rare and constant companion to walk through life with. Lara had, through the death of her aunt, inherited the material wealth needed to live comfortably, but there was so much more she had been hoping to have one day. And none of it could be gained by an exchange of coin.

Lara might have remained lost in thought if not for Shani's prompting. Now a few minutes after seven o'clock, Lara found herself rushing to get dressed. The most important decision at this particular moment was deciding what to wear. She stood in her underwear in front of her open wardrobe. Pushing aside one dress for another until she decided upon a charcoal colored, cotton day dress suitable for church. Its sleeves were puffed from shoulder to wrist in a long tapering billow. The dress was simply cut with a high neckline. Other than the usual piping at the bodice seams, there was nothing in the way of decorations and trimmings. Even the hooks and eyes were hidden, set closely from the collar down to the waist. A conservative choice, quite plain one might say. The skirt was fashionably wide with precise pleats folded from the waist. Twice she thought of wearing a fourth petticoat to hold out the skirt, but then decided against the idea. It would be too hot a day to bear the weight of another layer.

The last of the hooks on Lara's bodice was being set into its eye when she heard the faint knocking on the front door. Lara looked at the mantle clock: seven-thirty. It was so very much like Kyle to be spot on time. Lara twirled in front of the tall mirror to make sure the hems of her skirts flowed to the floor. Her image reflected a prim and proper appearance, one correctly appropriate for a woman in mourning. Shani handed her the matching bonnet and handbag. She took a deep breath and was ready!

The sound of Lara's footsteps brought a smile to Kyle's face. "Good morning, Lara."

"Good morning, Kyle. Am I appropriately dressed?"

"Simple yet charming," Kyle complimented. "Even in black."

"It's getting rather tiresome," Lara admitted.

"I think Lyddie, of all people, would understand if you decided to discard the mourning garb," Kyle proposed. "She often found such customs boring and tedious. Of little value or consequence, she would say."

"Yes, she would," Lara agreed. Once again Kyle had surprised her with how well he had come to know her aunt.

Minutes later Lara was seated comfortably beside Kyle in the open landau. The morning air was refreshingly cool and the floral fragrances of late spring surrounded them. Their carriage moved along slowly for Meeting Street was busy with the many faithful proceeding to church. Kyle steered the shay into a field to join the other black carriages parked there. A large crowd had already gathered and was mulling around in front of the church. All were waiting for the bell to summon them in for prayer and worship. As Kyle jumped off the landau, Lara sat admiring the narrow building. Various shades of grey stone trimmed the red brickwork. The colors were a pleasing contrast to her eyes. The entrance was awe-inspiring with its steep bell tower rising several storeys high towards the heavens. Multi-colored, stained glass adorned the tall arched windows above the double doors of the main entrance.

"Is this a new church?" Lara asked.

"It was built almost four years ago."

"Very impressive," Lara stated. "The sloping lines are very Gothic."

Kyle turned around to take a good look at the masonry structure as if seeing it for the first time. "Yes, they are," he replied, impressed by her comment. "I wasn't aware of your interest in architecture."

"Not mine, Aidan's. He enjoys roaming about the larger cities. We could spend hours at a time in a carriage; up one street and down another, stopping to look at the different architectural forms. He loves churches the most. I suppose I picked up a thing or two."

"So it seems."

Heads turned their way as Kyle assisted Lara down from the landau. He kept a respectable physical distance and together they joined the crowd. Kyle stopped now and then to greet friends. Lara smiled sweetly as she waited and returned the kind greetings after Kyle's introductions.

"Good morning, Lara. We're happy to have you join us this morning."

Lara turned towards the welcoming voice to see Jenna's bright face.

"Good morning, Jenna."

"What about me?" Kyle asked. "Are you not happy to see me?"

"Never," Jenna teased, then opened her arms wide.

Kyle greeted Jenna with a hug and a brotherly kiss on each cheek. As Lara looked on, she wondered if perhaps at one time Jenna and Kyle might have been more than good friends.

Bryce Landon freed himself from a trio of men to greet Lara and Kyle. "First the aunt and now the niece. You are the luckiest fellow."

"First the aunt and now the niece?" Lara repeated, wanting an explanation.

"I would accompany Lyddie to church whenever she felt the spiritual need to attend," Kyle replied.

"Did she come often?"

"She would every now and then, mostly when she was preoccupied with worry."

"Was she welcome?"

"There were always those who did not approve of Lyddie," Jenna replied, "but she was not one to be bothered by the pretentious beliefs of others."

"And the Pastor?"

"Pastor Thomas and his wife, Ally, would never turn anyone away. Every soul needs friendship and compassion."

"Amen to that." Pastor Noland Thomas had overheard Jenna as he came up from behind to join the foursome.

Kyle was quick to make the introduction. "Lara has only recently returned from Savannah."

"We're pleased to have you join us today, Mrs. Quinn. Service will begin shortly so I will leave you in the company of these fine folks."

A few minutes later, the double doors opened with the ringing of the bell. Jenna and Bryce led the way to the Landon family pew near the front of the church. Inside, Lara estimated that the nave could accommodate a few hundred parishioners. Its size seemed overly large, but Lara attributed this to the elongated roof span and the curved ribs of white oak. The hall was painted a bright white and everything sparkled as rays of sunlight streamed in through the windows. A stove sat in each corner of the room for these were deemed a necessity during Charleston's winter months.

Lara's eyes were drawn high above the chancel. There they rested upon a stained-glass image of Jesus with his arms extended to each side, his body in the shape of a cross. She stared at the mosaic. Déjà vu. She had seen a similar image somewhere before. She thought hard, trying to remember as the feeling of familiarity grew stronger and had become hard to ignore. The artist had used the leading very effectively to create lines radiating from the body. Combined with various shades of white glass, an ethereal light surrounded a robed figure. A bright, angelic light. Like the light in her dream! Yes, her dream. It all came back to her! The vision of her walking to the end of the church aisle where she was ready to take the hand of the man she was about to exchange vows with. She remembered the organ music, the patchwork glasswork, and the strong masculine hand. Although astonished by the parallel between reality and her dream, Lara decided it was nothing more than a striking coincidence, for what more could it possibly mean?

Bryce leaned over to whisper softly into Jenna's ear. Jenna turned to take a sweeping glance around the room. Her smile was broad and sweet as she leaned over towards Kyle. "It seems Lara has captured the attention of the congregation."

Like Jenna did a moment before, Kyle turned and quickly glanced over the crowd.

His movements woke Lara from her thoughts. "Is something wrong?" she asked, totally unaware that she had become the center of attention.

"Nothing out of the ordinary," Kyle answered.

He was not convincing enough. Lara turned to catch one or two people watching her while others turned away quickly. Still, there were those few who met her gaze while continuing to speak in hushed tones with their companion. No doubt she and Kyle were the topic of their conversation. Immediately, she remembered what Kyle had said on the way home after the Music Academy: *If people are going to talk, I would prefer we give them something to talk about.* Dare she?

Lara reached up to smooth the underside of Kyle's collar. She then gently brushed the imaginary specks of fluff off his broad shoulder. Both motions were completed in a casual, but wifely manner.

Kyle raised a curious brow as he glanced down at his shoulder. He wasn't able to determine any reason for Lara's actions, especially since he had given extra care and attention to his attire that morning. Puzzled, he leaned closer to whisper ever so softly into her ear. "Madame, what are you doing?"

Lara grinned. Those observing the pair could only agree that the two were in the midst of sharing some sort of intimate exchange. "I'm giving them something to talk about."

Kyle caught on immediately. Playing along, he placed his hand around her waist and brought her to him until their bodies touched. His words tickled her ear. "No longer worried about your reputation? What would Aidan say?"

Lara caught sight of Pastor Thomas as he entered and approached the altar. She nudged Kyle gently in his side with her elbow, forcing him to back away. She continued to face the front of the church with an impish grin on her face.

Pastor Thomas stood tall at the podium as he delivered his message with passion and great enthusiasm. The undulating tones of his deep voice commanded the attention of his followers. His discourse was separated into short, purposeful lessons with the unifying moral of staying true to one's faith. In between his recitations, he led the congregation in song and prayer, all the while coaching and inspiring those who wanted to believe, and raising thought-provoking questions in the minds of those less devoted.

The loud notes of the pipe organ rang through Lara's body. Moved by the music and the lyrics, Lara followed along in the hymnal. She lifted her sweet voice, joining the congregation in harmony for the closing song of praise. This service had reaffirmed some of Lara's beliefs and helped re-instill her faith. Many times since Aunt Lyddie's death she had experienced moments of weakness, finding herself temporarily lost in grief and self-pity. Now, with a bit of confidence and determination, she felt she could finally let go of all the sadness that had come to fill her heart.

~ . ~

"Do you ride much, Lara?" Jenna asked.

"I go riding at least once a day when I'm at home. Aidan gifted me with a Pinto a few years ago."

"Bryce thought it a fine morning to take the horses out along Ashley River. Would you and Kyle like to join us? Of course you'll stay and lunch with us afterwards."

"I'm sure I'd enjoy the ride, but I have no riding habit and I don't know what Kyle's plans are for the rest of the day," Lara answered.

"The clothes shouldn't be a problem. My sister-in-law, Sarah, visits so often that she keeps a few of her things here for convenience's sake. I'm sure she will have something suitable. Other than Sarah being a bit taller, I would think you are both near the same size. I'm sure she won't mind. Will she, Bryce?"

"Not at all," Bryce confirmed. "Where did Kyle get to?"

"He was pulled away as we came out of Church. Someone mentioned mulberry trees," Lara revealed.

Bryce chuckled.

"Is there something amusing about mulberry trees?" Lara asked.

"There is a consortium of merchants and bankers that have been working to establish a silk industry here in South Carolina. They have been trying for some time to get Kyle and the Planters

Bank of South Carolina to join in their efforts. They corner Kyle at every opportunity, I'm sure he keeps putting them off."

"I didn't know silkworms thrived here in the Americas."

"They don't," Jenna confirmed. "It has been suggested that silkworms could be interbred with gypsy moths, but first they are trying to establish a healthy growth of white mulberry tree cuttings from the Orient. They say that silkworms feeding off this variety will produce a finer thread of silk."

"The first cuttings were planted earlier in spring and have faired well," Bryce explained. "Silkworms are said to be voracious eaters. The consortium expects to plant two more groves in addition to the three already started. If all goes as planned and the initial eggs survive the trip from China then silk production might begin as early as next year."

"A new industry would reduce the need to import silk. How exciting! But Kyle isn't convinced?"

"It's not a new industry to the Americas. A small production has established itself in the northern states, but it hasn't gained the recognition that our Consortium is hoping to achieve. As for Kyle, he's invested personally in the venture although he's not completely on side with the project. It's on his advice that the Planters Bank has not joined in. He thinks there are too many risks."

"Then why would he have bought in?"

"Kyle is not one to turn down an opportunity where money is to be made. He's convinced there's profit somewhere in this venture and there has been thus far. The price of mulberry cuttings were pegged at a few dollars per hundred at the outset. They're now at twenty-three. However planting of the groves is only the first step. It will be quite sometime before we know with any certainty whether a silk industry can survive here. Even if the trees do well and the silkworms survive, there are economies of scale to consider and that's where many of Kyle's doubts lie. It may take a tremendously large operation and a huge investment before any sizeable profit is realized."

"And he thinks the risks are too high for the Bank?" Lara asked.

"So it seems," Bryce answered.

"We've bought stock as well, haven't we, Bryce?" Jenna asked.

"Some. They were initially offered at seven-fifty a share and have since risen to over twelve. On Kyle's recommendation, Pierce and I each went in for a thousand shares, but I believe Kyle had joined in for twice that much."

"He tends to be more conservative with the Bank's money than his own," Lara realized aloud. "Who is Pierce?"

"Pierce is Bryce's brother. He lives in Hamburg, but comes to Charleston fairly often. In fact he and his wife, Sarah, will be visiting us in time to join us for the orphan's ball. Would you and Senator Palmer care to join our little party?"

Bryce raised a brow. "Cameron Palmer?"

"Mr. Palmer has extended an invitation for me to accompany him, but I declined," Lara answered. She was grateful Kyle was not there to be part of the conversation and did not want to elaborate any more on her association with the Senator.

"Cameron is one of the founding members of the consortium," Bryce revealed.

"Then I'm not surprised Kyle hasn't joined in. I gather the two do not get along."

"They were like brothers when they were young boys," Bryce stated. "Now they are more rivals than they are cousins."

"Kyle and Cameron Palmer are cousins!"

"First cousins," Jenna confirmed. "Kyle's mother and Cameron's father were sister and brother."

"Curious that he's never told me of his relation to Cameron. What happened between the two of them?"

"There is less than a year's age difference between Kyle and Cameron," Jenna surmised. "One day while swimming, the playing got overly rough. They must have been fourteen or fifteen years of age then. Cameron had grown taller and stronger than

Kyle. In fun, Cameron had held Kyle under water for longer than he should have. Cameron didn't realize his strength and had lost himself in the moment. Kyle panicked and took in some water. The entire incident put quite a scare into Kyle. Cameron tried very hard for a long time to make amends, but Kyle never was able to trust him after that. They keep out of each other's business for the most part, but cannot be avoided altogether. The Senate, as you know, drafts the laws that govern the running of the banks."

And then there was Faye Carin to further the rift between them, Lara reminded herself.

"Did you learn much about mulberry trees?" Lara asked when Kyle rejoined her.

"More than I ever need to know," he quipped.

"How about taking the horses out along the river?" Bryce asked Kyle. "We can go up to the ridge to see how the mulberry orchard is coming along and then back to Landon Oaks for lunch."

"That sounds good to me. Lara, are you up for a gallop?"

"I am."

"Then so it shall be," Kyle confirmed. He let Jenna and Bryce lead the way to the carriages. Kyle held Lara back for a moment. He spoke softly with a twinkle in his eye. "A ride along the river… perhaps we might even stop for a bit of a swim."

Lara's face lit up as the vivid memory of her falling into the river flashed through her mind.

~ · ~

The Landon estate stretched on for thousands of acres beyond the cotton, tobacco and rice fields. Large warehouses appeared every so often. These were not only for the crops, but also for storage of tools and lumber from the Landon's mill in Hamburg, and for goods brought home from abroad by the six merchant ships belonging to Warren Enterprises. Space was also available during the fall and winter months for rent by neighboring planters while they kept their harvests in storage in hopes that crop prices would increase. Although the slave cabins never fell within sight, Lara assumed they were probably within a mile of the main house. The only hint of their existence was a wide, well-trodden footpath that the foursome had crossed earlier on.

Jenna and Bryce led the way up the river with Lara and Kyle lagging behind. The two stopped at the river's edge to await their guests.

"Lara's quite charming, isn't she, Bryce?" Jenna initiated. "They seem comfortable around each other. Even at church this morning they seemed to be more than acquaintances. Did Kyle tell you how they met?"

"He said they met through a mutual friend when he was still in Brooklyn."

"He's been home now for almost six years and she's been in Savannah for about the same length of time. They've known each other at least that long. Doesn't it seem odd that he's never mentioned Lara before?"

"Perhaps there was nothing to mention," Bryce reasoned. "She is, after all, married to another man."

"Or perhaps they've shared more than they are willing to let on." Jenna broke into a smile as Lara and Kyle ambled closer towards them.

"We're at the edge of the property," Bryce announced. "Why don't we take this trail? It leads to the top of the ridge overlooking one of the mulberry groves."

"Good idea. I'd like to see how the cuttings are coming along," agreed Kyle. "A little further, Lara?"

"You lead and I'll follow."

Jenna fell back to accompany Lara so that Kyle and Bryce could lead the way.

The women kept their eyes on the men ahead. Both were silently admiring the masculine figures of their riding partners.

"They are a pair, the two of them," Jenna stated.

"Are they?"

"Oh, very much so. Each can send a girl into a tizzy with the slightest hint of a smile or the most innocent of compliments. For the most part, their words are measured. Certainly their thoughts are logical and methodical. They both analyze everything to the end, seeking out the gains and the risks. Shrewd, I'd say." Jenna then laughed, "And it frustrates them when they can't find the reason in something."

"You seem to know Kyle as well as you do your husband."

"Kyle is family to us. He and my stepbrother grew up together. They were the best of friends."

"Were?"

"Christopher died two and half years ago," Jenna replied.

"Was he your son's namesake?"

"Yes." Jenna's sorrow was reflected in the wavering tone of her voice.

"I'm sorry, Jenna. I didn't mean to stir up painful memories."

"I miss him dearly. Sometimes I need only say his name and the emptiness returns."

"Or picture him in your head. Or think of him when you come across one of his favorite things."

Jenna looked to Lara to see the empathy reflected in her companion's eyes. Lara's distant expression was a clear reminder that she had also more recently lost one of the last members of her family. "It does get easier with time," Jenna offered.

There was some comfort in Jenna's words, but it wasn't just Aunt Lyddie whom Lara was thinking of. Gavin was in her thoughts more and more each day. Had he stopped pulling the ponytails of the little blonde girl, Jeanette? How was he progressing with his numbers and letters? Were they still having a difficult time in getting him to eat his vegetables? Had he grown much in the weeks she had been away?

"Jenna!" Bryce called back. "We're riding ahead to the first grove."

"Alright with you, Lara?" Kyle turned.

"We'll meet you there," Jenna confirmed for both the ladies.

In the next instant the two men had set their horses into a gallop. Within seconds the thundering of the hooves died down as the men put distance between them and the women.

"Don't they both look magnificent on their mounts?" Jenna asked proudly.

Lara laughed. "They do indeed!"

By the time Lara and Jenna reached the top of the ridge, Kyle and Bryce had dismounted and were surveying the orchard before them. Kyle was pointing, drawing a line from where they were standing out to the far edge of the grove. Bryce nodded his head in agreement with whatever Kyle was saying.

"Kyle's not happy about something," Lara stated.

The two women watched Kyle as he knelt down at the foot of one of the trees.

"He's taking something awfully seriously," Jenna commented.

"Business has always been a serious concern with Kyle, perhaps too much so."

"Not at all," Jenna came to Kyle's defense. "He's proud of his career, but his dearest friends and family mean everything to him. He would abandon all and traverse the world if it meant he could keep us safe from harm. No," she continued, "his priorities between work and play have always been well-balanced. When he returned to Charleston he labored long and hard, but such dedication and commitment is not unheard of. There was much criticism and doubt. Many voiced their concerns, believing him too young to be managing the assets of such a large bank. There were quite a few he meant to prove wrong."

"And has he proven himself?"

"Several times over. The Bank of the State of South Carolina was having a rough go of it when Kyle joined them. Their bank notes had been discounted to ninety percent by many merchants, even lower still by a few other tradesmen. I even recall one run that was started by rumors of the bank being overextended. Fortunately it was late in the day. The bank was able to close and remained so until some state bonds were redeemed. Rough days followed, but the bank made it through. Kyle stayed in the position to tackle what no one else dared to accept. It took some time, but somehow he was able to turn things around. There were some who argued that his methods were extreme and unconventional, but I think the panic warranted such action."

"How did he come to the Planters Bank of South Carolina?"

"A few banks started pursuing Kyle as soon as it was clear that the Bank of South Carolina had made it through the storm. Owen Landrey and his two partners eventually won Kyle over with quite a generous offer, but then I'm sure the Planters Bank has profited from several projects since for which Kyle has arranged financing. He's worked hard for them."

"That's the Kyle Harrison I know. He's always putting his work and career above all else."

"I don't see that in Kyle at all," Jenna contradicted. "Family and friends have always been most important to him. He would never let us down."

"Except Cameron."

"Even then, Kyle might have had just cause."

"What do you mean?" Lara asked, once again becoming intrigued.

"Let's just say that there has been more between Kyle and his cousin since that one swimming incident."

Lara waited for more details, but Jenna remained close-mouthed. Jenna must have been thinking of Kyle's relationship with Faye Carin. Or could there be more about Kyle that she had yet to learn? "It seems I don't know Kyle as well as you."

"He's quite taken with you," Jenna suggested. "I've never seen him so mindful of any woman before."

"Kyle and I met years ago in New York. We now have the opportunity to become reacquainted, but there will never again be anything more between us than friendship."

"Then you did care for him at one time?" Jenna wanted so much to learn more about their relationship. She had often wondered why Kyle never married and had suspected that he had fallen madly in love at one time. Could Lara have been that One?

"Kyle and I parted on bad terms. It's nothing that can be easily reconciled. There were words spoken that should have been left unsaid, and silence when communication would have been best." Lara shifted in her saddle to adjust her balance, securing her legs against the prommel horn. "We met in Brooklyn City. Kyle was assistant manager at a New York bank then and I was studying at the seminary there. We were introduced at my friend Irina's wedding. She had married a good friend of Kyle's. Kyle was so charming and devilishly handsome. He was everything a woman could want in a man... and a husband."

"He proposed marriage?" Jenna's immediate response and the pitch of her voice betrayed her surprise.

Lara was taken aback by Jenna's reaction. Perhaps she had revealed too much.

"I'm sorry, Lara. I'm prying into your personal affairs and it's awfully rude of me. I'm curious. I can't deny that. Kyle is like a brother to me. We can talk about something else if you'd rather."

Lara's gaze was on Kyle. He and Bryce were in animated discussion as they led their horses between the rows of the mulberry trees. "He proposed and I accepted. I handed him my heart and it was broken that same night."

"What happened?" Jenna couldn't resist asking.

"I had told him Lydia Randall was my aunt. He wasn't able to accept that given who she was and how she made her living. He was to come home to Charleston within the month to take the manager's position at the State Bank of South Carolina. In his mind, Aunt Lyddie was not the right sort of woman to be associated with in any way. He forced me to make a choice and I did. Aunt Lyddie was the only family I had left. I couldn't turn my back on her. Not for him, not for anyone or anything. If he truly did love me, then my connections should not have weighed so heavily against me."

"You never saw him after that?"

"He came to the seminary every day for the next while, but I had refused to see him. Eventually he had to leave for Charleston. I left for Savannah a short time later. I never spoke to him again until my first evening back when we chanced to see each other at The Charlestown Hotel."

"What made you decide on Savannah?"

"I spent my childhood there. Aunt Lyddie begged me to come back to Charleston to stay with her, but I couldn't, not with Kyle here. Savannah was close enough for visits, but still a comfortable distance away."

Jenna paused, wondering if she should be so bold as to say what came to mind. Then stated decidedly: "He's still very fond of you."

Lara stared back at Jenna. She had uttered those words with such certainty, but what did it matter when nothing could possibly become of it.

~ · ~

"You're sure of this?" Bryce asked again. "You want to sell all our shares."

"Quite. Would you rather stay in?" Kyle asked.

"No, you've convinced me. I'll follow your lead."

"Leave it to me, then. I'll take care of it," Kyle offered.

"You never did believe in the sericulture venture," Bryce guessed.

"Not entirely," Kyle admitted as he took a sip of his whiskey. "Parts of the plan seemed sensible enough, but overall it's too ambitious a scheme. Too much of it relies on luck, and a great deal of it at that. They'll be hard pressed to meet their production targets even if all goes well."

"No matter. From less than eight dollars a share to nearly thirteen. Thank you, my friend!" Their two glasses clinked as the two men shared a toast to the healthy profit they were about to make.

Kyle savored the rich spicy character of the malt. "There are few things in the world better than a good scotch whiskey," he grinned.

"With your profits you'll be able to fill your cellar," Bryce predicted.

"True, but a good spirit is not what I have in mind," Kyle mused.

A smile came to Bryce's face. He knew that look on Kyle's face. His friend was already thinking of another investment. Simple math told him Kyle would walk away with more than nine thousand dollars in profit from this venture. What scheme would his friend come up with next? And would Kyle be generous and offer to include him again?

Bryce had come to rely on Kyle's advice since settling in Charleston. He quickly came to admire Kyle's ability to analyze situations and decipher the numbers. Kyle seemed to have a sixth sense in matters relating to finance. Some had called it luck. Bryce likened it to instinct. Whatever it was, Kyle seemed to enjoy taking the risks. Somehow he knew when to stay clear, when to throw himself into a deal, and then when to abandon it.

"You two look like you're celebrating," Jenna commented as she and Lara entered the room.

"You'll be glad to know that our banker friend here is on the verge of making us a healthy profit. We're selling our shares of the mulberry groves," Bryce revealed.

"Are you planning to sell Aunt Lyddie's shares as well?" Lara asked, convinced this decision was based upon whatever the two men were discussing earlier on their ride.

"Unless you instruct otherwise," Kyle confirmed.

"I'm not in a position to question your decision," Lara stated. "I suppose I'll just have to trust you."

Chapter 11

A Splendid Race

C ameron Palmer stood at the mantle in the front parlor. His eyes wandered from one corner of the room to the next. He had expected Lara to trim her home in a more feminine fashion. Instead of an abundance of frills and florals, she had chosen cool colors and complimented them with varying textures and subtle patterns on the furniture and fabrics. Altogether, she had been successful in creating an inviting and soulful atmosphere.

The ticking of the clock caught his attention. He reached into his vest pocket for his own watch. He was surprised to find himself more than a few minutes early. With most appointments, whether social or business, he usually found himself late. He wondered if Lara would be one to play games and keep him waiting.

Cameron picked up the magazine that lay waiting on the table before him. He flipped through the pages of the popular *Godey's Lady's Book*. He scanned the hand-colored fashion plates and health articles before coming to a piece of sheet music tucked neatly inside. The sound of footsteps prompted him to return the magazine to its place. He smiled with confidence, almost certain that would be Shani sent to tell him Lara would be down shortly.

The surprise was his when he turned to see Lara with purse and parasol in hand. His eyes swept over her. His facial expression was clear indication that he was pleased with what he saw. Lara had been sensible and was dressed in lightweight traveling clothes as his last note to her had recommended. Her long linen skirt was simply cut without any frills and layers to camouflage her slender figure. The jacket with its tapered collar was fitted to the curves of her upper body. Her white blouse was of fine lightweight cotton. Its bodice precisely pleated to bring detail to an otherwise simple summer beige suit

"Good afternoon, Cameron. I trust you had a pleasant trip."

Cameron took her hand in gentlemanly fashion. He was pleased that she remembered his request to use his given name. "My trip was all business with little time for pleasure. It was rather boring, in fact. I'm glad to be back in Charleston."

"I was told Columbia has as much to offer as Charleston, if not more."

"I disagree. There isn't anyone as lovely as you in Columbia."

Lara returned his compliment with a cautious smile. Beware the wolf, she told herself. "Are you always this prompt?"

"Always when calling upon such a charming lady," he lied, taking advantage of the situation to paint a more appealing picture of himself. "Are you? Many women prefer to test the patience of their menfolk by keeping them waiting."

"I never understood the purpose of such games. Aunt Lyddie taught me never to be late. She believed it to be a sign of disrespect."

"Lyddie knew how to treat a man well. She had much to teach, especially to any willing young lady. Were you a willing pupil, Lara?"

"I listened well to anything Aunt Lyddie had to say," Lara replied innocently.

"I'm curious to know how well you adapted to Lyddie's household and lifestyle."

"Mr. Palmer, your words of praise and admiration flow too freely as do your sly intimations," Lara confronted tactfully. "A true gentleman would be much more discreet."

"Then you still think me a gentleman?"

"I am making a concerted effort to do so. I have to admit, however, that I'm finding it to be quite an arduous task. It seems you also enjoy a good scuffle with words."

Cameron burst out laughing. In one breath Lara had mocked and reprimanded him, and let him know that she had not forgotten their first encounter. "I do," he admitted without hesitation or embarrassment. "Something tells me you would be a formidable adversary. I must keep my guard up."

Lara paused. Here stood a man whose poise and self-confidence allowed him to acknowledge his achievements with pride. Yet he possessed a self-image strong enough to recognize and accept his own shortcomings and mistakes. He had a venturesome spirit and a teasing, playful manner. If caution was not foremost on her mind, Lara might have let down her guard to challenge his innuendoes with allusions of her own. Astonished by the similarities, Lara decided that Cameron was very much like Kyle!

Cameron realized he had lost her. "Is something wrong?" he asked.

Lara tossed aside her thoughts. "Nothing at all," she smiled sweetly. "I was trying to guess what plans you have for us this afternoon."

"Then I won't keep you in the dark any longer. Lara, have you ever been to a horse race? I admit that it's not the usual kind of place for one to take a lady. If you'd prefer we go elsewhere then I will gladly accommodate, but I think you'll enjoy the excitement of it all. What do you say, Lara?"

~ • ~

"There's quite a crowd," Lara commented, as she let Cameron lift her from the shay.

The grandstand of the Washington Race Course stretched down the length of the racetrack. The many long rows of filled seats were testimony to the popularity of the sport in Charleston. On a serious race day, Lara imagined there would be a horde of spectators crammed into the structure. All would be exuberantly loud as they cheered their favorite horse on to victory.

"Nothing out of the ordinary," Cameron informed her. "My horse, Hurricane, is running today. It's a preliminary race before the state trials. For fun, you might say. Those with a bit of money to lose will be over by the stables. They will have their eyes and ears open to catch any omen, good or bad, which might help them decide on how to place their wager. Would you like to meet Hurricane before the race?"

"I would."

"The stables are located at the far end behind the grandstand. Shall we?" Cameron motioned for her to lead the way.

Lara scanned the surroundings. Her eyes followed one length of the racetrack then back along the other. "This is a sizeable parcel of land to be set aside for the occasional race."

"At one time it was a tobacco field. It had been over-planted and the soil depleted of its nutrients. It would lie fallow if not for the track. This is a good alternative, don't you think?"

"So it seems. How long is the track?"

"Total length is four miles, but the race today will only be for two."

"I didn't realize horse racing was so popular here."

"Horse racing has been deemed the sport of kings. It's a serious pastime and anyone with any wealth will own a horse. It's been this way since the first colonists arrived from England."

"Does Kyle or Bryce Landon own a race horse?"

"They both do. No doubt Kyle will be running Aglaia today. Bryce has two horses: Euphrosyne and Thalia. We'll have to wait to see if he's running one or both."

"It's interesting that they named their horses after the three Graces."

"You know your Greek mythology," Cameron remarked.

"Splendor, Mirth and…," Lara was hard-pressed to think of the third.

"Good cheer. Very good, I am impressed! Kyle and Bryce purchased the steeds at the same time from a Virginian breeder two or three years back. Remember though, you are here with me today so you mustn't cheer for any horse other than my Hurricane."

Taking Lara by the hand, Cameron led her through the crowd. He tipped his hat to those who acknowledged their presence, but declined their invitations to stop and chat, explaining that he wanted to look in on Hurricane before the start of the race. There were the usual inquisitive and scrutinizing glances. Lara searched the gathering, looking for Kyle and the Landons. They were nowhere to be seen. Perhaps they were over by the stables.

"Come, Lara, we don't have much time before the race."

At the opposite end of the grandstand, many of the owners had gathered around their four-legged beasts.

"We're over there." Cameron pointed to a dapple-grey stallion being led forward by his jockey. Lara saw a spirited, majestic beast. Hurricane held his head high, his neck in a swanlike arch. Muscles rippled through his long legs and torso. There was no doubting the animal's power and speed.

"Cameron, he's magnificent!"

The Senator beamed with pride. "He is, isn't he?"

"Horses and dogs. You have a love of animals."

"For the domesticated four-legged variety, I'd admit to that."

"Good afternoon, Senator Palmer," greeted the jockey.

"Good day, Josh. Hurricane looks to be in fine shape." Cameron took the reins from the jockey. The horse snorted. Cameron loosened his grip to allow the animal some freedom to move as it tossed its head high to one side.

"He is. He'll be more than ready for the state trials next month."

"That's good news. Lara, this is my rider, Josh Fenn."

"I'm pleased to meet you, Mr. Fenn. Is Hurricane as much of a threat as his name suggests?" Lara reached up to pat the horse.

"He's slow out of the gate," Josh admitted, "but he has a powerful stride in those long legs and he'll recover quickly. He likes the dirt track better than the greens so he's sure to give the other horses a good run today."

"He always does," came Kyle's familiar voice. "Josh, Cameron," Kyle acknowledged the two men before turning to Lara.

Lara's heart leapt when she heard Kyle's voice, but that elated feeling was short lived. She felt the weight of his cold, piercing stare and knew immediately that Kyle was not at all pleased to find her there. Was he perturbed because she was with Cameron Palmer, or was he more upset that she was not in his company?

Kyle's low patronizing voice was paired with soft unhurried words. "I'm surprised to see you here, Lara. I didn't know you enjoyed the races. Or perhaps this is another of Aidan's interests that you've become enamored with?"

Kyle's deep, derisive tone grated on Cameron. The Senator moved in closer to Lara. He placed his hand at the small of her back as if to declare himself to be her protector. "I invited Lara to watch Hurricane run," Cameron volunteered. "You speak as though you ought to know of all Lara's likes and dislikes."

Kyle forced a slight smile as his cousin hovered close over Lara. Kyle couldn't help but notice how relaxed and comfortable Lara was in Cameron's presence. It was unsettling. Never had he known feelings of jealousy so intense. "It would surprise you as to how much I do know of her preferences. Yet she is cunning, able to keep her secrets deeply hidden."

Lara's eyes shot up. She was perplexed by Kyle's allusion and his strange mood. He seemed purposefully antagonistic towards her and Cameron, and there was no reason for his rudeness.

"I'm sure you know nothing that I won't soon come to learn myself," Cameron stated confidently.

Fully aware of their surroundings, Kyle fought off the urge to strike out at Cameron. "Dear cousin, one of your faults is that you are often times too sure of yourself."

"Then it must be a family trait." There was something irksome simmering beneath Kyle's somber facade. Cameron decided then that there had to be some other undeclared attachment between Kyle and Lara.

An awkward, resentful silence fell among the threesome.

Lara stood between the two men. Their tall, broad frames towered over her, closing her in. The more she listened to their sparring, the more uncomfortable she became. She was the object of their exchange and they were speaking as though she wasn't there. Each rebuttal only made her feel smaller and more uneasy. She remained silent, unable to think of anything tactful to say. She tried to distract herself by centering her attention on Hurricane, but found her thoughts and emotions were as clouded as the varying shades of the horse's coat.

"I've been told you've sold your shares of the groves." Cameron was too curious not to ask.

"I did," Kyle confirmed with a frown. It was annoying how quickly the word had spread for he had only completed the transaction late that morning.

"Rumors say you think the trees won't survive a storm."

"Not a strong one," Kyle confirmed.

"Even if that proves to be true, it's a little too soon to be cashing in," Cameron surmised.

Kyle gave his cousin a cold, hard stare, annoyed that his cousin would question his judgment. "As far as I'm concerned, it's never too soon if you can make a decent profit." Kyle cast his gaze back to Lara who stood silent, stroking Hurricane's mane. Kyle waited for her to speak, but she seemed intent on ignoring him. With the passing seconds it became obvious that she had no further intentions of speaking to him. Vexed even more by her disregard, Kyle excused himself. "They'll be ready to start soon. I should rejoin my party."

"You should," Cameron dismissed him flatly.

Another forced grin from Kyle. "Good luck in the race, Josh." He turned his back on Lara and walked away without another word.

Josh had stepped back, feeling uncomfortable when Cameron and Kyle began their bout of words. He was caught off guard when Kyle addressed him and could only respond with a stutter. "Sir? Yes, sir. I mean thank you, sir."

Cameron kept his eyes on Lara as she looked up to watch Kyle leave. Her heavy-hearted expression told Cameron that his speculations of Lara and Kyle had to be correct. "I've never known him to be so confrontational before."

"He doesn't approve of me being here with you," Lara confessed, totally dejected by Kyle's affront.

"That doesn't surprise me."

"I shouldn't have come."

Cameron was determined not to let Kyle spoil their afternoon. "He's being overly protective. I must admit that if our roles were reversed, I would do and feel much the same. Come, let's forget about all this. We have a horse to cheer for."

～ ∙ ～

Nine horses bolted from their positions at the loud blast from the starter's gun. Immediately, the rumble of the horses' hooves sounded, only to be drowned out by the deafening roar from the impassioned crowd. Startled, Lara covered her ears. Her reaction prompted a lighthearted chuckle from Cameron before he redirected his attention to the race.

Never before had Lara witnessed anything like the sight of those magnificent animals racing down the straightaway. She had often been impressed by the horses Aidan had raised and trained, but this was different. The speed of the horses was incredible, their strides unfaltering as they raced down the track. Seconds into the contest, and even at such a splendid pace, the pack was beginning to thin out. Lara was able to keep her eyes on Hurricane only because of his mottled coloring. Hurricane had proven Josh right in that the horse was slow to start, able only to maintain sixth position. It seemed to Lara that it would take an enormous effort for Josh and Hurricane to close the gap and catch the leaders.

The spectators bellowed, their excitement unrestrained as the racers sped forward down the stretch, vying for that advantageous position before entering the first turn. Hurricane responded quickly to the feel of leather as Josh applied the thong. Together they closed the gap on the leaders as they hugged the inside rail. The crowd roared a mix of cheers and hollered foul language as the horses rounded the turn.

"Let him run!" Cameron shouted. "Let him run!"

Josh must have had the same thought for he shifted lower into the saddle. Lara didn't think it possible, but Hurricane broke into a longer, raking stride as he came out of the corner to surge forward to join the leaders.

"He's coming up on Mosey," Cameron hollered.

Hurricane flew like Pegasus. If not for the flying clumps of dirt, it would seem his hooves barely touched the skinned track. Within seconds he was head to head with Mosey. Josh applied the thong: once, twice. Hurricane responded again, outpacing Mosey to gain fourth place. It was electric! Lara could feel the excitement pulsating through her body. The rush fueled by Hurricane's magnificent burst of speed and Cameron's own boisterous cheering.

Cameron leaned down to Lara. "Euphrosyne is out front, then Maverick and Aglaia."

Lara could only nod for the noise was too loud for her to be heard above this crowd.

Euphrosyne's lead was shortened to a half-length when the four horses came out of the second turn. Before them was the straight stretch paralleling the grandstand. Lara felt the pounding of her heart in her chest to be matched only by the sound of thundering hooves in her ears. The crowd came alive yet again to cheer their favorite horse on to the finish line.

Cameron grabbed hold of Lara's arm. "Wait."

Wait? Wait for what?

"Josh!" Cameron shouted.

"Now, Aglaia! Go! Go!" It could only have been Kyle yelling from somewhere behind them.

Each horse felt his rider's whip. It was the jockeys' last desperate attempt to spur their mounts forward to the finish line. Euphrosyne, Aglaia and Hurricane burst forth, each summing up all their strength and that last flash of speed. Maverick could not match the rapid response of the other three horses and started to lose ground. He would have to settle for fourth place. Hurricane fought with Aglaia for second position, both only a head behind Euphrosyne. Suddenly the three were matched head to head, stride for stride. The din of the crowd rose to deafening new heights with only a handful of lengths left to go.

Mass confusion reigned at the end of the heat. Spectators scrambled to the finish line, converging en masse to surround the horses and their jockeys.

"Aglaia!" one man shouted.

"No, Euphrosyne!"

"Definitely not! It was Hurricane!"

Shouts rang out as gamblers quarreled over the winner.

A shot was fired from the starter's pistol, the unexpected blast startling those closest. The impassioned crowd calmed, eventually quieting, anxious to hear the judge's verdict. "Aglaia! I declare Aglaia to be today's winner!"

Hurrahs and congratulatory sentiments could be heard along with the groans and profanity from rude tongues. Gleeful smiles mocked as many long faces while the winners sought out the losers to collect on their wagers. Not often had the Washington Race Course seen such an exhilarating contest!

Lara held tightly onto Cameron's hand as he led the way through the heavy crowd, both anxious to get to Josh and Hurricane.

"A fine race, Josh!" Cameron complimented as he held his hand out to the jockey. The Senator was clearly pleased with Hurricane's performance. He patted the horse. Hurricane blew strong, but otherwise seemed unaffected by the physical stress of the heat. "You did well, Hurricane!"

"He did!" Josh agreed. "Another couple of lengths and we would have had them both!"

"I know, Josh. Hurricane prefers a longer race, but you can't fault him for today. Fine show it was! Wouldn't you agree, Lara?"

"It was exhilarating!"

"You were cheering for Hurricane, weren't you?"

Cameron beamed with Lara's emphatic nod. Overcome with excitement, and without warning, he wrapped his arms around her and effortlessly swept her off her feet into a tight hug before setting her back on the ground.

A roar rang out from the group gathered a little further down the track. In the middle stood Aglaia and Euphrosyne surrounded by Kyle, Bryce and their party.

"Come, Lara. We must be good sports and congratulate the winner."

Aglaia was being led away by her rider as Lara and Cameron came up to Kyle.

"Splendid race, Kyle! Congratulations!"

Kyle turned with a smile to greet his cousin. Clearly Kyle was in much better spirits than prior to the race. He took firm hold of Cameron's extended hand and the two exchanged a friendly handshake. "Yes, indeed it was. Hurricane helped make it so."

"Congratulations, Kyle." Lara offered out of politeness for she was unsure of how Kyle would respond after their earlier exchange.

Kyle might have stepped forward to steal a congratulatory hug from Lara, but Morgan rushed in between them.

"Darling, that was grand!" Morgan's sugar-sweet voice chimed in.

Like blood running through her veins, jealousy ran through Lara as she was forced to step back and make way for Morgan. Lara could only watch as the beautiful strawberry blonde flung herself into Kyle's arms. Lara turned her back on the two of them. She allowed Cameron to lead her away from the couple. She knew her heart and resolve were not strong enough to bear witness to the hugs and kisses that Morgan was eager to congratulate Kyle with. Nor could she stand by to watch Kyle take another woman in his arms.

~ · ~

Morgan Landrey sat poised and confident as she watched and waited. Kyle seemed to be having some difficulty with formulating his answer to her proposition. He shifted in his seat. Such a tentative and indecisive response was unlike Kyle, and Morgan found herself silently questioning her approach. Clearly her offer caught him by surprise. Perhaps it was going to be more difficult than she had originally thought to convince Kyle of the merits of her plan. She knew she was being bold, but this was not a situation in which she could remain passive.

Kyle had become more and more distant over the many weeks since Lara Quinn arrived in Charleston. At first, Morgan ignored the telltale signs and closed her ears to the gossip. She had allowed herself to be blinded by faith that she and Kyle belonged together. However, it became too obvious at the racetrack that Kyle did not care to be in her company. Morgan had acted quickly at the end of the race. She purposefully threw herself into Kyle's arms. Although her intentions would have been clearly understood by Lara, Morgan knew she had to do more if she were to hold on to Kyle. She had to make him understand that she was the right woman for him. She had done so where Faye Carin was concerned and she would be successful again with Lara Kendrick.

"Morgan, I'm fond of you, but marriage." Kyle was still stunned by her forthright offer.

"Darling, there's no reason why we couldn't," Morgan answered calmly. "Father will offer you a position on the Board. I know he will, especially if I suggest it. He thinks so very highly of you. Oh, Kyle, we'll have everything: money, connections, social status. Together we will have it all!"

Not everything, Kyle told himself.

Morgan joined Kyle on the settee. She purposefully bent over further than she needed to in order to move a pillow out of the way, thus granting him a teasing view of the deep cleft of her bosom. She took her place, pressing up to him. She rested her hands upon his chest then swept them over his shoulders and around his neck as she moved in. Her lips were parted, eager to taste his kiss.

"I love you, Kyle. We'll be happy together. I know we will."

Morgan's flirtatious tactics were nothing short of astonishing. This was a side of her Kyle had never witnessed before nor would he ever have believed her capable of such bold measures. How far was she prepared to go to get what she wanted? He was about to speak when her mouth covered his again. She ran her hand down over his chest, then boldly to the inside of his thigh where she let it rest intimately for the remainder of another long exchange. This time Kyle responded, slowly tasting her kiss.

"I love you, Kyle," Morgan whispered, knowing he was aroused and wanting more.

A rap upon the door brought an abrupt end to Morgan's advances. She rose quickly from her seat. The interruption came at a perfect time, eliminating the need to carry on seducing him. For now, her performance was enough to make Kyle think seriously about marrying her. She would give him time to consider her offer. Only if absolutely necessary would she resort to more provocative tactics and daring measures.

~ . ~

The morning spent with Morgan had been full of surprises while the afternoon at the bank had been chock-full of problems. First, Kyle had been greeted by an irate customer after the bank foreclosed on a property. Then there was a second loan account on the verge of default. Just when the work day seemed to be settling down, he was rudely interrupted twice by investors who wanted confirmation that he had cashed in his shares of the mulberry trees. The day was nearly at an end when the exchange report came in. A quick look at the numbers confirmed that the Planters Bank was still uncomfortably overextended on its specie reserve despite earlier measures to hedge the risk.

With old worries renewed, Kyle gathered the bank's journals and hid away in his office. He spent the next few hours pouring over the ledger entries in search of anything peculiar. In his mind he had almost convinced himself that it was useless, looking for that single clue as to why the bank's notes were not being returned for deposit, but he had to try. The volume of notes that had come in over the last three months was below normal levels. This had been going on much too long to reason it away as some extraordinary fluctuation. Someone was hoarding bank notes and nothing good could come of that! Who? How and how much? And equally as important, why?

The exchange reports gave no evidence to support the theory that a competing institution was working against the Planters Bank. It had to be some commercial entity, he reasoned: one with a steady reliable cash flow in which to have an influx of Planters Bank notes. He would start by reviewing a list of the bank's own customers. That would have to wait until tomorrow, he decided, for he had to leave early to get himself ready for tonight's charity ball. Arrangements had been made to have the Landreys meet him at his home. Knowing Morgan, she would be overly excited. She wouldn't be able to wait and the Landreys would arrive early.

Although Morgan's offer of marriage did not come as a complete surprise, her tactics did. She was serious, of that there was no question. Another situation to be resolved, thought Kyle. How was he going to turn Morgan down without damaging his business relationship with Owen Landrey and without risking his position with the bank? Or perhaps he should consider her offer more seriously.

Morgan had not lied. Kyle knew that their union would secure for him the board position he had worked so long and hard for. Owen had hinted of such two or three times over the past year. With that would come the political and social connections that would open up greater opportunities for him. However now, with his feelings for Lara renewed and stronger than ever, Kyle wasn't sure if he was willing to settle for "enough". Could all that status and prestige fill the void of a loveless marriage? However, that wouldn't be the case. There would be love in the marriage. Morgan loved him and he knew that. What he didn't know was whether or not they would be able to build on that.

Chapter 12

∞

A Night of Games

A mix of anticipation and anxiety had the butterflies fluttering rampant in Lara's stomach. Even with Aidan on her arm, touching him, standing beside him, she still couldn't believe he was there with her.

Lara was flabbergasted when Aidan walked through her door late that morning. After the initial flurry of excitement and disbelief, Aidan explained his compulsion to come to Charleston after receiving her letter. In those seven pages she had relayed all the events from her arrival: her first encounter with Kyle, the horrible incident with Cameron at Haven Manor, and the terms of her inheritance. There was also much unwritten in her letter, too much for him to be able to read between the lines to know what she was actually thinking or feeling. Lyddie's death had far reaching implications. Lara was now an independent woman. Their quiet and comfortable existence in Savannah had suddenly turned upside down, becoming quite unsettled. Now with Kyle intruding in her life, the stage was set for a reconciliation between those two, just as Lyddie had always hoped for. By the time Aidan read her last sentence, he had realized that all would never be the same between him and Lara.

A hush fell over the crowd nearest the entrance. Curious glances were cast upon Mr. and Mrs. Aidan Quinn as they caught the attention of those around them. Immediately the whispers started to circulate. It was the ripple effect that Lara had expected and often encountered whenever she entered a room full of strangers with Aidan by her side. Tonight was no exception. The two exchanged a glance and Lara returned Aidan's reassuring smile before making their way through the crowd.

"Are you ready, Mrs. Quinn?" Aidan's dark brown eyes were aglow with admiration as he gazed down at Lara.

Lara's eyes smiled back at him. It was one of those rare occasions on which he had addressed her with that possessive, attaching the title of a married woman to his surname. Now standing there, ready to enter the Great Room of the Exchange Building, the butterflies multiplied and she couldn't help but wonder how this night would unfold.

"Be good," Lara forewarned. That sly, playful look upon Aidan's face made her nervous. She knew he was intending to have as much fun as he possibly could from this evening. No doubt he planned to bestow some kind words of flattery upon the womenfolk to send their hearts aflutter. With his good looks and his sharp wit, there would be few, if any, who could resist his black Irish charms. He might also throw out one or two bold allusions to purposefully start their tongues wagging even more. And if Lara knew Aidan Quinn at all, he would have much more in store than a simple exchange of how-do-you-do's when he finally comes face-to-face with Kyle.

"No such promises," Aidan responded. "I'm surprised you would even ask that of me."

It was the light-hearted, tease of a response Lara had expected. She shook her head. Her nervous smile broadened in response to Aidan's own roguish grin. "You can't fault me for trying."

Aidan would have his innocent fun and part of that would be to keep Lara in suspense and make her wait for whatever he had in mind. It would all happen soon enough and, short of going home, she knew there was nothing she could do to curtail his mischievous plans. Lara brushed her thoughts aside to quickly scan the ballroom.

"Is *he* anywhere in sight?" Aidan asked, knowing exactly whom she was looking for.

"Not that I can see," Lara replied easily. There was no point in trying to be secretive or discreet for there was very little that she could keep from Aidan.

"Come, my darling wife," Aidan invited. "The music beckons and we *must* make an impression."

~ . ~

Jenna immediately sensed Kyle's abrupt change of mood. Even under the most stressful conditions he was always one to remain calm and level-headed, seemingly unaffected by the goings-on around him. Now suddenly quiet, completely distracted and withdrawn from conversation, such a transformation was quite uncharacteristic of him. She looked ahead searching for that which had bewitched her friend and stolen his attention.

"There's Lara," Jenna voiced aloud. Everyone in her party turned, focusing their attention on the couple strolling onto the dance floor. "She looks exquisite tonight! I wonder who she has with her."

"That's Aidan Quinn," Bryce announced, still able to recognize the man from their first encounter years earlier.

"I didn't know her husband was here," Jenna commented, now aware of the reason for Kyle's change in temperament.

"He's a devilishly handsome fellow, whoever he is," Sarah Landon decided easily. "They make for a striking couple, don't you think?" she asked her husband without realizing the stirring effect her words had upon Kyle.

"As do we," Pierce commented. "Come, Sarah, we can't let them have all the fun."

There was a chuckle from Bryce before he followed his younger brother's lead and escorted his own Jenna to the floor. Kyle turned to Morgan. "Shall we?" he asked. It came to him then that it might prove difficult to keep his eyes off of Lara. He would have to make a concerted effort to do so for he couldn't be rude and ignore Morgan.

The musicians played the first introductory notes of a slow French waltz as the couples greeted their partners. Two quadrilles and another waltz later, Lara and Aidan stepped off of the floor and soon after found themselves in the company of the Landon party.

Introductions were made to Pierce and Sarah Landon, Bryce's brother and sister-in-law. The pair was most certainly a fun-loving couple, both possessing a sharp sense of humor that easily matched up to Aidan's. The cajoling and light-hearted fun seemed to indicate that Bryce and Pierce shared a tight bond as family, and a friendship based upon mutual respect and admiration for one another. A similar relationship seemed to exist between Sarah and Jenna, and Lara found herself admiring the foursome for such strong and healthy relationships were rare.

Pierce stood taller than his older brother and with a slightly leaner build. However, like Bryce, he shared the same dark hair and deep brown eyes. A chiseled jaw line set off his clean-shaven face with a single dimple marking an irresistible smile. With Pierce standing beside his wife, it was true that the two made for a stunning couple. Sarah stood taller than most women, but still paired well beside her husband with her height and svelte figure. She had a glowing ivory complexion that required little in the way of powder or rouge to accentuate her naturally healthy features. She moved with a fluid sensual grace; motions which most men, no doubt, would find alluring.

"Aidan, this is Miss Morgan Landrey," Lara continued the string of introductions.

"The pleasure is mine, Miss Landrey." Aidan's smooth, deep voice rang like a song in Morgan's ears. All watched as he placed the most tender of kisses upon Morgan's hand. "I would be honored if you were to save me a dance or two," he requested as his thumb softly brushed the top of her hand.

"I look forward to it," Morgan responded, both delighted and intrigued by Aidan's suave, gentlemanly ways.

In response to her acceptance, Aidan raised her hand to his lips once again.

Without waiting for Lara, Aidan turned quickly to face Kyle. "You must be Kyle Harrison." Aidan offered his hand. "I recognize you from a miniature likeness Lara has—" Aidan was quite ready to refer to Gavin's portrait and the resemblance between father and son, but broke off when he felt Lara tighten her hold around his arm. He took heed of Lara's warning and finished wisely. "… of you from Brooklyn City."

Aidan's attempt to allude to Gavin had not been overlooked by Kyle. There had been no likeness taken of him when he was in Brooklyn. Thus, Aidan could only mean the picture of Gavin that Kyle had taken from Lara the day she told him of his son. The same framed image that now lay hidden in the drawer of his tall chest at home.

Kyle exchanged a wary look with Aidan Quinn along with the firmest handshake.

"We are indebted to you, Mr. Harrison," Aidan acknowledged. "I understand there was an unfortunate incident at Haven Manor in which you were able to assist Lara."

It seemed Lara kept no secrets from her husband. Silently, Kyle wondered if Aidan Quinn would prove to be a friend or a foe. "I must admit I was partly to blame."

"The fault was all mine," Lara interrupted. "It was a reckless decision on my part." It had been her decision to send Addison away when they were out at Haven Manor. It wouldn't be right if she were to let Kyle take any responsibility.

Kyle could sense his companions becoming intrigued by their conversation for all were unaware of the particular event being discussed. He cast a cautious glance to Lara whose expression indicated her unwillingness to continue discussing the topic. "Lara was caught up in the excitement of coming home to Charleston," he offered. "Regardless, I was glad to be of service."

"I don't think I've ever heard Lara refer to Charleston as home," Aidan mused aloud. "We're quite happily settled in Savannah. I must say, though, our son Gavin is looking forward to meeting you."

Kyle raised a curious brow. Why would Aidan want to introduce Gavin into their conversation? "Why would that be?" he dared to ask in the presence of his closest friends.

"A natural curiosity. You've come suddenly to share much with the boy. You are, after all, a friend of Lara's from her school days in Brooklyn City. And as I understand it, are now in charge of his mother's finances."

"I am to provide advice and assistance, not to dictate her spending," Kyle felt compelled to clarify.

The rest of the Landon party, and those in close enough proximity to overhear, were suddenly fascinated with a most interesting and telling conversation. Lara remained close to Aidan's side to witness what was to come. She had expected Aidan to take every opportunity to test Kyle right from the very start. Thus far, he did not disappoint.

"Not to worry, my man," Aidan continued on. "I believe Lyddie made a wise decision."

"I was concerned you might resent my involvement," Kyle challenged.

"Kyle," Aidan started again, "I hope you don't mind me dropping the formalities. It seems awkward to continue on with protocol in the presence of friends, don't you agree?"

Kyle chuckled at the man's abilities to keep the situation light and under control. Decidedly, he would continue to play along, preparing himself for whatever Aidan Quinn had planned for him.

"I know horses best, investments and finances least," Aidan admitted. "Lyddie recognized your talents and believed you would do well for Lara and Gavin. I would be a cad to question Lyddie's decision and a fool to disregard your experience and expertise. Lara needs someone like you. She has been known to get carried away at times and make hasty decisions."

"Yes, Aidan, but only when it comes to accepting marriage proposals." Lara was quick to take advantage of the opportunity to quip back. Her innocent voice was laced with just enough sarcasm to catch Kyle and Aidan off guard for they knew she was referring equally to both of them.

"You are full of praises for Kyle," Morgan joined in.

"He is deserving of them," Aidan countered, not at all affected by Lara's slight. "I understand he has worked hard for the Planters Bank. Your father's bank, isn't it?"

"It is. Father is one of three partners," Morgan acknowledged, surprised that Aidan was interested enough to have expended the effort to find out about her connections.

"Did Gavin accompany you to Charleston?" Kyle asked, most curious as to the boy's whereabouts. He had not intended to broach the topic, but now felt confident that Aidan would take care in disclosing any information that might put Lara in an awkward position.

"He's still in Savannah. I haven't had a chance to discuss with Lara yet, but I'd like to send for him soon, along with my daughter, Abigail. I'm sure Lara will want to be with Gavin when he celebrates his birthday."

"An upcoming birthday. How old will your son be?" Morgan inquired.

"He'll be five in a few weeks," Aidan answered.

Kyle exchanged a quick glance with Lara. Silently they both hoped no one in their party would know enough to think anything improper. If anyone, it would be Jenna who would be sharp enough to put two and two together, to do the simple math that would put he and Lara together in Brooklyn City at the time when the child would have been conceived.

"I'm surprised you left your children in Savannah," Kyle commented quickly in an attempt to distract any further discussion on Gavin's upcoming birthday.

"With Lyddie's death, this has been a terrible time for Lara. Now with having to stay in Charleston for an extended period of time, I wanted to come ahead to help her sort out a few things," Aidan forewarned. "Besides," he directed his gaze to Lara, "this will give us the rare chance to spend some time together."

"It's true there have been one or two unforeseen circumstances," Kyle admitted while wondering how much interference there would be from Aidan. "I'm sure there's nothing that Lara and I won't be able to come to terms with."

The two men locked gazes. "I'm glad to hear it," Aidan replied. "We don't want this to be any more complicated than it needs to be."

"Lara, you didn't tell us you had a son and a daughter," Morgan interrupted with renewed interest. The new information left Morgan feeling confident in that Lara would pose no threat in disrupting her own relationship with Kyle.

Lara hesitated, unsure as to how to answer. She didn't want to divulge much about the children, but if too vague Morgan might press on to try to learn as much as she could.

"Aidan was lucky enough to have found two loves in his life," Kyle offered quickly.

"My first wife, Chelsea, passed away years ago," Aidan explained.

"I'm sorry for your loss," Morgan sympathized, making the wrong assumption that both children were from Aidan's first marriage.

"Your sentiments are appreciated, but the time for such sympathies have long passed," Aidan responded. "I have, as Kyle has rightly noted, been fortunate to find my second love, one as cherished as the first." There was a playful glimmer in Aidan's eyes as he brought Lara's hand up to receive his kiss. The look on Lara's face was the reaction he had expected. He was encouraged and silently he wondered if perhaps he and Lara might yet be able to have something more together.

Kyle, too, was waiting for Lara's response. The glimmer in her eyes was enough to spark unfamiliar pangs of jealousy. These grew more intense as he continued to look on. Finally, he forced himself to look away. The stinging feelings became too intense and he couldn't bear to witness any more husbandly affections of which Aidan had every right to bestow upon Lara.

It was only when Kyle turned away that Lara became aware of the unnerving effect Aidan's game seemed to be having on him. She sensed his discomfort and this, she decided, would be quite enough for now. "Aidan, I think it's time we find something to quench my thirst. We must see what treats await us at the tables."

"Anything for you, my Sweet," came Aidan's casual reply as he wrapped Lara's arm tight around his own.

With that, Lara made their excuses and pulled Aidan from the Landon party. "I've forgotten how well you can carry this charade," Lara commented when she was certain they were no longer within hearing distance of anyone around them. "You almost had me believing."

"You needn't worry. Kyle has just saved you from an embarrassing moment by not having to explain Gavin. He is mindful of how far he is willing to let this go."

"Yes, but are you?" Lara asked nervously. "Perhaps, you're having a bit too much fun."

"You needn't doubt my good intentions," Aidan reassured her with another kiss to her hand. "I only want to know that Kyle is worthy of your affections."

"I don't need your services as a matchmaker. I am content to leave things as they are."

"That would be too easy. Progress cannot be made without change, and nothing worthwhile comes without risk."

Lara knew Aidan meant well. He had been the best of confidants and could always be relied upon to look out for her best interests just as she would for his. "You're making ridiculous assumptions. Besides, maybe it is I who is not worthy of him." Aidan stopped mid-stride to scowl at her. "You are! And you must never think otherwise," he chided. "There is nothing ridiculous about my assumption. I can tell your heart still yearns for him. Lyddie was right. There will never be anyone else for you. Now let's get you that drink. Then I think I shall have Miss Landrey keep her promise of a dance. And I insist you take the opportunity to escort Kyle to the floor, otherwise I will have to think up some brilliant plan to see the two of you together."

"You disappoint me, Aidan. I expected you to have some devious scheme concocted already."

"You know me all too well," Aidan replied, his mischievous grin pasted upon his face.

"Yes, I believe I do. You, Aidan Quinn, are a first-rate cad," Lara accused.

~ · ~

Lara watched Aidan lead Morgan to the dance floor, then turned back to give Kyle her full attention.

"She's beautiful," Lara commented.

"She is," Kyle agreed.

"Thank you for saving me from an awkward moment," Lara started. "I didn't know what to say when Morgan asked about the children."

"Not at all," Kyle responded, thankful that he had finally been able to have some time alone with Lara. "I owe you at least that for my behavior at the racetrack the other day. It was rather—"

"Uncouth," Lara offered quickly, not having to think too hard for what she thought was the right descriptive.

"It was that," he had to admit.

Lara held his gaze. "You're staring."

Kyle struggled to find the perfect compliment only there were no words to justly describe how radiantly beautiful she looked. Instead he brought the palm of her hand up to receive his kiss. For anyone looking on, his actions would have raised questions of impropriety. However, for Lara, his silent gesture of admiration spoke volumes, and such a compliment from Kyle was the only praise she wanted.

The long, silky lengths of Lara's hair had been coiled into a series of ringlets that teased as she moved about. He couldn't resist. He reached out to play with a soft curl. Totally entranced by the vision before him, he had never known any woman as ravishing as Lara. These sentiments were not reserved for only tonight, but each day. Lara carried with her a quality of grace and elegance, whether clothed in the richest of silks or the roughest of cottons. She was even more enchanting this evening, adorned in a soft flowing mass of luscious armure silk, goldenrod in color and distinctively French in design. The bodice was cut low, displaying enough cleavage to warrant any man's attention. Sleeves puffed at the top clung to bare shoulders, tapering down to her elbows from which a generous span of the finest lace flowed. The gown must have cost Aidan a good coin or two. Worth every penny for what man wouldn't be proud to have Lara on his arm?

Lara blushed under Kyle's long hard stare. It seemed she had made the right choice in gowns after all. Lara would have opted for another color if not for the seamstress's convincing argument. The woman had admitted the shade was unusual and not at all popular, but only because not many could carry such a rich golden hue. She had unraveled several yards of the fabric from its bolt and draped it over Lara's svelte body to prove how its deep iridescent color enhanced her ivory skin, the dark auburn undertones of her rich brown tresses, and accentuated the curved lines of her slender body. Now standing before Kyle and seeing the glowing admiration in his eyes, Lara knew the gown had had the dazzling effect that she had hoped for.

"May I have the next dance?" Kyle finally asked.

Lara remembered back almost six years to Irene and Adam's wedding reception. "Isn't that how we started?"

Kyle held her gaze. He needed so much to hold her, to have her in his arms, but that would be impossible amidst this crowd and under Aidan's watchful eye. He would have to toss aside his desires and hope for nothing more than a dance. "I thought we could capture another extraordinary moment. Please join me."

Lara hesitated, unsure of herself.

"Circumstances are different now and it can never be as it once was," Kyle reminded her with her own words. "But we shouldn't let that stop us from enjoying ourselves. Lara, I'm only asking for an innocent little dance. Nothing more."

With his hand extended in invitation and that daring look of anticipation in his eyes, Lara could not find it in herself to deny his request. Hand in hand, they ventured onto the dance floor. She held out her skirt and returned Kyle's formal bow with a deep curtsy. Held captive by his longing gaze, Lara had already lost herself when their bodies began to move. Their movements flowed as one in time with the swaying rhythm of the music. Lara was carried off, swept across the floor in Kyle's strong arms. Their steps were smooth and naturally light. It was like stepping back into time! The feelings and memories from their first dance came flooding back with each step and with each turn as they twirled across the dance floor. And when the hypnotic melody stopped, the two stood before one another. Still in each other's arms, still entranced in the other's presence. Lara could only wonder if, perchance, Fate might be kind and allow it to be as wonderful as it once was almost six years ago.

~ • ~

Many eyes in the room were centered upon Lara, and rightly so for she looked exceptionally beautiful tonight. He would have to remember to tell her so, Aidan told himself. Aidan Quinn stood silent as he watched Lara and Kyle with an overly keen interest. He watched, not with jealousy, but empathy for he was able to appreciate the tender moment he had just witnessed between the two of them.

If Lyddie were here, she would be ecstatic to see the two together. She might even have shed a joyful tear. Through all these years, she had been right in her bold assumption. Lara was still in love with Kyle Harrison and, whether Lara was willing to admit to it or not, she would always be forever his.

As Aidan had planned from the start, his so-called "marriage" to Lara had been nothing, but a lie. It had been a ruse successfully played out for those around him. To have those closest to him stop their persistent matchmaking so he could come to terms with Chelsea's death on his own and in his own time. For Lara, the deal struck with Aidan had secured a home for herself and her son for as long as she wanted. She would play the role of mother to Abigail, and that of the loving and attentive wife to Aidan with the promise of separate bedrooms. Sheltered within the Quinn household, Lara could protect Gavin from the cruelties society would lash upon a bastard child, and Lara would be saved from the prejudices cast upon an unwed mother. In hindsight, it had been a wise and creative solution for Lyddie to convince Lara to join Aidan and move to Savannah.

One day soon, Aidan told himself as he continued to watch Kyle escort Lara off the dance floor, Lara will come to him and he will have to keep his promise and let her go. He loved her enough for that. And if Lara could find the courage to give her heart to Kyle again, then perhaps he could also let go of his own grief and come to terms with Chelsea's death. Then, maybe, he also might find love again.

~ · ~

Crossing the room took more time than it should have for another string of introductions had to be made along the way. Many of these were unavoidable as ladies and gentlemen alike boldly stepped forward to introduce themselves to Lara Quinn. Just as audacious were the questions that followed the preliminaries as everyone seemed keenly interested in anything Lara cared to divulge about the Quinns and their plans to stay on in Charleston.

"They have all heard of your return and can't resist the opportunity to learn more about you," Kyle half-teased as he continued to lead Lara through the crowd and back to Aidan.

"What could they possibly want to know?" Lara asked.

Kyle chuckled, amused by the naïve innocence of her question. "There is much that needs to be answered before their wagging tongues will rest. Isn't it obvious that they all want to meet you? What is of utmost interest is your inheritance. How large a fortune did Lyddie leave you? What about the two properties? And let's not forget that treasure trove of fine jewels. No woman here can resist eying that string of diamonds around your slender neck or those sparkling stones dangling from your ears. Were they part of your inheritance? Perhaps they were trinkets bestowed upon Lyddie by a rich and anonymous patron. Certainly that makes for a much more interesting tale than if an overly generous gift from your wealthy husband. And, utmost on their minds, their fierce curiosities are wondering what the terms of your inheritance are."

"And what role you play," Lara added in fun.

"And what's to become of Haven Manor. What are your intentions, they are all asking themselves."

"My intentions?" asked a puzzled Lara.

"Are you planning to make Haven Manor your home? Are you to become the next Madame of this fine city?"

Lara threw her head back as she burst out laughing at Kyle's outrageous notions.

Kyle grinned ear to ear. Clearly he was enjoying Lara's reaction as he voiced his rambling thoughts. "You find all this absurd, do you?"

"Quite ludicrous. Much ado about nothing," Lara quoted.

"Beth didn't think so and neither do these fine citizens. Look how they seek you out, and once they have your attention, observe how they hang on your every word as you answer their probing questions. And the men here, which one of these fine gentlemen wouldn't want to be in your company?"

"And which one of these fine ladies wouldn't want to be in yours?" Lara countered.

"Let me remind you that more than half these women are married."

"As it is with the men. A married man finds as much solace in a discreet tryst as a single male. Do you think it different for the fairer sex?"

"Hmm, if I didn't know better, I would think you've had some first hand experience in the matter."

"You only need to examine Aunt Lyddie's list of clients. She would have been hard pressed if she had to rely only on the single men of the community."

"You truly believe I could have any woman here?" Kyle mused aloud.

"Any woman here," Lara replied, confident in her assertion.

"Married or single?"

"Married or single," Lara confirmed. She started to take a long, scrutinizing glance across the room. "Who will be the lucky lady? Whom would you choose?"

Kyle leaned in close to whisper in her ear. Her perfume filled his nostrils with a fragrant floral scent. His voice was soft and tender when he spoke. "No one, but you."

Lara could only stare into the depths of his blue-grey eyes. She had forgotten herself and let her guard down. "Don't be ridiculous!" she responded.

"I'm being honest. What do you say, Lara? Will I ever have you again? Will we ever share another discreet tryst?" he whispered. "Perhaps another afternoon in the woods somewhere."

"There you are." Aidan's voice surprised them both. "I was wondering where you had gotten to."

Lara turned away from Kyle, flustered by his sudden and suggestive proposition. "Were you starting to worry?" she managed while struggling to collect her thoughts.

"I know you well enough not to worry," Aidan replied. By the delicate blush on Lara's cheeks he knew he had interrupted some sort of intimate exchange.

"I was in good hands," Lara stated.

"Of course you were," Aidan replied, all the while keeping his watchful eyes on Kyle.

"Good evening, Lara," came another familiar voice.

"Good evening, Cameron," Lara returned the Senator's greeting.

"Senator Cameron Palmer!" Aidan presumed upon hearing the man's name.

Kyle stepped in between the two men, deciding it best to stay put and make the introduction himself. "Cameron, allow me to introduce Lara's husband, Mr. Aidan Quinn of Savannah, Georgia."

Aidan seized Cameron's hand to give it an iron-tight squeeze. "My wife has told me much about you, Senator Palmer. We were even talking about your first chance encounter."

"I regret we started off on the wrong foot," Cameron acknowledged without taking any of the blame. "We had an unfortunate misunderstanding."

"A brash assumption on your part that led to a harrowing experience for my wife." Aidan was not willing to let the matter rest.

"I had hoped I had set things right," Cameron responded with a quick glance to Lara for some sort of reassurance.

"You were generous to have brought Shani and Avram to me," Lara acknowledged. "I'm grateful to have them."

"I'm pleased to hear it," Cameron replied.

"Come, Lara, the Senator's gesture was nothing more than an extravagant bribe," Aidan challenged. "Everyone knows that even a hint of a scandal might be enough to ruin the career of a man in politics. Silence is golden, is it not, Senator?"

Cameron forced the shallowest smile. "As your wife has assured me, all is forgiven. In fact, we even enjoyed an afternoon at the races together, didn't we, Lara?"

"My wife has a heart of gold. She finds forgiveness much too easily. I doubt anyone else would be so generous."

"Both Cameron and Kyle race their own horses," Lara explained to Aidan, in the hopes that some mutual interest would be enough to change the topic to provide for more pleasant conversation. Lara's nerves were becoming frayed. She had barely been able to cast aside the thought of a discreet tryst with Kyle when she was force to deal with Aidan confronting Cameron. "I was fortunate enough to see them run."

"Women for hire and horses for racing. Can a state senator afford such wanton interests?" Aidan was bold to criticize. His eyes were dark and piercing as he glared at Cameron.

Lara became concerned with the look of dislike on Aidan's face. He was sure to pursue the matter of Haven Manor, and Cameron was not the sort of fellow to make an effort to smooth things over or bow out gracefully if provoked. And Kyle seemed quite content to let Aidan and Cameron continue with their verbal jousting. Not wanting to be the reason for any sort of embarrassing incident that might taint the evening, Lara decided it best to separate Aidan and Cameron. She slipped her arm around Aidan's. "My apologies, Cameron, but the music is much too lively to enjoy from the sidelines. It's time for my husband to join me on the dance floor."

"I would have liked to exchange another word or two with the Senator," Aidan told Lara as he was pulled away.

"Yes, I was sure of it. Although I can't imagine you would have had anything pleasant to say to the man," Lara commented stiffly. "I was afraid one of you might end up on the floor."

"I assure you, it would have been the Senator," Aidan replied with confidence. "But you needn't have worried, I'm sure Kyle would have intervened on Palmer's behalf."

"I doubt that since Kyle hasn't much use for his cousin. Besides, you needn't worry about the Senator getting his due. Kyle has already drawn blood and shown him the floor."

"Has he?" Aidan inquired, surprised by the discovery of Kyle's relation to Cameron, and that Kyle had taken it upon himself to defend Lara's honor. "If not for the circumstances, I'm sure I'd find your Mr. Harrison to be quite a likable fellow."

"He is not *my* Mr. Harrison," Lara disputed.

"Oh, but he is," Aidan replied, a knowing and confident smile wide upon his face. "You're in his blood and it's driving him mad."

Chapter 13

The Truth Be Out

*L*ara let the shawl slip from her shoulders. The Great Hall had suddenly turned stuffy and she had escaped outside on her own to the grounds for some fresh air and peaceful solitude. The roses scented the air as she followed the winding garden path, wondering if it might lead her out to a view of the harbor. Coming up to a bend, Lara stopped upon hearing low, unfamiliar voices.

"He was locked up in his office for hours this afternoon. If he continues his examination of the bank ledgers he'll be sure to find us out." The words were anxiously spoken and the serious undertone of the stranger's voice confirmed the gravity of the situation being discussed.

"His intuition may tell him something is wrong, but that's all he has to go on—intuition," a second voice responded, seemingly unconcerned in comparison to that of his companion.

"We can't afford to underestimate him. Damn it, we could be ruined!"

"Calm yourself, Granger. You're getting carried away. Someone might hear you."

Lara covered her mouth with her hands. She couldn't believe her ears. Was the other man Granger Wilkes?

"Calm myself? The only thing keeping Kyle from reconciling the deposits is his misguided trust in us. When he finds nothing in those journals he will take count against the ledger and it will be plain as day that someone has been embezzling funds. That will leave him to point the finger at you and me. You and me! Mark my words! He is not one to give up on something as serious as this. We have to do something!"

Lara was too shocked and frightened to listen to any more. She turned to run back to the Great Hall, trying to be as quick and quiet as possible. In her haste to rejoin the gathering, the fringes of her shawl became tangled in the bushes. She tugged, not caring that the fine cloth was now ruined, but terribly worried that the rustling of the branches would give away her presence and she would be caught. Freed, Lara dashed ahead without looking back. As she neared the Hall, she collided with a man she recognized as Matt Stevens, one of the other partners of the Planters Bank.

"Whoa, there!" Matt held her firm by the shoulders.

"Mr. Stevens!" Lara nearly screamed.

"Are you alright, my dear?"

"I-I'm fine," she stuttered. "Excuse me."

Lara brushed passed the man. She was too flustered to worry about being rude. Was he out for a breathe of air or was he intending to meet up with his partners in the garden? Could it be that Matt Stevens was also mixed up in their scheme?

~ • ~

The night was coming to a close. The raffle dances had long since been completed, and the crowd had already started to thin out. Aidan had disappeared somewhere, leaving Lara in the company of the Landon party. Full of worry, Lara grew restless. She found it increasingly difficult to concentrate on the conversation taking place. Her tactful attempts to pull Kyle aside to tell him about the discussion she had overheard in the garden had been spoilt each time by Morgan. Now, adding to Lara's insecurities was the fact that Aidan had been gone much too long for her liking.

The musicians started to play the last song, but the notes trailed off for no one dared to venture out onto the dance floor for the polka. Suddenly a short series of notes rang out from the musicians to catch everyone's attention. Like everyone else, Lara turned to find Aidan commanding attention.

"Good evening, fine citizens of Charleston. For those of you whom I have not yet had the opportunity to meet, I am Aidan Quinn and I have experienced, for the first time tonight, some of the finest hospitality in these southern states."

A short round of applause broke out.

"The purpose of tonight, I am told, is to raise money for the orphanage. In an effort to help achieve this worthy goal, I would like to propose that a very special lady come out to receive bids on this next dance."

Lara cringed. What was Aidan up to now? She was about to turn and leave when Kyle took a firm hold of her arm to stop her retreat.

"I'm sure Aidan would like you to stay for this." Kyle was not going to let her get away so easily. "Let's see what your husband has planned for us."

"Please Kyle, I need to speak to you," Lara tried again, unable to put aside all that had transpired outside.

"It's just starting to get interesting," Kyle noted, thinking that her growing anxieties were a result of whatever surprises Aidan was in the midst of conjuring up.

"I'd like to ask Miss Morgan Landrey to come out onto the floor to take bids for the last dance," Aidan announced.

Morgan blushed, both astonished and excited to suddenly find herself the center of attention.

Aidan started the round of bidding and Kyle joined in for fun. Quickly the bid rose to an impressive ten dollars, but, as

Lara had expected he would, Aidan forced the win by doubling the last bid.

"As I had come tonight with Miss Landrey on my arm, my heart was set on sharing the last dance of the evening with her," Kyle addressed Aidan in front of the remaining crowd. "As you have left me without a partner, I think it only fair that we're given the opportunity of winning a round on the dance floor with Mrs. Quinn as well."

A hush fell over the crowd again. Lara cast a quick glance to Morgan whose mood shifted with the turn of events. Aidan had set the stage and Kyle had proven his willingness to play along. Aidan would not refuse Kyle's request. Rather he would force the decision upon Lara. She only wanted a quick end to the evening. It annoyed her more to be pulled unwillingly into his game and into suddenly becoming the center of attention.

"Lara?" Aidan asked.

"I'm sure any gentleman here would prefer the lively steps of an eligible young lady to those of mine," Lara responded. For certain, she knew any attempt to bow out gracefully would be for naught.

"I can only speak for myself," Kyle started. "Let me prove you wrong by matching your husband's offer of twenty dollars."

A round of chatter was coupled with an enthusiastic round of applause for Kyle's generous bid.

"It's a night for the orphanage, my dear," Aidan reminded Lara.

Lara could only relent as those gathered around waited for her response. "Then it would be heartless of me to refuse."

"We start with a generous bid of twenty dollars from Mr. Harrison," Aidan declared.

"Twenty-one," a bid was shouted out from the side.

"Twenty-two," came another.

Kyle chuckled before throwing out his second offer. "Twenty-five dollars for the honor and the privilege."

The crowd fell silent as everyone waited to see if anyone would counter.

"Thirty," came another deep, familiar voice.

The room buzzed as everyone's attention turned. Cameron Palmer suddenly appeared at the edge of the dance floor, his face shining with a mischievous grin.

"Thirty-two," Kyle nodded in acceptance of the new challenge.

"Thirty-five. Will you go another two, cousin?" Cameron dared.

Kyle smiled, able to guess his cousin's strategy, but uncertain as to how far Cameron was willing to go. "No, I think not."

Cameron's grin broadened.

"Forty," Kyle offered instead, satisfied by the look of surprise on his cousin's face that he had ended the bidding war.

All eyes were upon Cameron. Knowing he had once again been bested, Cameron chuckled good-naturedly. He strolled casually across the floor and bestowed his attention onto Lara. "As usual, it seems Kyle is not to be outdone. Just the same I ask you to accept my donation to the orphanage." Cameron lifted her hand to his lips. With his polite kiss, he left her holding a neat roll of bank notes.

The crowd was amazed. Lara, too, was left flabbergasted. "Your generosity is overwhelming."

A small peck on Cameron's cheek would have been acceptable, but everyone guessed more was forthcoming when Lara reached up to wrap her arms around Cameron's neck and bring him down to receive her kiss. As she had expected, the Senator was bold enough to take advantage and she could sense the reaction of those around her as soon as Cameron's lips covered hers in a bold exchange. He held her tight, forcing her body into a graceful arch. Her token gesture of gratitude was enough to shock their audience.

Cameron held her in his arms for a little longer than was necessary. All eyes were upon them as he whispered in her ear before releasing her from his embrace. "You're a naughty little vixen, Lara Quinn."

Lara laughed.

Astonished and somewhat amused by Lara's audacity, Aidan brushed it off in good humor. In contrast, Kyle was anything but pleased. He scowled at Lara. His feelings were more intense, having been roused by such a brazen public display of impropriety.

Lara glared at Aidan as he stepped forward to escort her to the center of the dance floor.

"I wouldn't have guessed you would be so bold in front of all of Charleston, and under Kyle's critical eye," Aidan noted, his voice soft and low.

"I can be as bold as you are incorrigible," she scolded with a trite smile for their audience.

"So I've just discovered." With a broad grin, Aidan handed her over to Kyle.

"You are as daring as your husband," Kyle scolded as he accepted Lara's hand. "You both like to take risks."

"He enjoys his games, especially when he has nothing to lose," Lara replied. "And you are as much a cad as he is for playing along. You're both rakes! Was it necessary to put on such a show with Cameron?"

"It was much tamer than the performance you just put on. Besides, he seems happy with the outcome. I expect I'll be just as pleased."

"You won this next dance," Lara reminded him. "Nothing more."

"No warm and tender affections to show your gratitude over my generosity?"

"You will have to be content only to have me as a dance partner," Lara reaffirmed.

"I was hoping not," another voice was raised.

Lara turned. Her heart jumped as Granger Wilkes approached. "The bidding is still open, is it not? Forty-two for the orphanage," the man offered with an overly confident smile.

Lara held her breath, praying that Kyle would counter.

"When you get to be as old as me," Granger started to explain, "you will find that it takes more than charm to win even a few moments with a woman as lovely and fair as Mrs. Quinn."

As Lara had feared he would, Kyle politely conceded. Lara found herself partnered with Granger Wilkes for the last dance.

"Did you enjoy our gardens?" the man asked as he brought her into his arms.

"The gardens?"

"You were out on the grounds a short while ago, were you not?"

His question made Lara uneasy. She tried to disguise her distress and remain relaxed in his arms. How could he possibly have known anyone was in the shadows let alone her? She was sure she had been quiet enough. "Long enough only for a few breaths of fresh air. I'm afraid I didn't get much past the veranda."

Granger returned her cautious smile with a shallow one of his own, and Lara was left wondering if he believed her lie.

~ . ~

After the fundraiser, it seemed the most sensible thing for Harlene and Owen Landrey to have taken their daughter home rather than having Kyle complete the nicety. Kyle was grateful as this would save him not only the long trip out to the Landrey plantation and back into the city again, but from having to listen to Morgan and her mother recount the endless details of the evening. Surely that would include a flourish of critical comments regarding Lara's brazen display with Cameron, and this was something Kyle would rather not have to endure.

Despite the late hour, Kyle decided to walk home and sent Eaton ahead with the carriage. At the bottom of the steps of the Exchange Building, Kyle looked up into the dark endless heavens. He took in a deep breath of the cool night air. His eyes swept once across the harbor before starting for home. He had always enjoyed his walks for he used this time to sort through his jumbled thoughts and put his concerns into perspective. Lately though, this was not the case; at least not with anything to do with Lara. His musings of her worked only to confuse him more. Try as he might, he was unable to make sense of her actions and her words. It was nights ago when she had declared her love for him. One could argue that she had been pressured to do so, but he knew her words to be true. He felt it. Falsehoods could not come from emotions so passionately powerful. And yet tonight, seeing her with Aidan by her side seemed to reinforce the fact that Lara would never again be his. Aidan and Lara: husband and wife. Nothing could be more difficult to accept.

The slow rumble of another carriage over the cobblestones interrupted his thoughts. Kyle frowned as he watched it turn into Lara's lane. There he stopped to stand in the shadows to spy on the couple now standing at the door. Kyle watched with curious disbelief. There was an innocent peck on the cheek from husband to wife, but no other physical contact between the two. And instead of going into the house, Aidan returned to the coach only to be driven elsewhere.

Kyle watched Lara. She stood on the porch to wait until Aidan's carriage turned onto Wentworth Street. She hesitated at the door. Then, turning abruptly, Lara started running down the lane. Kyle stepped out of the shadows when she reached the street and Lara screamed with fright.

Kyle caught hold of her and held her firm until she recognized him. "Where are you going this time of night?"

Lara drew in a deep breath. "Oh, Kyle, you scared me near to death!" she declared, still feeling her heart pounding and the hollow in her stomach.

"Where were you going?" he asked again.

"To find you," she answered. "I've been trying to tell you of a conversation I overheard. I think it's important. They were talking about ledgers and bank notes."

That was enough to ignite Kyle's curiosity. "Who was talking?"

"I don't know for certain. I got tired of listening to you and Aidan banter on so I left the hall for some fresh air in the gardens." Lara shivered.

Kyle pulled her wrap over her shoulders. "Your shawl, it's shredded. Are you hurt?"

Lara shook her head. "I was afraid of being discovered. In my rush to get back, it got caught in the rosebushes."

Relieved it wasn't anything more serious, Kyle turned her about. "Come, let's get you out of the cold."

Once inside the house, Lara told Kyle of all she had overheard. "They were talking about how you had been looking over the bank ledgers, and that you would eventually find out they've been embezzling funds!"

"They used those words?"

"Embezzling funds," Lara repeated with certainty. "After reconciling the deposits against the journals. Does that make sense?"

"Did you recognize either of the men?"

"I didn't see them, but I heard one of them call the other, 'Granger'. Kyle, I think one of the men was Granger Wilkes. After that last dance with him, I'm sure of it. He was asking me how I enjoyed the gardens. I'm sure he was trying to find out how much I had overheard."

"Lara, whether it's true or false, the slightest rumor of this sort could ruin the bank. You mustn't mention this to anyone, do you understand?"

The tone of Kyle's voice was enough to confirm the seriousness of the situation. Yet still, Lara was surprised at how calm and composed he was.

"Have you mentioned this to anyone else?" he asked.

"No one," Lara replied.

"Not even Aidan?"

Lara shook her head.

"Where was he off to?" Kyle questioned, his curiosity finally getting the better of him. "I saw Aidan leave. Where was he going?"

Lara didn't want to answer any questions about her and Aidan. It had been a long evening. She wanted to feel the comfort of her own bed with the warmth of a light blanket snug over her shoulders. Aidan's taunting games with both Kyle and Cameron had exhausted her patience, and her attempt to find a few minutes of relief and solitude in the gardens gave her even more to fret about. Certainly the last dance with Granger Wilkes did nothing but unsettle her nerves even more.

"Lara," Kyle prompted again.

Knowing how persistent he could be, Lara finally answered, "Aidan is staying at The Charlestown Hotel."

"Not here with you?" Kyle's voice was controlled without any hint of surprise.

"No."

"Did you two quarrel?" Kyle probed further, wanting to know what had come about to keep such an affectionate husband and wife apart.

"It's best you leave now," Lara insisted, not wanting any more of his questions.

"Why is Aidan staying at The Charlestown?" Kyle tried again.

"It doesn't concern you. Please, Kyle, it's very late and I'm tired." Lara started walking towards the parlor door, but Kyle took hold of her to stop her retreat. The next instant she found herself in his arms, his lips pressed hard against hers.

"Do you know how irresistible you are?" His voice was soft and low as he spoke in her ear. He closed his eyes as he breathed in the intoxicating scent of her perfume. "If you were mine, there wouldn't be a single night without you feeling the warmth of my body next to yours. Do you remember how it was when we were together? How you cried out for my touch, how our bodies melded together, and how we couldn't bear to be apart? It could be that way again."

"Stop it!" Lara demanded. She couldn't stand hearing any more and tried to push him away. "Stop your games! You can play them with Aidan and Cameron, but don't try them on me. I don't want any part of them."

"I was playing along at the fundraiser tonight. I admit it." He brought her closer, his body pressed hard against hers. "But not now. Not here with you."

Again his mouth came down over hers. His kiss, a display of unrestrained passion, took her breath away. And yet, somehow, she was able to conjure up the willpower to push him away. Lara tried turning her back to him, but he refused to let her go. His strong arms encircled her waist tight to keep her to him.

"You're so beautiful," he repeated, his words a seductive whisper in her ear. "I always believed myself immune to jealousy, but I was proven wrong tonight. It was torture to have to stand by and watch Aidan hold you and shower you with his kisses. I wanted to be the one by your side, to dance with you in my arms, to be able to share your kiss. Can't you see, Lara? There is nothing I want more than to be with you."

Lara felt his kiss at the base of her slender neck. His touch left her weak. She closed her eyes. She rested her head upon his chest, enjoying the feel of his hands as they moved freely over the curves of her slender body, from her hips, over her stomach, then up to fondle her breasts. Shivers ran through her as he nibbled her ear lobe. Each sensuous touch kindling a desire that left her wanting more.

"Please stop." Her eyes flashed a jumbled mix of emotions when she turned to look up at him. "I can't. Aidan's been good to me. He deserves better than this."

"Then why isn't he here with you. Why are you in my arms and not his?"

Lara stared at him while keeping her silence. It would take nothing to give in to her desires.

"Because it's me you love," Kyle reminded her. "You belong to me, Lara. You've been mine since the night of Adam's wedding and I will never let you go."

Lara mistook his confidence for arrogance and his words were quick to ignite her temper. "How dare you! What makes you think you have any sort of claim over me? I belong to no one. Not you, not Aidan, not ever!"

Kyle was bold and sure enough of himself to prove her wrong. His lips were hard upon hers as he forced himself upon her.

Lara remained strong. She was determined not to waiver in his arms. She threw her hand up quickly, striking him across the cheek.

"If I didn't know better, I'd think I was witnessing a lover's spat," the voice came from across the room.

Startled, Lara and Kyle both turned to find Aidan standing at the door.

"A gentleman would have knocked." Lara managed to catch her breath.

"Now Lara, you know I've never considered myself much of a gentleman," Aidan replied with a broad smirk upon his face. "Besides, why would a husband need to knock when coming to his wife?"

Lara was totally flustered by the turn of events and couldn't think. Drained by the events of the night, she could only wonder why Aidan had bothered to return. "What are you doing here?" she demanded, her tone evidence that her patience had finally run out.

"That would be my question for Mr. Harrison." Aidan took strides into the room. He centered his attention on Kyle. "It's rather an obscene hour to be calling on another man's wife."

Fearing that Aidan would lash out at Lara, Kyle stepped forward, ready to intervene. "Lara asked me to leave. I was—"

"An explanation is not necessary!" Lara cut Kyle off, her patience lost.

Kyle was stunned by Lara's abrupt and rude response. She showed no fear and no hesitation after being caught in his arms. As her husband, Aidan Quinn had every right to an explanation if not to some sort of retribution.

"Get out! Both of you!" Lara pointed at the parlor door. "I've had more than enough of the two of you for one night. Get out of my house!"

Aidan waited for Kyle to make the first move. Neither man budged. Exasperated, Lara brushed past them to escape upstairs.

Baffled, Kyle was left standing face to face with Aidan who seemed unperturbed, perhaps even somewhat amused by the situation.

"What the hell was that all about?" Kyle managed.

"Come on, we better get out of here," Aidan directed as he grabbed hold of Kyle's arm.

But Kyle was not ready to leave and he waved his arm free. "How can you be so calm after catching your wife in another man's arms?"

"Would you rather I take a swing at you?" Aidan chuckled. "I doubt finding the two of us in a brawl would impress Lara much."

Kyle stood dumbfounded. Confused by all that had transpired in the last few minutes, he couldn't understand Aidan's reaction. No fisticuffs, no rage, not even a heated exchange of words. What kind of loving husband would be so indifferent?

"Don't you care about Lara? Don't you care about your marriage?"

Aidan laughed aloud. "I would be if there was one."

Kyle couldn't believe his ears. "What did you say?" he asked in stunned disbelief.

Aidan waited for his answer to sink in.

Aidan's answer struck Kyle like a thunderbolt. "You, Aidan Quinn, are a bastard! You've been playing me all evening."

"You think this is my game?" Aidan asked, not completely sure if Kyle had come to the right conclusion.

"What are you saying?"

Aidan laughed again.

"Lara?" Kyle realized.

~ · ~

Lara watched the lone figure leave the house from her bedroom window. At the same time, she could hear footsteps approaching her bedroom door. Hadn't Aidan had enough for one night? Why couldn't he just go away and leave her alone?

Three loud knocks.

Lara closed her eyes and heaved a heavy sigh in frustration. "Go away!" she commanded with as much grit as she could muster, but even as she spoke she knew her attempt to put Aidan off would be for naught. If only there was a lock on the door. She waited and watched. The doorknob turned. Her heart jumped when it was Kyle, and not Aidan, who stepped into her bedroom.

"We're not finished," Kyle declared. His voice was firm. He was determined to have his say. He closed the door behind him and approached. "You need to clear something up for me. You've accused me of playing games and yet it seems you've concocted a grand deception of your own."

"I don't know what you mean." Still stunned by his presence, Lara could barely get the words out. Now, standing before him, she found herself weak, further shaken by his commanding tone. His moods throughout the evening had been unpredictable and quick to change. He was casual and easy-going one second, serious and determined the next. Lara found herself cautiously on guard as she searched the depths of his dark, brooding eyes.

Kyle took a firm grasp of her left hand and held it up to bring attention to the wedding band that encircled her finger. "Tell me. What does this ring mean to you?"

Lara pulled her hand from his.

"What does it mean to you?" Kyle repeated his question, his voice louder as she continued to test his patience.

"It's a wedding ring," Lara answered softly, too tired to give any serious thought as to what Kyle was after or what his motive for questioning her might be.

"When a women wears a wedding ring, does it not symbolize her love and fidelity for the man whom she calls her husband? *A wedding ring*," he quoted, "but not *your* wedding ring."

Lara cast her eyes down to the plain, gold band. The one her mother put in her hand fourteen years ago when they said their last good-bye on the Savannah docks.

"Am I right? Is it your wedding ring, Lara? Do you wear it as a symbol of your love and fidelity for Aidan?"

Kyle knew! Did he figure it out for himself or did Aidan say something to him? Feelings of guilt and doubt confirmed she had been caught in her charade. Now what? What could she possibly say to save herself?

"You said it yourself. Several times in different ways, in fact," Kyle continued. "I just didn't put it all together until now. You love Aidan like a sister would her brother. He enjoys his games and has nothing to lose. You belong to no one. Not me, not Aidan, not ever. Your words, Lara." He stepped within reach, his tall, masculine frame hovering over her. "I'm not asking for anything, but the truth. Are you married to Aidan Quinn?"

Lara summoned all her courage. Bravely, she looked up to address Kyle. "No," she answered. "I'm not married to Aidan, nor to anyone else."

The words had barely escaped her before she was enveloped tight in Kyle's arms and returning his kiss. Long, passionate, it was an honest declaration of how much he had needed to hear that answer, and how alive and strong his love for her still was.

"Gavin, and now Aidan. Is there anything else you need to tell me?" Kyle asked half-jokingly, his head bent down to hers.

"You know everything. I have no more secrets."

"Then tell me again you love me."

"I do love you," Lara whispered.

"Heart and soul?"

Lara laughed, not altogether surprised that he had remembered her words from before. "With all my heart and all my soul," she declared.

There was relief and hope as Kyle drew his next breath for no words could have been any sweeter to his ears. "Let me love you. Let me show you how much you mean to me."

Lara's hands reached up to caress his handsome face. His kiss was warm in the palm of her hand. Lara gathered her long curls together to bring them over her shoulder. She turned to display the row of dainty buttons running down the back of her gown. She felt the cool air against her soft skin as Kyle worked to unfasten the buttons. As each was undone, he placed a gentle kiss on her back that sent a shiver running like a wave through her body. His strong, loving hands swept over her delicate shoulders to bring the loosened gown down over her arms. With a soft rustling, the garment crumpled to the floor. His arms encircled her, his thumbs brushing over her nipples before his hands began to massage her breasts. Lara leaned back against him, her senses alive, her body yearning for his loving touch.

One by one, she was freed from her petticoats, each layer joining the puddle of luscious, goldenrod silk that lay at her feet. A pull of the hair ribbons and the loops slipped out of their knot. She felt his fingers combing through her curls, the long tresses unraveling in thick, silky waves down the length of her back.

Lara was swept up in Kyle's arms and carried off to her bed. He lay her down gently. There, he finished undressing her. His fingers were nimble, working quickly to roll the fine cotton to uncover long shapely legs. Kyle's touch was amazingly gentle for his strong hands. They moved in one long caress from her ankles, over her calves and to the inside of her thighs, his touch fueling a desire from deep within.

It had been years since she last shared such intimacy. Without any inhibitions, Lara lay naked as she watched Kyle undress. He came to her, his eyes alive with a burning desire of his own. She lay waiting to receive him. Voluptuous, seductive, sultry. Needing him to make love to her, to show her how much she meant to him.

Lara reveled in Kyle's lovemaking. Every touch was a sensuous delight. His tongue teased the nipples of her breasts, his suckling sending titillating shivers throughout her body. Each caress of his hand, each kiss from his lips worked to heighten her senses and fuel her burning desire for more. Lara responded with a heated passion of her own, and Kyle's fondling turned into bolder strokes as he continued to explore the most intimate parts of her body. His hands were gentle, his massaging touch sending her mind reeling with carnal pleasure.

A different sensation began to overpower her as Kyle entered her body, his bold rhythmic thrusts exciting her more, fueling the passion burning deep inside. Moans of pleasure escaped her as the fire intensified, a wild sensation mounting uncontrollably. A pulsating surge emanating from deep within exploded. Lara clung tightly to Kyle, calling out to him as the rush enveloped her in its long, sensual wave.

Basking in the afterglow of their love, Lara lay wrapped in Kyle's loving arms. His body snuggled up to hers, each keeping the other warm. She placed a loving kiss on the lean, muscular arm that held her tight for, in that moment, she had everything she wanted and needed, and the world was all that she had ever hoped it could be. Lara was more than content to lie still, enjoying Kyle's long and gentle caresses. Her eyelids soon grew heavy and his soothing touch lulled her into a deep and peaceful sleep.

~ • ~

Kyle woke to unimaginable happiness! The gods had smiled upon him and turned his living nightmare into a living fantasy. Astonished by the sudden and fateful turn of good fortune, he could only stare at the beauty lying next to him. Enamored. Enthralled. Entranced and bewitched. Lara had worked her magic to turn him into all those things. Unable to restrain himself, he woke Lara. With tender kisses and long strokes of a loving hand, he roused her gently from the subconscious world of Hypnos.

A slow smile came to adorn Lara's beautiful face. Her grin broadened when Kyle's nibbling of her earlobe sent a tingling sensation through her body.

"Good morning, my love." Kyle's playful greeting rang like a song.

Lara opened her eyes to find Kyle leaning over her. His blue eyes were alive with love and passion.

"Good morning," Lara answered in a lazy drawl.

"A good sleep?" Kyle asked.

"A wonderful sleep." Her arms went about his neck and she brought him down for an amorous exchange of affection.

Kyle tugged at the bed sheets trapped between their legs and threw them aside. The cool morning air kissed Lara's skin. Almost immediately she was enveloped by Kyle's warmth as he wrapped her tight in his arms. She felt her own temperature rising with a rekindled passion as his bold caresses swept over the sinuous lines of her nude body. Her silken limbs became entwined with his and their bodies melded together. Lara pressed her lips to his, her fiery kiss demanding an immediate response.

Kyle did not disappoint.

~ · ~

Lara pulled on the reins to command her horse to a stop. She looked ahead, wondering where in this world Kyle was leading her. There was no path to follow and the slope was long and steep. She had only Kyle and her renewed faith in him that he knew where he was going as he and his mount continued to follow the curve down the narrow ravine.

"Not much further," Kyle promised as he stopped to look back to make sure Lara had not fallen behind. "Are you sorry I took the day off?"

"It might have been more fun to stay in bed," Lara teased.

"Do you doubt me? Oh, ye of little faith!" Kyle chided.

Nearer the bottom, the ravine took a turn and the gulch opened up to reveal a small sheltered bay. The secluded cove lay before them with a somewhat rocky beach save for a patch of fine beige sand that stretched into the sea. Here, Lara dismounted. She strolled to the edge of the water to take in the natural, unspoiled view. The horizon was marked by the deep, blue-green expanse of the Atlantic Ocean meeting the cloudless sky. Shimmers of silver danced upon the distant waters as the sun's rays reflected off the crest of the ocean's waves. The light sea breeze was enough to temper the heat and make it comfortable enough to be out enjoying the midday sun.

Lara spread their blanket over the sand, leaving Kyle to fetch the basket lunch she had prepared for them. There she settled to watch the waves lap one over the next while listening to the soothing sound that could only come from the ebb and flow of the waters. She closed her eyes and tilted her head skyward to feel the warmth of the sun upon her face. She took in a deep breath to fill her lungs. The smell of the sun! The air was hot and dry while fresh and exciting all at the same time. Only wonderfully good things could happen on such exceptionally beautiful days!

"Hungry?" Lara's idyllic moment was broken by Kyle's deep voice.

Lara opened her eyes to find he had dug into the sweetgrass basket and found himself a wedge of cheese. He held it out, offering her a bite.

"No, but it seems hunger has found you." Lara withdrew the carefully wrapped stem glasses from the basket then retrieved the bottle of wine and the corkscrew to hand to Kyle.

"Famished," Kyle admitted, "but not just for food." He winked at Lara, his suggestive tone enough to prompt a laugh.

Kyle gave the T-shaped handle of the corkscrew a clockwise turn into the wine cork, then a quick twist and pull and the plug popped out of the bottle's neck. Zealously, he poured wine into two glasses, almost to overflowing.

"Do you mean to make me silly?" Lara chided in fun.

Her question prompted a hearty chuckle from Kyle. "My love, we both know you possess a natural talent for silliness. In that respect, you need no aid from wine or any other such intoxicant."

"Then your intention must be to get me drunk so as to have your way with me."

"After last night, I didn't think I needed to resort to such crude tactics, but if that's what needs to be done." Kyle raised his glass. "To drunken bliss."

Lara found Kyle's dimpled grin and winsome manner totally irresistible. She threw her head back and burst out laughing in response to his toast. Her reaction caused a sprinkling of wine to splash onto the bodice of her dress. Instinctively, she quickly moved her glass away. In so doing, hers clashed with Kyle's with an overly loud clink and another slosh spewed out from both goblets to douse them both.

"Oh, no!" Lara held the cup of her chalice in both hands, now dripping with wine as she tried hopelessly to control her laughter.

Kyle shook his own hand dry. "Give me that," he directed, wearing his own broad grin. Shaking his head, he seized Lara's wine glass to set both his and hers firmly into the sand.

"I'm—" Lara couldn't finish her apology for all her giggles.

On his hands and knees, Kyle started a slow, stealthy crawl towards her.

"Kyle!" she managed, fully aware that her playful warning would do nothing to put him off. She tried to retreat backwards, but found his hands heavy on top of her skirts. Pinned and unable to withdraw, Lara could only fall back on top of the blanket where she lay completely at his mercy.

Kyle's eyes reflected his own lustful thoughts as he glanced down at her chest wet with the last spill of wine. He gave in to temptation without a second thought. His breath was hot against her skin. His kiss was light and tender. The fruity flavor of Chardonnay was sweet as his tongue brushed over her breast, his touch quick to rouse desires of her own. Instantly, her big, brown, sparkling eyes had bewitched him again. Eyes like an angel. Never before had any woman been able to possess him like Lara. How seductively ravishing she was with her mahogany tresses strewn all around her, framing her beautiful face.

"Kiss me," she bade.

Kyle's kiss was bold and demanding, leaving no doubt in Lara's mind that he would make love to her again, here and now. This outing was going to be much more exhilarating than staying in bed! She would never doubt Kyle again!

Chapter 14

Something Had To Be Done

"And where is your Mr. Harrison tonight?" Aidan asked before taking another sip of cognac.

Inwardly, Lara smiled, deciding she liked the idea of Kyle being "her" Mr. Harrison. "He has a meeting with Matt Stevens, one of the partners from the bank."

Aidan watched Lara carefully. Despite her calm, reserved behavior he could tell her spirits were high. Although he still had reservations of his own, Aidan was glad for Lara. Of all the people he knew, she deserved most of all to be happy. "How do you feel now that it's all out?"

"Relieved, but I'm not sure it changes anything."

Aidan raised a curious brow. "I would have thought it changed everything."

"I don't want to rush into anything."

"Perhaps you should learn to be a bit more spontaneous."

"I have to be practical and sensible. I have Gavin to think about."

"What are you going to tell him? Then again, what am I going to tell Abi?"

"Abi already knows about us. You and me, I mean," Lara declared. "She came right out and asked me whether or not we had truly married."

"When was this?"

"A few months after we made our announcement."

Aidan shook his head.

"She's a very bright and observant young lady," Lara added. "She has a good head on her shoulders. You should be very proud of her."

"I am," Aidan confirmed. "Abi is very much like Chelsea that way."

"It would go a long way if you told her so. She wants so much to be able to share with you."

Aidan nodded. He loved his daughter, and yes, he should start sharing more of himself with her. "Well, with all your secrets out, I'll only be in Kyle's way." He chuckled at his own joke. "I'll stay for a couple days. Try to sell a horse or two. Then I think it's time I went home to Savannah where I belong."

"Aidan, what made you come back the other night?"

"I didn't get a chance to tell you how beautiful you looked, and how much I enjoyed the evening. I thought maybe, if ever we were meant to be together–" Aidan stopped himself. He had said too much. He smiled. "But I knew as soon as I saw him with you."

"Then you meant it when you said not having the children along would give us a chance to spend time together?"

"I did."

Lara came to his side. Her hand went up to caress his cheek before she stood up on tiptoe to give him a kiss. "Gavin and I, we love you and Abi both. You've been so good to us. I'll always be grateful."

"You needn't be. You saved me from myself, and you were there for Abi when I couldn't be. Kyle will make you happy, Lara. He deserves a second chance."

"I'm not convinced he wants one. There is Gavin to think about," she repeated. "I don't think Kyle is ready for that kind of responsibility."

"A lot has happened," Aidan reasoned. "The man needs time."

Yes, Lara told herself, but with the goings on at the bank, where will Kyle's priorities lie?

~ · ~

Matt Stevens sat at his desk. He had been pouring over the ledgers for almost thirty minutes now while Kyle waited quietly and patiently for the man to come to his own conclusions. Kyle's own examination had already confirmed what Lara had overheard that night at the fundraiser. Both Owen Landrey and Granger Wilkes had been defrauding the bank for some time. Between the two of them, more than a thousand dollars had been diverted into their own personal accounts over this last month alone. Kyle had not yet been able to determine how long this had been going on, but he had no doubts that the actual sum embezzled would be mind-boggling. He needn't go any further, at least not yet. The evidence contained in these few journals would be enough proof for Matt, and for the law if that should be what Matt chose to do.

"It's so simple," Matt finally spoke calmly and without any doubts as to what Kyle had uncovered.

The deception revolved around the deposits made by both Owen and Granger. The incoming cash entries were itemized correctly to balance to the bank notes received, however the amounts recorded against the depositor's account was purposefully and erroneously written as a higher entry simply by transposing two of the numbers. If any single record had been caught, it could easily be reasoned away as an innocent mistake.

"How the hell did you figure this out?" Matt asked, still shaking his head.

"I wouldn't have if I didn't know where to look. I was concentrating so hard on the reserves that I didn't think of anything else. Lara Quinn told me of a conversation she had overheard between Granger and Owen outside the Exchange Building. It seems Granger was getting nervous when he found me examining the journals. He was worried I would reconcile the deposits against the journal entries. So I did. From there I was able to trace the falsified figures back to Owen and Granger."

"When did Mrs. Quinn hear all this? Was it the night of the orphan's fundraiser?" Matt inquired.

"It was. How did you know that?"

"I had gone out on the terrace to get some air. She literally ran into me as she was coming back in from the gardens. She had quite a look on her face and turned white as a sheet when she recognized me. That must have been immediately after she found Owen and Granger. She probably thought I was mixed up in the scheme as well."

"What do you want to do?"

"Granger doesn't have the guts to do something like this on his own. Owen must have put him up to it!" Matt thrust the books off the desk, his temper finally getting the better of him. "Twenty-three years Owen and I have been partners, and seventeen with Granger! Through good and bad. After all this time, how could they do this to me... to a friend!"

Kyle stood in shock, stunned by Matt's sudden reaction. Never had he been witness to Matt's temper before. Of the three partners, he was the most level-headed, always able to remain focused and composed.

"Who else knows about this?" Matt demanded, his voice more controlled, but still gruff.

"No one else. I instructed Lara not to say a word to anyone." Kyle responded calmly with hopes that his own controlled voice might help pacify Matt's anger.

"Can we trust her to keep quiet? Even from her husband?"

"I'm certain we can," Kyle replied.

"How can you be so sure?"

"I just know," Kyle answered, not wanting to explain further.

Matt stared hard at Kyle. "This could bring us to ruin. Not just the bank, but each and every one of us."

Kyle nodded, fully aware of what was at stake.

"I can't believe it." Matt shook his head as he glared at the books lying on the floor. Yet he had seen the entries himself, scrawled in those pages, in both Owen and Granger's own handwriting! Matt sat up straight as he remembered the events of the fundraiser. "Granger and Owen were right behind Lara when she came in from the gardens. I wonder if they know she overheard."

"Lara's positive of it. She thinks Granger partnered with her for the last dance to try to find out how much she knows."

"Granger will be close to a nervous breakdown if he thinks their secret is about to come out. You know how he buckles under pressure. The mere thought of losing all he has could drive him mad."

Matt was right for they had both witnessed it before. Could fear of being caught embezzling drive Granger Wilkes to insanity? Could the man be capable of more than stealing? The room fell deafly quiet. Morbid thoughts continued to fill Kyle's head and he found himself worrying for Lara's safety. He debated silently, wondering if the situation could deteriorate to the point where Granger would lose all sense of morality.

"We're both tired," Matt stated. "We'll continue tomorrow. Leave the journals, I may want to take another look at them."

"They should be returned before anyone finds them missing." Kyle reminded him.

"Not to worry. I'll go in early tomorrow, long before anyone else starts. And Kyle," Matt met his gaze, "I know this wasn't easy for you."

~ · ~

"He's going to keep digging until he finds something." Granger Wilkes continued his pacing back and forth in front of Owen Landrey's desk. His anxious words and the serious undertone of his voice were teamed with the deep crease of his brow.

"He knows nothing and he's found nothing. He still thinks there's a problem with the specie reserve," Owen responded calmly, knowing he had to maintain his composure for fear of Granger losing his.

"Now we have that Quinn woman to contend with. She heard every word we said. I'm convinced of it!"

"Yes, that is most unfortunate," Owen agreed, but did not want to delve into the matter of Lara Quinn any further.

"Quite," Granger quipped with sarcasm. "And what of Matt? He's been a good friend to both of us over the years. Seventeen years of friendship. Do you think he's going to accept a simple apology if this all comes out? I doubt very much."

"The answer is simple," Owen voiced. "We must return the money. Some of it at least. If Kyle continues scrutinizing the books, he will find nothing. Maybe one or two simple recording errors, but nothing of consequence. Certainly nothing that would call for any serious reconciliation."

"Ha! I have little left," Granger admitted, "and that is tied up in stocks. What about you?" There was only silence from his long time friend and partner. "Well then, what do you suggest?"

"We'll cash in some shares," Owen replied quickly. "Enough to convince Kyle and Matt that this problem has taken care of itself. Some nominal amounts over the next month or so should help make the numbers look better."

"A few hundred or so," Granger agreed, his voice sounding more confident than minutes before. "At least those mulberry trees are doing well. We'll see some profit from that at least."

"There might also be something else worth considering. Morgan has approached me with a request. I was going to discard the notion, but given the situation it might work to our advantage. Sit down Granger and hear me out." Owen waited for his partner to settle into the seat across from his desk before expressing his thoughts. "Morgan has had her sights on Kyle since he came to the Planters Bank. The two have discussed marriage, but Kyle seems to be in need of some incentive. She believes he would agree to marrying her if we were to make him a partner in the Bank."

"That would mean a seat on the Board. We'd have to give up some control of the bank."

Owen nodded. "We've always been worried that he would leave us for a better position elsewhere. Such an arrangement would tie him permanently to the Planters Bank. Think also of our current dilemma. Perhaps we need not be so hasty in liquidating our stocks. Kyle would be much less inclined to reveal any of our misdeeds, should they ever be discovered. It would be suicide for him as well as for us."

"Brash assumption, Owen, on the point of marriage and on disclosing our misdeeds as you put it. Kyle is very much his own man and not one to be easily swayed or bribed."

Owen Landrey and Granger Wilkes spent the remainder of the hour discussing the possibilities. The option of dismissing Kyle altogether was raised, but discarded just as quickly. There were no reasonable grounds on which to terminate his employment. As a result any such action would raise more than a few hard questions. It had taken a great deal of effort over recent years to build up their client portfolio and many of their new account holders were loyal to Kyle. It would seem an easier task convincing Matt Stevens that a partnership with Kyle was in order.

Owen remained secluded in his study after Granger left. Their pilfering of the bank's coffers had to stop. He knew it and Granger knew it, but both were in the same position of owning large, labor-intensive plantations with little cash flow. They would have to wait until after their crops sold at market before any profits would be realized. With tobacco prices still relatively low, the returns on a good crop were expected to be fair at best. So how would they manage until then?

Owen's thoughts were interrupted with a light rap on the door.

It was Morgan who opened the door and stepped in. "Father, may I have a few minutes of your time?"

"What is it, Morgan?"

"I was wondering if you had given any more thought to Kyle. You and Mother approve of my choice, do you not?"

"Kyle would make you a fine husband."

"I'm glad you approve." Morgan paused briefly to gather her thoughts. "I bid good night to Mr. Wilkes in the hall. He seemed preoccupied. I thought you might have spoken to him about the matter we discussed."

"I have," Owen confirmed. "Yes, we both can see our way into offering Kyle a partnership."

Morgan beamed, running to her father to throw her arms around him.

"Now, child, don't get too excited," Owen cautioned. "We need to have Matt agree to it as well."

"Father, that won't be difficult. Mr. Stevens thinks very highly of Kyle."

"Yes, he does," Owen confirmed. "And when he agrees, we must take care as to how we present this to Kyle. He is fond of you, but he's also very proud. I wonder, too, if he's ready to settle down just yet."

"He is Father, I know he is!"

Overcome with happiness, Morgan ran out of her father's study. It didn't matter if Kyle might still have feelings for Lara Quinn. Kyle would never refuse a partnership in the bank and that was the one gem that Morgan had secured for him.

~ · ~

After leaving the Landrey plantation, Granger Wilkes had every intention of going back to the bank to review the journals. The entries were penned in ink, there would be no rewriting them, but still he felt a need to go through the ledgers. There had to be something else they could do to get themselves out of this chaos. And what of Lara Quinn? Neither he nor Owen had been able to come up with any ideas as to what to do about her. What to do? What to do?

Gazing out the carriage window, he was distracted from his troubled thoughts at the sight of Kyle leaving Matt's rowhouse. What possible reason could Kyle have for meeting with Matt so late into the evening? Fear struck Granger at that instant, fear of the unknown, fear of his nightmarish thoughts coming true.

Granger Wilkes poked his head out the window to instruct his driver. "That's Harrison up ahead on that mount. Follow him slowly and not too close. He's not to know he's being watched."

Granger's nerves grew increasingly frayed as his carriage followed Kyle through the business district. Then, as Kyle passed the Planters Bank and turned onto Wentworth Street, Granger relaxed, convinced now that Kyle was headed home for the evening. Granger was ready to give new instructions to the driver to take him home as well when Kyle unexpectedly turned into a strange lane.

Stopped at an inconspicuous distance away from the Italianate style house, Granger watched, peering out of the carriage window to spy on the couple at the door. In each other's arms, the exchange of affection between the two was enough to convince anyone that Kyle Harrison was having an affair with Lara Quinn. Granger sat in stunned silence, paralyzed by fear; panic-stricken at seeing the two together. Suddenly he was certain. She had heard everything! And seeing the two together, he was able to easily convince himself that she had also told Kyle!

Suddenly Granger Wilkes was certain about one other thing. Something had to be done! Lara Quinn had to be silenced!

"This may be the one time in which I might have preferred the company of young Mr. Addison to yours." Lara finally spoke out, partly in jest. She was able to sense Kyle's troubled thoughts from the first moment he wrapped her tight in his arms. His short and trite answers were becoming tiresome as were her attempts to coax a reasonably intelligent conversation from him. Never had she known him to be so preoccupied and unresponsive.

The exasperated tone of Lara's voice broke Kyle's silence. "I'm sorry, Mack. I didn't mean to be rude." With his apology came an encouraging smile and wide open arms.

Lara gladly accepted his invitation to join him on the settee. "Your thoughts have been elsewhere. How did it go with Matt?" she finally asked.

"As expected," Kyle replied. "He feels betrayed, and rightly so."

"What's going to happen next?"

"I don't know. Matt will have to make that decision," Kyle replied. "But it's not as though there are many options available. You will be careful not to say a word to anyone about what's going on, won't you?"

Lara looked up, meeting his gaze. "Not a single word."

His lips came down to hers. His arms were tight around her. His head filled with concern for her safety.

"You're tired," Lara noted. "You should get home to bed."

Kyle stared down at her, disliking the thought of having to leave. "I was hoping to stay longer."

"I don't think that's a good idea," Lara admitted, knowing they would be saying good morning instead of good night if he did stay. "These last few days and nights with you have been wonderful, but I don't think we should go on this way."

"No?" Kyle responded.

"No," Lara confirmed. "It's late and you're tired."

"And I should get home to bed," Kyle repeated.

"And you should get home to bed," Lara confirmed again.

Kyle hovered over her as he lay her down along the settee. "And what if I want you to tuck me in."

Lara turned her head and laughed at his childlike thought.

Kyle cast his admiring eyes down upon the curve of her slender neck. Lara was irresistible. He leaned forward to plant a kiss at the base of her throat. His other hand moved freely over the curves of her svelte body. His fingers worked quickly to undo the top buttons of her day dress.

Lara moaned with pleasure as his hands fondled her breasts free from beneath her undergarments. She closed her eyes, completely lost in the ecstasy of the moment as she relished in the power of Kyle's love. She felt the light touch of his lips against hers, then tasted his kiss. She responded, unable to muster the strength to deny him, but neither did she want to try.

~ · ~

Charleston woke to rain the next morning. Unexpectedly it turned into a torrential downpour. The large raindrops pelted down hard against the glass panes while an endless sheet of water flowed down the cobblestone streets of the business district. The wind whistled as it blew.

Kyle stood staring out his office window. He watched the branches of the strongest trees being thrashed about in the wind. Was this the start of the first hurricane of the season?

A hint of a smile came to his handsome face as he thought of the profit he had made from selling off the shares of the mulberry groves. It seemed the sale of his shares was completed with not much time to spare. His eyes gleamed with self-satisfaction as he remembered what he had told Cameron: *It's never too soon if you can make a decent profit.* He had realized a profit for himself, for the Landons, and for Lara.

Kyle had been confident in his prediction and he might know soon enough if he was right. He had expressed his concerns to Bryce that day he and Lara were riding through the groves with the Landons. The roots of the young mulberry trees would not be able to withstand the force of a fierce wind. The saplings would be easily uprooted and toppled. Kyle had predicted they would fall like dominoes.

Kyle checked his pocket watch. 1:15 p.m. He was expecting Aidan Quinn at 1:30. Kyle's smile broadened. This time tomorrow, Lara will have put Aidan Quinn on the train to Savannah. With the man out of the way, he would start seriously courting Lara. Together, they would make plans for their future, a future together with their son. *My son, Gavin.* It was going to be more than he had ever hoped for. It was going to be perfect!

The knock on his office door interrupted his happy thoughts.

"Good morning, Kyle," came Morgan's familiar voice.

Kyle managed a smile. "I wasn't expecting to see you today. It's a wicked day to be out and about."

"It is horrid weather, isn't it? But I couldn't wait to tell you. Darling, I've spoken to Father, and I have the most wonderful news." The elation in Morgan's voice could not be denied. "He and Mr. Wilkes are both willing to make you a partner."

"Are they now?" Kyle raised his brow. It was difficult for him to imagine Owen Landrey discussing any business matters with his daughter.

In a wifely manner, Morgan ran her hands down the shawl collar of his vest only to rest them upon his chest. "Of course they are. They both know how terribly hard you've been working and how diligent and resourceful you are."

"That sounds quite promising, but you forget that the decision is not theirs alone," Kyle reminded her. He brushed aside her compliments altogether, but continued to wonder how much longer it would take for her to come to the heart of what was foremost on her mind.

"It wouldn't take any convincing to get Mr. Stevens to agree. Besides, Father would be only too happy to back you. Especially if—"

"If you and I were to wed?"

Morgan beamed. "Oh darling, you have thought about it! It's going to be wonderful! The two of us will get married, and you'll have controlling interest in one of the largest banks in South Carolina! We could build a house along the river to raise our sons and daughters."

Kyle removed her hands from his chest. Morgan waited expectantly while Kyle tried to come up with the tactful words. Not the whole truth for he wasn't prepared to reveal everything about Lara and Gavin. Neither, though, would he lie to Morgan. "I'm not the man for you, Morgan. You deserve someone who loves you."

"Kyle, you're speaking nonsense. I love you and I know you have strong feelings for me. Maybe not of love, but with a little time that fondness in your heart will grow into the most intimate and profound of feelings. We're meant to be together. I've known that from the first day Father introduced us."

"No, Morgan. You and I, that's your dream, not mine."

Morgan raised her hand to caress his cheek. She felt the sting of his rejection when he turned his head away. She braved another attempt. "Marry me and I can help you get everything you've always wanted. Father will grant you the position on the Board. You know he will. You've worked hard to prove yourself and you deserve nothing less. The opportunity is here within your grasp and for your taking. Don't throw it all away!"

"Morgan, it's not possible. I don't love you."

"Of course it's possible. I know you, Kyle." Morgan moved in close to wrap her arms around his neck. "I know your thoughts." She placed a tender kiss upon his lips. "I know your desires." There was a second kiss as she pressed her body against his. "And I can give you everything you've ever wanted—and more!"

Matt was tired and disillusioned by the end of his meeting with Owen and Granger. His two partners had put forth their idea of offering Kyle a partnership in the bank. The discussion open and straightforward, all as though nothing was wrong. There was nothing but logic and strength in their case. Matt had to admit that. Still, he was left with nagging suspicions. If his partners had made their recommendation even a month ago, Matt would not have hesitated. Now, after learning about their scheming, he could only wonder what ulterior motives they might have.

Matt had spent the last two days examining the ledgers. With Kyle's help, they had been able to complete a review back to the beginning of the year. Still they had no idea how long the pilfering had been going on, only that the final sum would be staggering. Was there any point in going further? It was time for action. Or was it even too late for that?

Matt rose from his chair. He needed to talk to Kyle. Even if he was to ramble on senselessly, he needed to get his thoughts out. He wandered down the office corridor, totally oblivious to those around him. His sights were on Kyle's door. It was open.

Good, he thought, Kyle was in.

Matt stopped suddenly as he approached Kyle's office. The door had been left ajar, wide enough for him to see the figures inside. Matt stood stunned, caught off guard at finding Morgan and Kyle in each other's arms. He turned quickly to retreat to the privacy of his own office. Matt Stevens was so distracted he didn't even bother looking up to apologize when he rudely brushed passed Aidan Quinn in the hallway.

Behind his own closed door, Matt could not get the image of Morgan and Kyle out of his head. As his thoughts continued to whirl, it came to him that Owen was unrelenting in his scheming. His partner had brought the bank to the brink of ruin, turned one of his best friends against him, and still he continued his plotting to gain Kyle on his side. The proposal to give Kyle a controlling interest in the bank now made sense. With that in place, and Kyle married to Morgan, Kyle would never turn on Owen no matter what the outcome of all this chaos.

"Not if I can help it, you bastard," Matt muttered, his normally complacent manner displaced by his growing rage. Something had to be done. He couldn't let Owen get away with it. Enough was enough and it was time he took something near and dear away from Owen! His thoughts went back to Morgan.

~ · ~

Kyle's story about Lara, Aidan and Gavin was all too mind-boggling. Morgan sat in stunned silence, staring at Kyle in disbelief. Kyle had told Morgan everything. He felt compelled to tell her the entire truth for it would have been more cruel to let her continue on with false hopes of the two of them getting married. As Kyle recounted his affair with Lara, Morgan sat solemnly still and quiet, hanging on to every word he had to tell her. With an honest effort, Kyle had chosen his words carefully. He was mindful of Morgan's feelings, but guilt still gnawed at him as he waited for her response.

Morgan looked up, her eyes glazed with tears. "Your son."

Kyle nodded.

"You still love her?" Morgan almost choked on her words.

"I always will. I hope you can understand why I can't marry you."

Morgan rose from her chair. She couldn't listen to any more of what he had to say. Suddenly it was all too clear that Kyle never loved her, nor would he ever be hers.

Kyle approached, ready to take Morgan into his arms, hoping he could do or say something to take away the hurt.

Morgan stepped away, refusing him. With her heart breaking, Morgan managed the shallowest of smiles as the first tear rolled down her cheek. She looked into Kyle's eyes with courage and an understanding beyond her years. "You will be happy, won't you, darling."

~ • ~

There was the initial disbelief followed by anger when Aidan Quinn peered through the partially open doorway to find Morgan Landrey in Kyle's arms. Like Matt Stevens had done, Aidan immediately retreated. He waited around the corner. Almost a half hour went by before Morgan came out from Kyle's office.

"You're a bastard!" Aidan accused as he stomped into Kyle's office. The door shook when he slammed it shut behind him.

Kyle had his wits about him and was able to hold Aidan off as the man approached. There was no mistaking the anger flaring in Aidan Quinn's eyes. "What the hell are you talking about?"

"Morgan Landrey. I saw her in your arms," Aidan declared.

Kyle pushed the man away. "Get a hold of yourself. It's not what you think."

"It doesn't matter what I think, it's what Lara would think. She's loved you ever since Brooklyn. She can't shake you and still you continue to treat her like dirt!"

"You've got it all wrong. Morgan's been trying for weeks to convince me to marry her. She was trying again to sway me with her… her tactics."

"It looks like she was succeeding."

"Go to hell," Kyle muttered, looking Aidan straight in the eyes

Aidan stepped forward. "I swear, if you hurt Lara again, I'll–"

Kyle's fist came down hard upon his desk. "I love, Lara!" he admitted truthfully. "I've almost won her back, damn it! Don't you think I know what's at stake? One wrong move, one wrong word from the likes of you and she'll be lost to me forever!"

Kyle opened the bottom drawer of his desk. He took out two small glasses and a bottle of whiskey. With the first glass poured, he pushed it in front of Aidan. His own glass was barely half filled before he gulped down the contents only to fill it to the top again. "I'm not such an imbecile as to do anything to lose her. I swear, not ever again."

To Aidan, Kyle's pledge was passionately genuine and his fears were quickly appeased. "You've got it bad, Harrison!" A broad grin was pasted upon Aidan's face as he raised his glass and then made himself comfortable in a chair.

Kyle was able to laugh at himself in response. "Yes," he finally admitted as he settled into his own chair. "I most certainly do. You, of all people, should be able to understand why."

"Then you're willing to accept Gavin as your son? You know Lara will have nothing less. That boy is everything to her and she'll sacrifice her own happiness for him."

"She won't have to. Gavin is mine and I'm ready to own up to the responsibilities. If Lara gives me the chance, I'll be a good husband to her and a good father to Gavin."

Kyle's pledge was filled with sincerity and it was all Aidan Quinn needed to hear.

"What time is your train tomorrow?" Kyle asked, wanting confirmation from the man himself.

"It's to leave at one o'clock. You'll be happy to see me go."

"Let's just say it's been awkward having you around," Kyle admitted.

Kyle's reply drew a slight smile from Aidan. "I was hoping to be more annoying than that," Aidan confessed, half-jokingly.

"Believe me, you did well enough," Kyle confirmed. "How did you meet Lara?"

"I met her when Dane delivered her to us after the fever hit Savannah."

"You mean to Lyddie."

Aidan shook his head. "Lyddie met and fell in love with me dear old Dad at one of the local gambling halls here in Charleston.

That was about eleven years ago. He was a decent enough fellow when things were going all right, but was the devil unleashed when the cards turned on him. Lyddie and I figured he must have racked up one very large debt. He left one night and never came back. From that day on, it was just me and Lyddie until Lara joined us."

"How did Lara end up in Savannah again?"

"After Brooklyn, you mean?"

Kyle nodded.

"Lyddie fretted constantly over Lara and the boy. She wanted them in Charleston with her, but Lara would have nothing of it." A slight crease came over Aidan's brow. "They had some pretty heavy arguments over you. Anyways, I wasn't coping well after Chelsea died so Lyddie convinced Lara to come stay with Abi and me. I guess she thought we could do each other some good."

"You two later decided to get *married*?"

Aidan chuckled. "It seemed like a good idea at the time. It's all been quite innocent." He withdrew his pocket watch to check the time.

"So it seems. You must have loved your wife a great deal."

"I did," Aidan replied. "You should know, Harrison, that if I ever get another chance–"

"Forget it," Kyle was quick to respond. "That'll never happen."

Aidan nodded. "Enough said. What is it you wanted to see me about?"

"Horses." Kyle reached over with the bottle of whiskey to top up Aidan's glass. "Lara told me she goes riding every morning with Gavin. I'd like to buy their horses from you."

"You know how to care for them and have a place to keep them?"

"I will have. How much?"

"Forty... each."

Without even thinking about the price, Kyle pulled out a bank draft and wrote in the amount. He handed it to Aidan without bothering to barter down the price.

Aidan glanced down at the check. "How do you know I'm not cheating you?"

"You buy and sell horses. You know your trade and, from what I understand, you're one of the best. You wouldn't ruin your reputation over a simple deal like this. After all, what would Lara think?"

Aidan picked up the draft only to tear it in half. "Consider them a gift. Just let me know when and where to deliver them."

A broad, infectious grin came to Kyle's face. "I have another favor to ask."

It was another half hour before Aidan left Kyle's office. There was no doubt Kyle Harrison knew what he wanted and knew how to get it. There was nothing to stop the man now. Like you once were years ago, Aidan reminded himself. Aidan shrugged off the thought, confident in knowing that Kyle would make both Lara and Gavin very happy.

~ • ~

Lara returned home from dinner with Aidan. The house was dark and quiet with Shani and Avram having retired for the evening. Lara ventured into the music room. She was full of energy and had the desire to play her violin. She searched through her bundle of sheet music, playing a few notes of one before discarding it for another. Unable to find that one piece that matched her mood, Lara put aside the papers and books.

With her violin raised and her jaw set upon its chin rest, she ran the bow across the strings. Closing her eyes, she tried hard to remember the notes to that first dance she had shared with Kyle. Again and again she put the bow to the strings. She played what she could remember, testing her tempo and rhythm. Each time she was able to piece together a few more bars of music until finally the notes blended harmoniously one into the other. The more she played, the more familiar the music, and the more she was able to recall. She continued on, pleased and inspired by her efforts. As the minutes ticked away, the melody grew sweeter and more soulful, a striking contrast to the sounds of the storm brewing outside.

Focused on her music, Lara was unaware of Kyle's presence. He stood in the doorway, listening, watching, mesmerized by the vision standing before him. He dared not move for fear of catching Lara's attention and breaking her concentration. Her movements were fluid and graceful. One motion flowed effortlessly into the next, just as one note blended into another.

"Don't stop," Kyle urged when the music suddenly stopped.

"Kyle! I didn't hear you come in."

"That was beautiful. Play it again for me, all the way through."

"I can't remember much more," Lara declared, almost apologetically.

"You don't have the music?" Kyle asked.

"Not anymore," Lara replied as she placed her violin and bow back in their case.

"You lost it?" Kyle came from behind to slide his arms around her waist. He pulled her to him. The sweet floral scent of her perfume was intoxicating.

"I threw it away," Lara answered truthfully.

"I was a fool, Lara. Can you ever forgive me?"

She turned in his arms. Her lips touched his for the most tender of kisses. "I already have," she replied, her heart overflowing with love for him.

With barely an effort, Kyle bent down to sweep Lara off her feet and into his arms.

Lara rested her head on his shoulder, more than content to let him carry her upstairs where they would once again share her bed.

The storm had grown in strength. The rain pounded. The wind screeched. Together, they muffled the loud ticking of the old mantle clock. The dark shadows in the den were cast from the glow of a single hurricane lamp.

A lone figure sat staring at the Patterson Colt pistol that lay on his desk. A box of ammunition sat next to the gun. It was growing late, but there was no point in going to bed. Like last night, he knew he would not be able to sleep. He would only toss and turn. His mind would not be able to find rest. Sinful thoughts had come to fill his head, the kind of thoughts that would send a man to hell. Still he couldn't stop from thinking them. He picked up the revolver to test its weight. The gun was heavy, but felt surprisingly comfortable in his hand.

He rose from his chair. His arm extended. He pointed the barrel of the handgun at the face of the mantle clock. He drew back the hammer and the cylinder of the gun turned. He squeezed the trigger. The clock would have been shattered, silenced forever had the gun been loaded.

His thoughts took him back to the last time he had used the weapon. Although years ago, the memory of the chase and the shooting were still intensely clear. His prey had been a runaway slave. He had the law on his side back then. This time, if he had the nerve to carry through with his plan and should he be caught, the law would see him hang. Hanged to death. Before his conscience could speak, his angst and anxieties reminded him that it was time for action. Something had to be done!

Undeterred, he withdrew five cartridges from the tin box. One by one, each bullet found its place in the gun cylinder. Now fully loaded, he carefully put the weapon back down on the desk. He stared at it, all the while wondering if he had the nerve to carry through with his plan. No, there wasn't going to be a slave this time. This time his prey would be a beautiful and vibrant, young woman.

Chapter 15

◌◌

What Gain Has the Worker?

It was early morning. A group of men had gathered at the top of the ridge. In silence, they gazed down upon the devastation. Torrential rains teamed with fierce winds had beat down upon the rows of mulberry trees. The young roots had been torn from the rain-soaked ground by the violent gusts of wind. Even after all had fallen and there was no damage left to be done, the storm had continued to rage on for snapped branches had been blown and scattered about everywhere.

As reality set in, the men became fully aware that below them was nothing more than a field covered with firewood. Acres of tinder. Tens of thousands of dollars lost. For those who had invested too heavily in the venture, there was the real possibility of financial ruin. Perhaps those were the thoughts running through the heads of the few who had to wipe their eyes dry or clear their throats. Too proud to show their emotions, the men climbed onto their horses to ride home in silence.

They had been beaten by Mother Nature who had been cruel and without mercy. It was in her power to nurture new life from the earth, so it seems it was also hers to take it away. As the Bible had foretold, there was a time for everything. *A time to plant, and a time to pluck up what is planted....* But this was not the fate these men had in mind for their investment. There was supposed to be a better outcome, a time when they would reap the rewards, not lament of their loss. *What gain has the worker from his toil?* For most of the men standing on the hill, there was none in this venture.

"We were lucky to get out when we did," Bryce acknowledged, grateful he followed Kyle's advice of selling the shares. Once again, his friend had proven his keen foresight.

Kyle didn't know what to say. It was one of those times when he honestly wished he hadn't been right. So many of those men who lost in the venture were his friends and business partners. Kyle felt their loss.

"There's nothing you could have done. You told them what you thought," Bryce offered. He knew Kyle well enough to know how much his friend cared. "We each have to live by the decisions we make. They chose to stay with it."

Kyle kept his eyes on the muddy trail as the two rode back to Landon Oaks for a late breakfast with Lara and Jenna. He knew Bryce was right, but hearing his friend say it didn't make him feel any better. The coming days would be difficult ones and there would be no satisfaction in knowing that he had saved himself from a huge financial loss.

"We better get a move on," Bryce stated. "We'll be late getting out to the orphanage."

The two men spurred their horses to a gallop. Their thoughts turned to wonder how well the orphanage and its wards had survived the storm.

～ · ～

It had been a difficult day spent at the foundling home. More than a foot of water had flooded the cellar. Several windows had been shattered by flailing tree branches, and the roof had sprung heavy leaks in more than a few places. Cold and wet, it would prove difficult to keep the rooms warm even with all the fireplaces burning. So even before they could start assessing the damage done by the storm, there was the decision as to whether it would be wise to stay in the house, such as it was, or move the children into a temporary residence. As soon as the question was raised, Lara became convinced that Haven Manor should be considered. It would certainly be large enough, but how well did her old home survive the storm?

They soon discovered that Haven Manor had weathered the rain and winds better than expected. One broken window was cleared of its glass panes and thick pine boards put up in its place. Dry firewood was scarce, but enough had been gathered to keep two of the larger rooms heated through the night. Feather ticks were brought in and placed on the floors. It was on these that the children huddled together to sleep, all happy enough to have a warm, dry place to sleep, no matter how temporary it might be.

The red-orange glow from the fire was the only light in the room. Its tall flames flickered and danced in the dark. Its heat radiated from the hearth. Kyle sat on the floor at one end of the room. He watched Lara stroll quietly among the children. She would stop to pull blankets up over small shoulders, say a few reassuring words, even give a hug or two to anyone who needed to feel safe and more secure. Lara had a way with these children. She could endear herself to them. She could understand their fears and insecurities. No doubt it was because she had been an orphan herself that she could feel for these young ones. A warm heart and a generous soul, despite the desperate times she had had to endure. Lyddie would be proud of her niece! *A woman of love, life and laughter.* Kyle remembered the words he had chosen for Lyddie's gravestone. Lara was so much like her aunt! If only he had been more sensible and given Lyddie a chance, then perhaps these last years without Lara would not have been wasted, perhaps he might even have come to know his son. Perhaps!

"Is everything alright?" Lara asked softly.

"As much as it can be," Kyle replied as he stood up.

It wasn't like Kyle to be so distant. Lara went to him. Her arms went about his neck to give him the hug he seemed to need.

Kyle released Lara from his embrace. "We better go see how Penny is doing."

They found Penny sitting in a rocking chair in front of the dining room fire. She greeted the couple with a broad grin, but even in the dim light it could be seen that Penny had been crying. "The children all settled?"

"All settled," Lara confirmed with a cheerful tone in an effort to boost Penny's spirits.

"It's very generous of the Planters Bank to open Haven Manor. Thank you, Kyle. I know it was your doing. It means a lot to us."

Kyle gave Penny a reassuring pat on the shoulder. "It'll be alright."

Penny nodded. "Yes, it will," the woman agreed, sounding quite positive. "Do you think we can stay here until the cellar's been cleaned out and the repairs done?"

"We'll see." He looked up to meet Lara's gaze before turning back to Penny. "Tomorrow, I'll go back to the orphanage with Bryce. We'll try to figure out the extent of the damage and what it'll take to get it all fixed."

"The money from the fundraiser was meant to keep the orphanage running for this next year. There wasn't going to be much left over for... for contingencies. Is that what you'd call this – a contingency?"

Kyle nodded.

"Don't worry, Penny. We'll find a way," Lara stated confidently.

"We have to," Penny agreed. "For the sake of the children."

Lara could see that Kyle was lost in thought. Immediately she knew that his mind was already churning, planning and plotting, trying to think of possibilities. He would consider each idea carefully, and only when the most appealing solution was thought through would he finally reveal his plan. If anyone could find a way to make everything right, she knew Kyle could, and indeed he would. And it wouldn't be for money, status or recognition, not for anything or anyone else except for the children.

~ · ~

The storm had lasting effects and difficult days followed. Lara's time was dedicated to the children at the orphanage. She, along with Shani and Avram, spent most of their time at Haven Manor doing what they could to help Penny establish some sort of routine and stability. Their days were long and tiring and each night Lara would come home alone, too tired to wait up to see if Kyle would come calling.

Thus Lara saw very little of Kyle in those days immediately after the storm. Despite what he had told Penny, he had not been able to make it out to the orphanage that next day. The bank was extraordinarily busy with a sharp decrease in deposits and a marked increase in loan requests and account withdrawals, all putting a strain on the bank reserves. With crops ruined, buildings damaged and hundreds of worthless shares in the sericulture venture, everyone was scrambling to fix one thing or another, needing money or credit for this or for that. It was a time to rebuild, and tradesmen, or even slaves hired out by their masters, were difficult to find. Everyone's attention was on their own problems. No one had time to concern themselves with anything else, least of all the orphanage.

The bank soon began seeing missed payments on their outstanding loans. Kyle and the three partners found it a struggle to have to decide what action to take. These people were not only clients, but also friends with families. In Kyle's mind there had to be a balance between what was good for business and what was right for the families. Such was not an easy task on one loan let alone the several that had crossed his desk for collection!

Kyle, Owen, Granger and Matt sat around the table discussing the current state. There was no good humor amongst the four men. Tempers were short for each had little patience in attending to business given their own financial concerns.

"Our reserves are too low," Matt spoke aloud what the others had been thinking. "How much longer can we keep our doors open? A few weeks, maybe a month?"

"Good God, do you really think it's that bad?" Granger asked as he took a handkerchief to his sweaty brow.

"All this on top of the problems we've been having," Matt reminded his partners, his own voice laced with impatience. "You're a fool if you think we've seen the worst of it?"

Kyle observed the partners carefully as Matt continued on. The man seemed intent on putting fear into his two partners.

"What do you say, Kyle?" Owen finally asked.

"Too soon to say, one way or another. We have to be patient," Kyle responded calmly.

"Easy enough for you," Granger grunted, thinking of his own situation. "You didn't lose your shirt with those cursed trees, nor do you have your whole life invested with the bank."

"The sericulture venture was for seasoned investors and high-risk gamblers," Kyle reminded Granger. "A large payout is what everyone was looking for and that came with a certain degree of risk. Everybody who went in knew how the game was to be played. Besides, only a fool would put all his eggs in one basket."

That was enough to silence Granger for he would never admit how close to financial ruin he was. He gazed across the table to Owen. At least he wasn't the only fool.

"Enough," Owen declared. "So what do we do?"

"Let's start with Sweetwater Plantation." Matt decided, wanting to take control. "Put it up for auction. We may not get much, but something is better than nothing."

Kyle waited for the nods from Owen and Granger. "We should section it off," he recommended.

"We'll get more if each parcel has both road and water access," Owen joined in.

"Agreed?" Kyle asked, getting the consensus he wanted. "I'll get started tomorrow."

"What about Haven Manor?" Owen asked. "Shouldn't we put that up as well?"

"I'm buying Haven Manor," Kyle announced. "I'm prepared to pay asking price. The papers are being drafted and should be ready for your signatures tomorrow morning."

"What brought this on?" Owen asked, pleased by the news for he knew Morgan had always been intrigued with Haven Manor and had commented before how she would one day like to have the place for herself.

"It's a good investment. Something for the future," Kyle responded. "Now, if you'll excuse me, it's been a long day. It's coming up eight o'clock and I'm to meet the Landons for dinner. It's time we all went home."

The men said their good nights quickly with Owen and Granger remaining behind with the door shut tight.

"Have you lost your mind?" Granger asked, remembering to keep his voice low. "I thought we decided no more. We were supposed to be putting money back and here you are at it again. How much did you take this time?"

"Come on, Grange. Kyle doesn't know what to look for," Owen countered. "Besides, with all the withdrawals over the last couple of days, it'll be that much harder to find. A hundred dollars, that's all. No one's going to notice a hundred dollars."

"You're forgetting Lara Quinn. He's been seen with her several times since the fundraiser. I've seen them together."

"It's been more than a week. If she was going to say anything, she would have already and we wouldn't be sitting here now," Owen reasoned.

"You're fooling yourself," Granger scoffed.

"Can't you see? Kyle's thinking seriously of settling down. Morgan told me she's talked to him. Tomorrow Haven Manor will be his. Mark my words. It won't be long before Morgan and Kyle are married." He gave his friend a broad smile and a pat on the back. "Nothing to worry about, old friend, everything's going to be fine."

"You didn't see Kyle with that Quinn woman. They're having an affair I tell you."

Owen laughed, quite sure of himself. "A minor indiscretion. A bit of fun before he settles down. Who can blame him? Besides, what could possibly become of it? She's married and Kyle's not going to let a sordid mess like that tarnish his credibility. He's much too proud."

Owen was overly confident. This made Granger even more nervous. Things had gotten out of hand. Uncontrollable. What worried Granger more was that Owen didn't seem to care.

~ · ~

Granger Wilkes stared at the clock: eight-fifty. He picked up the letter and folded it neatly into thirds. Crisp, clean lines. He tucked it into an envelope and carefully applied his wax seal. Who should he address it to? He had no wife, no children. To Matt or Owen? He wiped the sweat from his brow. With a shaky hand, he picked up the glass and took a long swallow of his favorite bourbon. He glared at the pistol lying on top of his figures. Desolate numbers confirming what he had known all along. There was nothing left. No land, no home, barely a few dollars to his name. Only huge debts, a stack of worthless stocks and a conscience filled with guilt and regret over how he and Owen had mistreated a friend – a very dear friend.

Granger left the envelope unmarked. He leaned it up against the inkwell in front of him. He allowed himself another dose of good bourbon with hopes the libation would give him courage. The clock started to chime nine o'clock. He picked up the revolver.

The barrel was hard and cold against his temple. Granger Wilkes closed his eyes.

"God forgive me my sins and grant me peace."

~ • ~

The sound of a gunshot sent a wave of fear through Owen Landrey and he immediately came running, bursting into his partner's office. The smell of gunpowder was strong. Owen stopped in his tracks at the sight of his long-time friend slumped over the desk. Granger's head rested face down on top of a pile of papers stained with a swelling pool of blood.

Owen took slow cautious steps to the other side of the room to view the lifeless body.

"Grange," he choked.

Silence.

He stared at the gun lying on the floor before glancing upwards through tear filled eyes to spot a long envelope set against the inkwell. Instantly he knew what it was. With a trembling hand, he reached for it. Taking it back to a chair, Owen opened it to read Granger's final and troubled thoughts. The suicide letter told everything: how both he and Granger had been embezzling funds for the last two years; how the pressure from poor crop yields, increasing debt and poor investments drove him to cheat on Matt Stephens, a friend whom he had loved and admired; how afraid he was of their secret coming to light; and how he could no longer suppress his fears, especially after being overheard by Lara Quinn. Such desperation drove him to immoral thoughts of murdering the woman. And finally how his guilty conscience had seized him and driven him to find peace only by taking his own life.

Owen Landrey wiped his eyes dry.

Lara Quinn! Only she would know the real reason as to why Granger killed himself. Only she could accuse Owen of partnering with Granger and committing fraud. If she hadn't said anything by now, she would most certainly come forward once learning of Granger's death. The secret of their scheme could die along with Granger if not for Lara Quinn. Think man!

Quickly, he tucked Granger's letter into his vest pocket. He would get rid of it later. Yes, he would burn the damning evidence. Without the letter everyone would think Granger committed suicide as a result of financial ruin. No one would be the wiser. No one except Lara Quinn! Think man!

~ · ~

Instinctively Lara knew something was wrong when Owen Landrey showed up at her door. It was odd for Kyle to have arranged for Owen to meet him here when Kyle lived just down the street. Still, she didn't want to be rude. She allowed the man entry into her home with the thought that she wouldn't have to entertain him long since Kyle, Jenna and Bryce were expected for a late dinner. Now Lara stood paralyzed as she stared down at the gun in Owen's hand.

"I don't understand. What have I done?" Lara asked, her voice shaking with fear.

"It's not what you've done," Owen Landrey explained. "It's what you overheard in the gardens last week at the fundraiser."

"I-I don't know what you mean," Lara stuttered.

"You're not a good liar, Mrs. Quinn. You know what I'm talking about. You heard Grange and I talking about the ledgers."

Lara shook her head in desperation.

"Don't lie to me!"

"I did overhear part of your conversation, but not enough to understand what it meant. Please, Mr. Landrey, you must believe me," Lara pleaded.

Owen's laugh was deep and evil. He waved the revolver as if to remind her of the dire situation she was in. "It doesn't really matter. We're beyond that now. Did you know Grange is dead? He killed himself because of you. He lost his nerve not knowing what you knew, or who you might have told. Who did you tell?"

"No one, there was nothing to tell," Lara lied, desperate to have him believe her.

Owen Landrey drew back the hammer. The sound of the gun cylinder turning filled Lara's head and she retreated backwards, her body shaking uncontrollably.

"Owen," a calm voice called out. "Put the gun down, Owen."

Lara looked over Owen's shoulder to see Kyle, Bryce and Jenna standing at the door. A revolver in Kyle's hand was drawn and pointed at Owen's back.

Owen Landrey didn't need to turn around to know whose voice that was. He kept his eyes on Lara as he spoke to Kyle. "Bad manners, Kyle. You've forgotten how to knock. I thought you were having dinner with the Landons."

"They're here with me," Kyle responded.

"So you've brought witnesses. A foursome for dinner," he stated rather calmly, realizing there would be no saving himself. "I guess Grange was right. You're having an affair. He's dead you know, slumped over his desk with a bullet through his head," Owen waved his gun at Lara. "She killed him."

The next seconds were filled with dread. Lara stood waiting. Frozen. Her back pressed against the wall.

"You've done a lot of damage for the short time you've been here," Owen accused Lara.

The blast of a single gunshot was overly loud as it rang through the house.

Lara screamed. Her adversary stumbled forward only to fall against her. She stared down into his eyes. They were dark and wide with the realization that it was not his gun that went off.

"Lara, step away!" Kyle called out to her. His voice was as calm and clear as he could manage. "Lara, come to me!"

Lara tried to step away, but Owen tightened his hold on her arm. He flashed Lara a broad, sinister grin.

"Please, Mr. Landrey, let me go," Lara pleaded for her life.

She felt the pressure of the gun barrel pushed into her abdomen. Lara saw Owen Landrey's pain through his eyes, then a glimmer. Immediately she knew his evil thoughts and fear paralyzed her. The man was intent on pulling the trigger. Her thought was barely realized before a second gunshot broke the ominous silence.

Lara's beautiful chestnut eyes grew large, filled with shock and pain. Instinctively she grabbed her stomach. She didn't need to look at her hands to know they were being painted with her own blood. Her mouth opened wide to call out for Kyle, but no sound escaped from her trembling lips. The pain was excruciating, too much for her to bear. Feeling faint, her legs crumpled and Lara fell to the floor.

"Lara! No!"

Two more shots were fired from Kyle's gun. Both hit their mark to take away whatever life remained in Owen Landrey's body.

Lara saw her assailant sprawled on the floor beside her before the room faded into darkness.

~ · ~

Suddenly there was no pain. Lara's fear had been replaced by a cleansing surge of peace and tranquility, and she found herself surrounded by darkness. A soft, angelic light appeared in the distance and she felt herself floating towards it. The light felt safe and familiar. Unafraid, she was drawn closer. It grew brighter and more compelling. She could feel its warmth and power and knew she wanted to be enveloped within it.

"Lara." Kyle's voice was easily recognizable. "Lara." She could hear him calling out to her from a distance, over and over again.

The light grew brighter to beckon her forward, but Kyle continued to call out to her. The two grew stronger, each fighting to win Lara's favor. One or the other with no turning back.

Chapter 16

∞

Ever After

Kyle was mentally drained and his body tired. He had been away at Haven Manor all morning and much of the afternoon, much longer than he had anticipated and he was happy to be almost home. He had spent hours talking with the trades, examining their workmanship and finalizing details, and settling payments. All of that was now finally over and done with. But he knew his efforts and the weeks spent planning would be worth every single penny, and more.

Kyle rode up to the Italianate across the street. Instead of passing the house by, he led his horse slowly up the lane. He commanded his mount to a stop at the foot of the wide stone steps that led up to 124 Wentworth Street. The building looked cold and lonely. He had ordered for it to be boarded up the day after the shooting. Left abandoned, no one other than the sheriff and his deputies had set foot inside since. A terrible shame for Lyddie had such high hopes for many wonderful years in her new home. Now put up for auction, Kyle's silent wish was for the new owners, whomever they may be, to find happiness in this house of hopes and dreams.

One long look at the dwelling was all Kyle could stand. The events of that horrible evening were still sharp in his memory.

The images were too fierce to even think they might one day begin to fade. It had been the most difficult decision of his life, whether or not to fire that first shot. But there was no hesitation, no battle with his conscience to take away Owen's life, not after seeing the pained expression on Lara's pale face. Owen had meant to kill. There was no doubt in Kyle's mind, nor was there any with Bryce or Jenna. And with those gruesome recollections Kyle would be reminded each time of his greatest failure: that of not being able to protect the woman who had filled his heart with love and his soul with life.

The vision of Lara covered in blood, lying on the floor, would continue to torment him, as would the anguish that filled those frantic moments. He had gathered her limp body into his arms and hugged her tight. He could still feel the shock and despair when he swept back her long tresses to uncover her ashen face. He had called her name over and over again, told her how much he needed her and how much Gavin needed her, all the while hoping and praying for her. Never had he felt so helpless as when he had tried to rouse her from her deep sleep: shaking her still body, squeezing her hand, desperately trying anything he could think of to bring her back to him.

Kyle closed his eyes and took a deep breath to quell the emotions surging within him. With such feelings of guilt and regret, Kyle commanded his horse into a turn. Suddenly he felt the overwhelming need to be home.

~ · ~

There was no one to greet Kyle when he came in the door. The Harrison household was peacefully quiet. Not a sound, only a tranquil calm to promote rest and healing. As it had been since that night Kyle brought Lara home.

He found his love sleeping soundly in his bed. He had left precise instructions that Lara was not to be left alone, and either

Casey or Shani was to remain by her side whenever he was not there to attend to Lara's needs himself. Today, Casey was seated nearby. The house servant rose quickly and quietly to leave the room as soon as Kyle entered.

Carelessly tossing his coat and vest aside, Kyle laid himself down beside Lara. He snuggled in as close as he dared, taking extra care not to wake her. He listened to her breathing, reassured by her soft and easy breaths that she was in no discomfort. Kyle closed his eyes to rest, but not before saying a silent prayer. Again he felt that overwhelming sense of relief. He would be forever thankful that God had spared Lara's life. He knew himself well enough to know that he would not have had the will and determination to go on living had she died in his arms that night.

It was another half hour before Lara began to stir. She opened her bright, sparkling eyes to the beautiful bouquet beside, what had suddenly become "her" side of the bed. These last days, colorful and fragrant flowers could always be found there, alongside Gavin's pewter-framed picture. These, as well as the portrait of her and Lyddie, which now hung over the fireplace, were all evidence of Kyle's endearing thoughtfulness.

Aware of Kyle's presence beside her, Lara rolled over. Careful not to stretch the stitches in her side, her movements were cautiously slow. Still they were enough to rouse Kyle from his light slumber.

"I didn't expect you home until much later," Lara said, pleased to have him there with her.

"I couldn't stay away." He took hold of her hand and brought it to his lips.

"I'm glad," she beamed. It was exactly what she needed to hear. She hugged his hand to her chest.

"Are you bored, my love?"

Lara nodded. "Quite. Dr. Daniels did say I'm well enough for some light chores, but Casey won't let me lift a finger. She's too afraid of your scolding. Kyle, won't you take me out for a bit, perhaps a ride in the country?" Lara suggested, her eyes twinkling at the thought of getting out of the house even for a short while.

"Maybe tomorrow."

To Lara, it seemed that Kyle had discarded the notion much too quickly and without any serious thought. Disappointed, Lara fell back onto her pillow. "You're treating me like an old woman," she pouted, letting go of his hand. "Soon my backside will be black and blue from all this lazing in bed and sitting around. Never in my life have I felt so useless."

Kyle hovered over her, unable to suppress a chuckle. "Well, we can't have that. If you're sure it won't be too much for you then maybe we can take the shay for a short ride this afternoon."

Her smile came as quickly as the sparkle to her beautiful chestnut eyes. "You do love me!" Lara announced playfully. She wrapped her arms around Kyle's neck. "Show me how much," she bade.

"My pleasure," Kyle muttered.

Lara brought him down to receive her kiss. Then another. Then still another. Longer, more passionate. And yet another until they almost forgot about their outing.

～ · ～

"Why are we going to Haven Manor?" Lara asked cheerfully, her mood very much improved with the fresh air, the warm sun, and the leisurely ride through Charleston.

"Penny and the children have been asking about you," Kyle answered, the stress of his day vanquished by Lara's infectious laughter and good spirits. "We can have a rest there before we return home."

The shay emerged from under the sprawling branches of the live oaks and out onto the open expanse of the yard. The grounds had been cleared of the broken branches and debris that had littered the homesite. Aunt Lyddie's prized camellias and rosebushes had been trimmed and reshaped. Buds and blooms dotted the bushes with their own splash of color and sweet fragrance. A fresh coat of whitewash brightened up the manor. Visitors were beckoned to the front porch laden with flowerpots scattered amidst several cozy wicker chairs and comfortable settees. The windows had been cleaned. They were sparkling and streak free. This was how Lara had always remembered Haven Manor – bright, cheerful, and most welcoming – a reflection of Aunt Lyddie's vibrant personality.

"It is a grand house, isn't it?" Lara commented with pride. "I hope Penny and the children will be happy here."

"Penny and the children have resettled into the orphanage," Kyle revealed. He brought the shay to a slow stop. He jumped down from the carriage and came around for Lara who was waiting for his further explanation.

Kyle wrapped his arms possessively around Lara's waist as they stood before the house. "I bought Haven Manor," he declared most casually. His kiss was tender upon her shoulder. "I think we need a larger home to raise our brood of sons and daughters." His voice was filled with mighty hopes and grand promises. "I couldn't think of a better place than here at Haven Manor."

Lara turned in his arms. Her face lit up, fully animated with surprise and elation.

"Haven Manor is yours, Lara. It's my wedding gift to you." Kyle then pulled out his mother's ring from within his pocket. Like years before in that cozy little parlor, the diamond solitaire sparkled its brilliance in the sunlight. "I had your initial added to mother's the day after our quarrel in Brooklyn City."

Lara glanced down to see her first initial engraved beside those of Martha Harrison.

"I've waited a long time to give this back to you," Kyle confessed. "I wasn't lying when I said I've never stopped loving you. I have always been yours, Lara." Kyle slipped the ring onto her finger then took both her hands in his. "Lara Mackenzie

Kendrick, you would make me the happiest man alive if you would spend the rest of your life with me in married bliss."

Lara didn't answer. She didn't need to for the glow upon her face reflected the fire in her heart. The flame would be eternal. Her love and devotion for him would be endless. The next instant, she was in his arms and delightedly smothering him with kisses.

"Do you think you could be happy again, here at Haven Manor? With me and Gavin?"

"Especially so, but I would be happy anywhere so long as the three of us were together."

Kyle beamed, unable to resist stealing another kiss. This time long and passionate, leaving her breathless.

"The trades have been in. I spent this morning here making sure everything was perfect. Shall we go inside?"

Lara nodded, giddy with excitement and anticipation.

With barely an effort, Kyle bent down to sweep Lara off her feet and into his arms to carry her across the threshold.

Standing inside the foyer, Lara took a sweeping glance across the room. The staircase had been redesigned and the results left her speechless. Amazed at the detail of work that had been done, she didn't need to see the rest of the house to know that Kyle had spared no expense. After realizing the time and planning that Kyle must have spent, Lara turned to confront him. "You knave!" she chided. "You've been at this for weeks."

Smugly satisfied with how well his surprise went over, Kyle walked over to the double doors that led into the dining room. He swung them open as if to lead the way.

"Mama!" The sound of Gavin's footsteps resounded through the foyer as her son burst forward from his hiding place.

Before she knew it, Lara was down on her knees with her son wrapped tight in her arms. "Gavin, where did you come from?"

"Papa sent for me."

"Papa sent for you?" Lara's eyes glistened as she met Kyle's gaze.

"Are you surprised?" the child asked, his sweet, dimpled face beaming with the widest and brightest of smiles.

"Oh, Gavin, Mama couldn't be more surprised!" She hugged her son again.

"Papa said you would be." The boy giggled as Kyle came up from behind to rough up his hair. "And guess what? Aidan and Abi are here, too!" Gavin declared. "We came last night. Know what else?"

Overwhelmed, Lara looked up to see father and daughter emerge from the dining room. Behind them, she recognized the faces of her newest friends from Charleston.

Gavin tugged at his mother's skirts to regain her attention. "Know what else, Mama?"

"No, Gavin, what else?" Lara asked, caught up in the excitement while trying to keep up with her son's chatter.

"Papa let me sleep in my new room last night!" the boy exclaimed.

"Did he? Here, in this house?"

Gavin's head bobbed up and down. "I get a big room because I'm a big boy."

"That's right," Lara laughed at her son's logic. "You're going to have to show me your room later," she suggested, her own voice filled with as much delight as Gavin's.

"We were told there's going to be a wedding," Aidan approached, his own broad grin pasted across his face. "I couldn't refuse when Kyle asked me to give away the bride."

Kyle returned to Lara's side. "You still haven't given me your answer, Lara. I hope I haven't been too cocky and presumptuous. Have I your promise to share your life with me? Is there going to be a wedding?"

"There most certainly will be!" Lara answered emphatically. She was now positive that "happily ever after" wasn't restricted only to little girls' dreams and fanciful fairy tales.

"Papa says we're going to be a family!" Gavin piped up again.

"Then maybe the three of you should become a family tonight." Aidan had dared to voice his thoughts. "There really is no time like the present, is there Pastor Thomas?"

The small gathering immediately fell silent.

Pastor Thomas beamed an infectious smile. He hesitated long enough to convince himself that he had performed many a wedding ceremony and would need no preparation. "No time like the present," he confirmed.

Lara looked at Kyle in disbelief. She couldn't believe what was happening!

"I didn't intend for us to marry today. Honest," Kyle professed. He was convinced that Lara would want time to sew her dress, pick the flowers, plan the reception dinner, and see to all the other intricate details of a wedding. "I'm most eager to have you become my wife, but I'll understand completely if you would rather we wait."

Eager faces surrounded Lara. Everyone waited for her reply. She looked down to Gavin. Each cheek was dotted with an adorable dimple. When she glanced back to Kyle, her answer was written clearly on her face, but she spoke for everyone else to hear. "I think we've waited long enough. Don't you?"

Kyle was delighted with her answer, but caution reigned. "There's been a lot of excitement already today. Perhaps we should wait until you're better."

"You're treating me like an old woman again, or maybe you're already having second thoughts," Lara teased as she stepped forward to wrap her arms around his neck.

Kyle laughed. In that moment he knew it was going to be difficult refusing Lara anything from now on. "It's going to be a wedding like no other," he proclaimed.

His answered earned him a kiss from Lara.

There started a flurry of activity. Everyone organized themselves and settled down in the main parlor. Simple words to love, honor and cherish were spoken, one to the other as Lara and Kyle exchanged their wedding vows. A short time later,

Pastor Thomas addressed the circle of family and dear friends to introduce them to Mr. and Mrs. Kyle Harrison. A long round of loud cheers could be heard throughout Haven Manor. With her heart overflowing, Mrs. Lara Mackenzie Harrison had finally made a promise of a lifetime to her one true love, Kyle Garrett Harrison, the overly thoughtful, generous, cocky and presumptuous man who possessed her completely, *Heart & Soul.*